# FACE OF THE EARTH

Andrew Klavan

*

# FACE OF THE EARTH

The Viking Press · New York

*For Treacy*


First published in 1980 by The Viking Press
625 Madison Avenue, New York, N.Y. 10022
Published simultaneously in Canada by
Penguin Books Canada Limited

LIBRARY OF CONGRESS CATALOGING IN PUBLICATION DATA
Klavan, Andrew.
Face of the Earth.
I. Title.
PZ4.K636TW [PS3561.L334] 813'.54 79-24072
ISBN 0-670-30440-9

Printed in the United States of America
Set in CRT DeVinne

# *Monday, December 19*

# · 1 ·

She'll be a breath; lovely. From her hair, and the plash and wave of her hair, to her throat and the ivory hollow there, to her chest and the delicate rise beneath to her breast and the mount to its nipple and peak and the peak's soft slope to her round breast's base and the plain of her stomach to the light-blond tangle at her fair-skinned groin and the coast of the profiled thigh to the crest and recession of calf to her ankle, buried in the grass. She will be, to all men, all; she will be, to him, all: Mary, she will be, with her breasts for milk and her thighs of honey, and her eyes with wisdom and proud wisdom's pain, and her face, before the good sun, hidden, and her features, toward the sky, arcane . . .

It's cold and it's dark and it's nearing dawn. Palmer Higgs curls in his sleeping bag and tries to get warm by the heat of his breath. The grass on which he lies is dead; the ground beneath the grass is flat, extending in a circle to a rim of bare-branched trees. Beyond the trees—somewhere beyond the trees—there is a lake, and from the lake a rustle comes, and then a wind: a bitter and a cold one; icy, dry.

Palmer peeks up through the bag's opening, and close to the circle of the clearing's edge he sees what seems a spark, what is a flame, fly upward; then the deep predawn falls slack, lies motionless, stays chill. Twisting for position, Palmer strains to see the flame again and sees, where it has been, a glow. And it grows brighter. A new flame licks forth, with a crackle, lifts higher until now it has the shadows of some tree trunks in it and bathes pale, dead grass in a pale, red flush. The flame seems to grow nearer as it grows to a blaze.

Palmer brings one hand from the sleeping bag to find his jacket and his shoes. His fingers grope and come upon them, grasp, and his whole body straightens out, prepared.

He kicks; his head emerges, then his other hand. Palms pressed against the ground, he quickly pulls his torso out. He kicks again and clears his legs, jumps to his feet, and, snatching jacket, shoes, and bag up, runs.

At first, out in the black freeze, dashing, he can't see the fire and jogs against the cold in wild patterns hemmed by the trees—they are tall, drear, phantom mourners and frightening bounds to overleap. But at last, he spins until he sees the light and heads toward it. A chill seeps through his shirt and his pores. He steps up his pace and with giant strides makes the fire and drops beside it, out of breath.

"God," he gasps, shivering.

Across from him, obscured by flame, the maker of the flame examines him:

Palmer Higgs is lank and small; he's young—just twenty—and his eyes are young. But his face, rutted by acne scars, seems rugged and sage, and his beard—if raw and scraggly, full—gives him an almost noble look, a look like Lincoln's, a gaunt, sad look.

Aware he's being watched, he pats his shoulders with his hands; he puts his hands inside his shirt and rubs his chest. He warms, and stretching forth his arms, he holds them at the fire, sees his fingers as, moon white, they glow.

"God," he says again. "It's cold."

Then he falls silent, never good at conversation, and staring at the staring man, he stares the firelight into diamonds, sees in the fire a fiery face like fate's, and looks away. Nervously he dresses, rolling up his sleeping bag, putting on his shoes, and stands.

He can see the fellow more clearly now: an old hobo left somehow out of the southern push. The bum lifts a sick glance at him, casts the glance from cuff to collar, noting Palmer's once-rich, now-worn clothes, and nods sullenly. Palmer walks off quickly to find his car.

The car is a Volvo; its color, deep green. Settling inside it, Palmer turns on the engine, hugs himself, shivering, as it revs and warms. He looks through the windshield and out to the lane that leads from the wood into the eastbound highway. The specter of the hobo and the burning specter of the hobo in his flame mingle at the mingling of his vision and the dark.

He whispers, "Mary."

Yes, my love, it is your name.

He puts the car in gear and lets it roll out past the trees. The land grows flatter, and the road grows wide, carrying him on into the interstate that will carry him on and toward Spokane.

As always, Palmer feels lonely driving by night. Nothing but a hush is in the full, soft dark. The air is silent and, with its silence, lush; soundless as when echoes still or when a small girl's furtive "shush" dissolves. The basin is unseen, and the quiet in a chill wind comes from off the sprawling, awesome plain beyond, as on that plain and at its rim the last of night dangles.

Now a glimmer cuts a cloud; electric, lit, it flits past, fades, and leaves its portion of the east cold, bare. And nothing but a hush is in it. Then a touch of gray along the distant border of the endless lea turns silver with a touch of light, and the sun's white edge arises.

The white turns yellow, and the gray sky blue, and the day's first breeze sways the dead maples gently. A great mosaic of wasted fields comes quietly to the winter dawn.

# · 2 ·

One pocketed, cock-scratching hand, one butt hung tough from the corner of a grim-set mouth, Janus Quintain leans against the peeling, pebbled wall, waiting for the bells. Not a giant, but compact and with a Johnny Pump build, he is massive, thick, and muscled—though there's some of a gut on him now, some fat—and seems to take up more space than his height allows. He huddles in his jacket from the cold, and except for something studied, it's a smooth, cool move that plucks the cigarette from his lips and flicks it to the ground.

They begin now: bells; a pickup truck first. It bumps over the rubber hose that sets them off. As it sidles to the island, Janus pushes from the wall and, with a lazy gaze along the road, begins a long-striding, hook-thumbed walk across the pavement.

"Howdy," says the driver, smiling. "Wanna fill er up with the reglar?"

"Sure thing," Janus says. He pulls the gas hose free, twists the gas cap off, sticks the nozzle in the pipe, and locks it on.

As he does: the bells; now a Chevy pulls up. Janus starts the gas on that one and goes back to the pickup to check the hood. Pretty soon he's got four cars going all at once, and his broad back's bent in a slavish curve, and his grim mouth's grinning howdies all round.

The bells keep ringing as the cars keep coming as the morning rush begins to pack the pumps.

On the wall where Janus was leaning before, another man leans, sipping coffee. He wears a straw, indented cowboy hat, has a broad, bare western face on a body running six feet to the ground and a belly nearly two feet from his back.

He goes, "Heh, heh, heh," in a round, deep voice, and he squints, watching Janus with the cars.

In a little while, when the rush is through, and the island clear, Janus tosses the windshield sponge into its bucket, wipes his hands, curses, and walks back toward the giant at the wall.

"Morning, Big Jim," he says.

"Heh, heh, heh," Big Jim goes again. "You must hear them bells in yer sleep, doncha, boy?"

"No joke," says Janus without laughing back. "I get out of bed to answer em sometimes."

"Heh, heh, heh. You ought to get a raise."

"Raise," says Janus. "Chuck fired the other jockey, and I got twice the cars now."

"Heh, heh."

" 'S Chuck here?"

"Nope," says Big Jim, crushing the cardboard coffee cup in his hand. "Chuck's got the jeebies some way. Don't know 'f he'll be in 'tall today."

Janus lights a cigarette and leans against the wall. He

looks down the road to the brown foothills at the edge of town. There's a haze above them.

"Gonna rain," he says.

Big Jim shakes his head. "Naw. Montana's a dry state. Hardly ever rains."

Janus starts to speak; then the bell goes off. He tosses his cigarette away and walks toward the pumps.

"Heh, heh, heh," goes Big Jim.

"Heh, heh, heh, you hick-ass zeppelin," Janus mutters under his breath.

But aloud to the customer: "Can I fill er up?"

More cars gather at the island, and Janus, growing busy, sees his breath come fast, forming white vapor in the cold air. He sees the boss drive in and sweeps through the smooth employee's arc from wave to smile to muttered curse. He plugs a nozzle in another car, and another, and, bent over, raises his eyes to the mountains and follows the heave and fall of land. Shaking his head, he whispers almost gently, "Man, oh, man."

Clouds are coming to the big sky now, covering it, darkening, misting the limits of the view. The far rises are slipping into wet gray, and the wet gray is deepening in the distance, cloaking the Great Divide.

Janus watches sadly. It is to the east he looks with longing, for it's from the east he came. From the east comes hazes and drizzly vision, and he sees the pass of a remembered feast and longs for the passage as he looks to the east:

It was pretty, beautiful perhaps, when the upstate landscape dawned at the window as the royalty flapped to place around the table round. The kings and queens and jacks settling before him: arms to heroes of a game of cards; chip-colored crests splayed over that felt made holy by careless cigarettes and table chatter worthier of bards; the pound of fists that beer or whiskey quells, the cool flip of a winning bluff face upward as in scorn . . .

But the picture disappears, becomes the gas, the dirt, their smells, and a customer who's leaning with impatience on his horn, and the shrill, the woeful ringing of the bells.

When the cars are gone, Janus walks back to the office. Here the boss is sitting on a stool, his wiry frame erect, his weathered hand upon the cash drawer of the register, pushing and pulling it in and out. His face is pale.

"You want the tire display up?" Janus asks him.

"Mm? Yeah, put it up." He pushes the drawer in, catches it, pulls it back.

"What about? . . ."

"Yeah, yeah. Go on. There's a car."

Janus strikes a rebellious, leg-bent, slant-hipped pose. "I asked you cause it's gonna rain," he says.

Chuck stands up, shouting. "It ain't gonna rain. We're in a dry state. Now go handle the customer."

Janus swivels, pushes out the door, muttering, "He's got a burr in his breeches, and I'm supposed to care, shit," and handles the customer.

After that he keeps clear of the boss for a while, is busy, anyway, at the pumps and with the morning cleanup. He is sweeping out the office when a brown Cadillac pulls in near the rest rooms. He stops and watches. A lanky, leather-skinned cowboy steps from the driver's door, and another from the passenger's. The first one dangles a billy stick, its strap around his wrist, its lead-filled tip tapping at his thigh. They stroll around the building, past the office, never looking in, and head straight for the garage.

Janus watches through the window of the connecting door, sees Chuck standing under a lifted car and Big Jim, on the far side, going through the toolbox. The two cowboys come in and head for Chuck, still strolling. One cowboy stands in front of him; the other moves behind.

Janus thrills. He listens. It's difficult for him to hear them through the connecting doors; their voices, soft, one plaintive, one threatening, never rise.

"Five letters, Chuck, three calls . . ." says the one with the billy.

"It's a ways from Philipsburg . . ." says the other.

Their voices sink. Chuck's hands are shaking, and he raises and lowers them over and over. He looks ridiculous. His face, pale before, is white; his eyes, which bulged from the pale face, burn.

"Men die for this in Granite County," says the boy with the billy.

Janus nearly laughs aloud to hear such talk. Excitement makes him tremble, and he wonders what to do.

Then, at the wall of the garage, Big Jim turns and takes a step forward. Janus, seeing him, gets tough and bursts into the room.

The unarmed cowboy glances at him. Big Jim has disappeared. Trying to stare coolly at the man, Janus's eyes begin to water, and looking through the water, he sees Uncle Death. . . . It's a bad moment. Big Jim steps out from behind the car.

The cowboys see him.

"Uh . . ." one of them says.

The armed man turns toward Jim in silence, lifts his stick, and, gripping it in one hand, taps it lightly on the other. He smiles, half a smile, a mean, perhaps a killer's smile.

Big Jim grins back, lifts his hand, too. It holds a tire iron.

"Heh, heh, heh," goes Big Jim as the cowboys drive away.

A weakling peace, a foolish silence follow. Everyone's ashamed.

"Well . . . You, Janus," Chuck says. "How about gettin us some rolls and coffee? I'll handle the front. C'mon, let's try and do some . . ."

He is saved by the bell and escapes to the island. For a moment after, Jim and Janus stand facing each other.

Then Big Jim shrugs, and the two men part. Janus goes for breakfast.

He dawdles at the diner, has a cup of coffee, smokes three cigarettes, toys with the waitress's memories of affection, and sits at last staring at the mirror on the wall. His eyes grow milky, and his face becomes a blank. *Through the door, the office door, he goes, again, again, unaided, unaware that aid is coming, and again and* layer after layer till the one swift deed imagined meets the fact of it and blends.

"Mary," he mutters softly.

Half a dead hour is behind him when he leaves.

He's walked a block when, at his back, he hears the siren of a police car. Its volume peaks and passes and declines; its lights go by him in a glow, recede before him to a flashing point. Then, only yards away, the lights die, and the siren winds down, whining; fades. The car turns into the gas station, pulls up to the garage.

Janus freezes, watches, sees Big Jim come running to the cop car's side. He sees two officers rise out, one stepping swiftly around the hood to follow Jim's pointed finger through the office door. The cars that come for gas are turned away at first, and then ignored. The cop still outside sinks down to use his radio.

Janus remains frozen, breathing fast. Then, with rigid movements, he turns and walks back a block to the highway junction. He puts out his thumb.

"Damn," he says aloud. "Damn all."

A car slows down beside him, stops; the door flips open, and he gets in, dropping to the seat without a word. As the car starts up again, there is a thunder roll.

It begins to rain.

# · 3 ·

From the swift rising of the sun, from the long shadows, Palmer takes heart. The road is peaceful. The earth is barren, beautiful, and bare. The light's undying, for it's cleared the horizon, where it splintered in the early dawn like gemshine.

Palmer has a passion for it all. There is an emptiness above his groin that takes for its contours the contours of the land. It feels like a grave, and it yearns for the soil to fill it. This is wanderlust. He has known it all his life, and he knows it now and knows it well, and for the past two years he's followed it and wandered. But while he knows it still, and still he knows it well, he is not the wanderer he was.

Now he charts his courses. Now he heads for Salt Lake City, one of the seven places, post offices, where he receives letters from his sister. Now he travels, in a chain of cities and days, for these.

His sister raised him and he loves her, and he thinks of her often, pictures her at their home by the western shore. He has haunting visions of her there sometimes and imagines some terror, in the sea engendered, in the sea to be entombed, as her familiar. There is his sister, and there is the water, and there's time in the ocean, out and back; there are dreams and memories, heaving and relieved. There is time in the motion of swell and slack; to the sand, to itself again, melodic, unperceived. There was his sister.

Younger, she was pretty as the plain, smooth as he'd seen it in the Mid- and Northwest; pure as it was out there was she then; lovely as the land he left her for.

Elizabeth Hayden, née Higgs, was born in Long Beach, California, the daughter of Frederik and Lillian Higgs.

Her father was a high school English teacher; her mother was a teacher's wife. They were not happy. Like many in his profession, Frederik Higgs had entered the teaching field because he believed himself a failure at something else. That is, he believed that the forces of evil, everywhere rife, had prevented him from doing what he truly wanted. To his mind, he had truly wanted to be a poet. He had even written a poem once: fourteen lines he trotted out for college love affairs and drunks, disclaiming it even then by protesting he had only written it for himself. The only other work of fiction he ever produced was a diary, and this he burned.

So one might think he had no reason to be bitter when he became a teacher. Not Higgs. He insisted on it, even while professing to believe that the past (which had never happened) was past, and the present (which was not at all what it appeared) was to be lived as if each moment of it were the last, which, if one thought about it and were an English teacher, it was.

He married and settled into a quiet existence as mentor of his students and master of his wife.

She, Lily Higgs, was considered by her husband a presentable woman, if something of a dud. To anyone else with half a cataracted eye, she was a beauty. She was auburn-haired and green-eyed and graceful and good. She believed in a few perfectly marvelous lies, and they decked her goodness like baubles on a tree. She believed in her husband, was almost in awe of him, and when, two years after they were married, she became pregnant, she was delighted.

Not Higgs.

The prospect of a baby made him angry and fearful. He was angry at Lily for the thing she did he couldn't, and he feared—and most of all he feared—that the outcome would be a man-child, a son of her flesh, who would usurp him—though in what way he wasn't sure—and upend the little kingdom he had built so well.

Elizabeth was born, the image of her mother, and the good teacher was reprieved. He had learned his lesson; let other lines seek heirs.

Not Higgs. Even now the great anxiety, the threat of sons over, he was not the man he was. His composure was gone. He sensed the averages in flux and, shortly after the birth of Elizabeth, moved his beddings to a hill, as it were. He deprived his wife by denial willed and denial willed upon him, and she, pulled out of mid-rejoicing to have her heart not broken, only slowly crushed, turned without complaint or understanding from the man she loved to her daughter, to transfer the life she was quietly losing to her.

Elizabeth grew, and she took on the mantle of auburn and beauty and marvelous lies. And she looked each day upon the mirror and she saw each day the growing flush of lady life, and she looked each day upon her mother and saw it fade.

Until one day—she was fifteen years old—her mother came up to her room and stood in the doorway silently. Each gazed at the other, and they were the same. Lily smiled, and Elizabeth knew right away that her mother was pregnant. She ran to her and hugged her and held her, but as they stepped from the embrace, the moment passed, the mother waned a little, the daughter blossomed some. Elizabeth knew right away that her mother was dying.

But this Lillian was none to disappear. She lasted through the pregnancy, which ravaged her; she willed herself through the ninth mean month, and she fought, screaming, through labor until out twixt piss and shit popped Palmer, named so, in a biblical moment, with her mother's last breath.

There was an heir to the House of Higgs.

The founder of that clan was shocked by this, more so than by the loss of his wife. He had tried, with the advice of doctor friends and with his own, to keep the birth from happening. But he had underestimated Lily. He had not known her power, and he hadn't counted on her will. In the woman he mastered, he met his match.

Over the years he had taken up the habit of drink. Over more years it had become a hobby. He turned to it now as his profession, and it was soon apparent that he was in no condition to care for an infant and a fifteen-year-old girl. Members of his own family begged him to give the children up to them. This, he said, was unthinkable, and he struggled desperately against their entreaties. Only after seven long days was he convinced to relent. While he could never part with his daughter, he said—she was all he had left of Lily—he would let them take the baby on the condition that they would never break a father's heart by bringing the child again before his yearning eyes.

So Palmer was sent to a cousin, an old spinster who was delighted to have a child to care for, and then wasn't and passed him off to a sister, whose husband spent the next year looking for someone else to take the baby off his hands until at last he found an aunt who said she'd try it for a little while to see how it worked out, but it didn't, and on the boy continued down a stream of indifference and hands.

Elizabeth wept when they took her baby brother away, wept openly many days and many days in secret. At last, she quietly resolved to keep track of his whereabouts and turned her attention to caring for her father. He was degenerating rapidly now, and though she watched over him tenderly and well, his own hand worked against her and was better at the game. Elizabeth could only look on, hoping in silence he might change his ways toward his own flesh and his mind toward his own son.

Not Higgs. That he had a flesh, that he had a son were past his understanding now. Now, for him, there was only an occasional confusion and a vague sadness. Of his wife he remembered little save that she died and that when she died, he missed her. He missed her terribly, as well he might, missed her nearly as much as she was worth missing. He didn't understand why she had had to go, and he wished she would come back as, after all, he loved her very much.

But mostly, to the last, he simply clung to his bitterness and his failure and his loss, for he was a man with a self to kill, and they were all his children, they were all he had. His face became like a barbut. He grayed; he wrinkled; he died.

Elizabeth saw him buried, then walked from the cemetery to the Greyhound station and boarded a bus to Illinois. There, in a suburb of Chicago, she found the people who were taking care of Palmer. She went to their home, knocked on their door, entered their hall, and, pointing at the six-year-old, said, "He's my brother. He's coming with me. Pack his bags."

To her surprise, they were only too happy to comply, and in a few days she was on her way back to California with the boy gazing up at her curiously from the next seat. He was a quiet charge, bearing the ride silently, reacting little to his new ward's henning. It was only after thirty hours on the bus, that he thought or cared to ask, "Who are you?"

"I'm your sister, Beth, Palmer Higgs," she said.

The boy nodded and lapsed back into silence. Two hours later he asked, "Where am I going now?"

Giving Elizabeth the opportunity to speak the lines she had been rehearsing for six years: "Home, Palmer Higgs. You are going home."

Home, however, as Elizabeth had known it, was gone. There was no money willed them, and the house was in second mortgage. There was a small life insurance policy, but it was hardly enough to insure subsistence, let alone life. In short, there was nothing for it but that Elizabeth go to work and try to make home afresh from whatever she could. She got a job as a bank teller, rented an apartment, and began to raise her little brother.

At first, it was simple. Frail and sickly, Palmer was rarely active and no trouble. He didn't speak much and—except for a phantasm named Smedley, the only faithful companion of his first six years—had no friends. Elizabeth was devoted to him. She nursed him; she taught him her books and her poets, and she read him Ovid's *Metamorphosis,* her holy writ. She kept his company, and she kept his confidence, and she gained, eventually, all his love. So, at first, it was simple. But they were young at first.

And things pile up:

Palmer grew. Elizabeth wanted him to go to college; she had missed it, watching her father die. Elizabeth, too, grew older and would soon be alone. There wasn't enough money anymore. It was not so simple now.

Palmer offered to find work, but Elizabeth wouldn't let him. In trust and laziness, he obeyed. Elizabeth met a man who could support them both, convinced herself she loved him, and married him.

A year later, when he was seventeen, Palmer saw his sister for the last time.

He was sitting, staring at the ocean from the widow's walk of his brother-in-law's house. His face, as he pictured it, was tragic with youth's parthian sorrows and their scars. In fact, it was only the acne and adolescence and a melancholy that was drama, at least in part.

Still, he watched the sea, and it, in fashion, splashed against the stony shore, wove between the labyrinths of rock, and half receded, half sank into the bubbling sand. Only the cold disturbed him as night fell.

After a time Elizabeth ascended, carrying a jacket.

"Palmer Higgs," she said, rounding the stairs. "There you are." She stepped out onto the balcony. "You'll freeze. Here, put this on."

"I'm fine. I don't need it."

"On," she commanded quietly, and draped the jacket over his shoulders.

He put it on without looking at her.

Elizabeth sat beside him.

"It is lovely," she said.

Palmer nodded.

"Richard says we can all take the boat out soon, when summer comes."

Palmer was silent still.

"Aren't you speaking to me, Palmer Higgs?"

"Beth?" he said. "I'll be gone when summer comes."

"Oh? And where, may I ask?"

"I don't know. All over. Anywhere."

"I see. And where will you be when school starts in the fall?"

"I don't know. Anywhere but in school on that bastard's money."

"I don't want you to speak of my husband like that," said Elizabeth, quiet and stern and kind.

Palmer stood up and quickly walked to the railing. He felt a terrible anger, felt it would burst him. Below, there was the crack of a wave and its slow, dying pull. Palmer swiveled to face his sister, and his voice was cruel.

"All right. Say that you love him, and I'll do whatever you want."

The girl's clear eyes went blank and turned toward the water.

"Say you love him, Beth," said Palmer.

Softly, Elizabeth said, "Don't leave me."

"We could have done it alone."

"Don't leave me alone, Palmer."

"It was an error, a mistake."

She looked at him. She smiled. There were tears in her eyes. "Now," she said, "what could I do with only a child when I was only a child?"

Palmer's eyes were swimming, too.

"Damn, Beth . . ." he said. And he broke down completely.

He knelt before his sister, and he laid his head upon her lap, and Elizabeth, as always, let him cry for them both. And so, with all their weeping in him, Palmer wept and couldn't speak. He sobbed and, in frustration, kept his clenched fist beating, mute and weak, against his dry-eyed sister's knee, clinging to her waist while she stroked his wet face and his hair, cooing, "Hush," and, "There, there, there . . ."

He is comforted by the scenery. There is an emptiness above his groin that takes for its contours the contours of the land. It feels like a grave, and it yearns for the soil to fill it. This is wanderlust.

# · 4 ·

The sky is dark at Coeur d'Alene. The darkness grows across the neck of Idaho until, above Montana's border and the Bitterroots, the sky is black. Soon after that, off a mountaintop, come a lightning flash, a thunderclap, and rain.

Palmer turns the wipers on. The blades cut the water with a quick tick-and-tick. The rain falls fast, and the road is misty, and the mist is empty of other cars. Palmer dreams. He drives slowly, and sometimes a truck, coming out of nowhere, tosses the Volvo in a suck of air and passes with a spray of water and dissolves in the water and the mist ahead. It takes Palmer a long time to reach Missoula.

This is a city deserted to the rain. Its roads are untraveled, and its buildings gray, and Christmas decorations hanging limp and wet from lampposts seem the trappings of a clown doll cast to the bad weather. A sign by the pavement reads: MISSOULA. FRIENDLIEST CITY IN THE WEST.

Palmer stops at a gas station here and makes a run from the car, through the rain, to the office.

"Howdy," the attendant says. "Help ya?"

"Hi. You got a map?"

"Sure thing."

While Palmer studies the map, the man leans against the countertop and stares out the window. He shakes his head.

"Quite a storm out there."

"Yes," Palmer says. He traces a finger along the drawn highways.

"Don't get many like this. Montana's a dry state, you know."

"Is it?" Palmer glances up and smiles but can think of nothing to say. Then he says, "Is this really the friendliest city in the West?"

The man laughs. "Not today it ain't." He is eager to tell something, eager to tell it to anyone.

"Well," says Palmer, "thanks a lot."

"You bet."

Palmer goes out, drives off.

The rain drops fast and it spatters now, heavier than the wind, and sheets of water hit the road and water hits the Volvo's windshield, where it is slashed away. Palmer leans closer to the glass, staring hard, squinting, but still cutting at a good clip along the street.

Outside the city he goes faster and he sees the road grow rougher, hears the rain, the wind, increase and slacken and blow back heavier than it did before. He hits a rut and curses. But he drives on.

And the road starts climbing, gently first, rising over long distances to the peaks of hills. The pavement has potholes and then deeper ones, puddled over, and the car splashes into them and grinds out slowly. At roadside and beyond, the ground, grassless, is becoming mud. It washes toward the chipped pockets at the highway's edge. The road starts climbing more steeply into the mountains.

No cars are on the road ahead; no cars pass Palmer as he drives. He senses he is lost, and he considers turning back.

But at this moment, right before him, here in the piedmont of the continent's divide, obscured, revealed, then gone again behind the rain, he sees the dead and sudden ending of the road.

It is all mud, all of it: a steep slope rising, swamped at each edge with a flooded ditch. The pools of water rise at either side and lick away the slush and, washing backward, swallow it into the pit.

Palmer hasn't time to stop, has only a second to put the gears in low. Then he's coasting forward over the wet ground.

At first, beneath the layers of mud there's broken road and gravel for the tire's treads to grip. A few feet more, and this is gone. The rubber slips. The car swerves left, sinks backward, aiming for the ditch.

Palmer hits the gas and turns away from the skid. It works; the tires catch, and he shoots forward. Now, not letting up the gas, he tries to take the mount with speed. The mud shoots up against the windshield and splats on it hard, covering it. The wipers fling it off. The car skids, forward, toward the pit again. Palmer throws the wheel; the car slides straight, then toward the other side. More gas, and the wheels steady, speed up, spit out mud from underneath. This time a sheet of sludge comes up. It jams the wipers, holds them fast. In desperation, Palmer pulls the door latch, slams his shoulder on the door. It swings out, and he leans out with it, gripping at the wheel with one hand, gripping at the window with the other, steering, staring out into the rain and mud.

Ahead he sees the mountain's top, and there he sees the road begin. Dirt hits him in his face and eyes; he tears it off, steps harder on the gas. The car strains for the top, nearly grabs it—and spins out of control.

The Volvo skids full around, and Palmer, in a final move, flicks at the gearshift, throws it in reverse, and jams down the gas. The car backs swiftly toward the top, grips pavement, loses it, and slides and skids and hits the edge and crashes over into the ditch, throwing Palmer from the open door, free through air and down, into the pit.

Palmer feels nothing, then hits: the water first, engulfing, and the mud beneath it next. It grabs. His head is underwater, and panicking, he pulls his sinking hands free and rises to his knees. He gasps and pulls his sinking knees free and rises to his feet. He stands atop a shifting platform made of silt, out of water from the waist up. He sees his car, its front end in the ditch, its rear wheels on the muddy path. He wades toward it.

The platform underneath him disappears. He drops into the grip of mud, the water at his throat. He sinks, and the water laps above his chin; across his lips; above.

# · 5 ·

The arms that draw him out are mighty. The face he sees at first is vague. All the world is shadowy, in matter and in meaning, and, chaotic and receding, pauses, throbs, focuses, and slowly clears before his eyes.

There's a laugh. It's a marvelous laugh. It's a god's.

Coughing, choking, spitting dirt, grasping at the shoulders of his savior, Palmer stumbles forth onto the path from which he fell. He sits down in the mud. Rain washes him.

It's a laugh without an echo.

"God Almighty," Palmer says; he chokes.

"Ha-ha."

"God."

"Ha, ha, ha, hee, hee."

Some vomit comes to Palmer's throat. He coughs it up and spits it out.

"Man, oh, man," he says; he gasps.

"Hoo, hoo, hee, haw!"

"Shit."

"Whoo!"

"God."

The laughter continues, and a bit annoyed, Palmer peers up through the rain at the man above him. He can't see much: a form foreshortened; it's like looking at a perched statue from its base.

Palms pushed in the mud, Palmer rises, brushes off his hands, dashes loose erupta from his neck and cheeks, and flaps it to the ground.

"Thanks," he says.

"Haw, haw, haw. Sure. Whoo! C'mon. Let's lift us up yer hot rod."

Expelling a long breath, Palmer follows the other man down the path to the car's rear end. They reconnoiter the Volvo's position. It's stuck on a delicate pit-to-path slant. Palmer shakes his head. The other whistles, humphs, laughs.

"Bogged as a bastard," he says. He holds his hands out as if to test for rain. Rain spatters on the palm. "Wulp." He nods at Palmer. Palmer nods.

They step to the pit's edge and to the car, each at one side, each at one door. They lean out over the ditch, and each grabs a window. The stranger leans out still farther, opens a door, and, barely holding the path with his boot heels, pushes the gearshift into neutral.

Now, Palmer at his post and the other again at his, they begin to tug.

As often happens in moments of shared physical strain, the two men's conversation acquires an instant intimacy and depth:

"Woh," says Palmer, flipping into the air and landing on his ass.

But, "Agh," rejoins the other, and he slips waist-deep in muck, then scrambles out and slides across the path.

"Shit," says Palmer.

"My ass, my ass."

"Gnah."

"Ark."

"Pull."

"Fuck."

"Whoop."

"Stand up. Woh."

"All right?"

"I'm gonna drown . . ."

"What?" says Palmer, standing and tugging at the car again.

The reply is garbled.

"Hello?"

Palmer looks over the Volvo's roof to try to find his comrade.

Sputtering up, the man appears, grit, muddy teeth spitting, spouting curses, water, mire, slime. Arms thrashing angrily, he wades through the flood, his feet uplifting with a plug-pulled sound, and seizing at the car door, he rips it open, jumps inside.

He grasps the key and heaves it over. He hears the engine groan and die. Again, and almost leaning on it, he turns and pushes the key around. The engine coughs, chokes, rolls over, roars.

Outside, Palmer grabs the door handle once more.

The man slams his palm against the gearshift, jabs it to reverse and hits the gas.

Higgs tugs.

And does it rise?

Like boys at birth and bombs from the bottom of the deep, blue sea, indeed it does, hurling Palmer to the ground, where he slides four yards along the path; spurting across the path itself to break just inches from the other ditch's edge . . .

"Yay," says Palmer.

The other man roars.

He jumps out of the car. Palmer scrambles to his feet and, digging through the rain, runs up.

They both climb inside, and the man puts the gears in drive and goes. The car skids, slides; then it shoots ahead, comes flying past the mountain's crest to land on solid, rain-darkened road.

Clasped hands spit mud, shaking.

"Palmer Higgs," says Palmer.

"Janus Quintain," the stranger says.

# · 6 ·

Along the road our grimy heroes go, and through the rain. Except for the fall of water and the wiper blades' tick and the beat of the engine beneath the hood, it is quiet inside the car.

The quiet is Palmer's way. He learned it in his youth—when to speak to no stranger was to speak to no man.

He remembers a prank played on him when he was young. Some boys dug a hole and covered the hole with paper and covered the paper with a sprinkling of dirt until it looked like solid earth. Palmer fell for it and in it then.

Now he is given to the watch, to the listen, to the watchful deduction of inner minds. He's a veteran of outward perfection and will truck with it no more.

So, in the silence, he looks at the man beside him and rates his features carefully:

Janus Quintain is handsome; is blond-haired, round-headed, and bare-faced, a young-looking twenty-five, yet possessed of a certain surface shrewdness which may or may not travel farther down. He is big, broad, and muscular, but Palmer notices that the muscles, like the looks, were once better kept and are going now to seed.

*And what may we deduce from this?*

Ah. Smedley! Here was a hero: given by greatness a grand conceit and by fame an hour all his own. Here was an eye with its white to the world and an ear hearing cheers, not listening. He'll be a talker, this one.

*Astounding, Higgs!*

Because this last is indeed the case. To Janus, quiet's a shuck, and he can't keep it. Here, at the wheel, in the natural silence, he curses and snorts, humphs and laughs loudly, loudly saying nothing while there's nothing to say, waiting till enough miles pass for chatter.

And enough miles pass.

"Sure damped up my smokes," he says. "Got some?"

Palmer shakes his head.

"Look at them." He throws the pack on the dash. "Ruined."

Palmer, not a huffer by habit, huffs politely.

"You ain't so dry yourself," says Janus, laughing. "Hell, I ain't exactly spruced. Look like I just gained ten yards on my ass."

*Football?*

Football or war, thinks Palmer.

*Ah.*

A physical moment, gone.

". . . that hill?"

"What?"

"I say, what made you think you could take that hill?"

Palmer shrugs.

"I don't know," he says.

"You damn near bought it."

"Yes. Thanks again." Then, figuring to assert himself, he says, "Why don't we stop and get cleaned up?"

And suddenly Janus gives a little whoop. "Looky that. Looky that Salmon River."

For here the river meets the road and travels with it for a time. Rain makes it rush and wash against its banks. It tears and carries stone and earth along. It flows and has no rhythm, but the rhythmic motion of the car, the steady rise to mountain, and the rocky fall away seem parcel of it.

Palmer looks to the water. He feels tired; he feels silt and clay and feels the danger that had caught him, passing. He slips in his seat a little, sleepy, and feels with his body the beat of the car.

There's a town on the road ahead, and he points at it. "That Salmon?"

"Eyup. All one horse of her," Janus says. "You know the place?"

"Not really. Let's stop there."

"Good, right. We'll get gas, get clean, and get going."

Palmer sighs heavily. "I have to get some sleep."

"Wu-hell, don't you worry at all, not at all. I don't mind driving one little bit. Why, I can . . ."

"No. No, let's stop at a motel."

Janus gives a big shrug, laughs. "Awright. Okay. Don't want you to be all mussed up. You got to get your beauty rest."

And, with an almost deadly wrench of the wheel, he swerves the car over to a motel.

Palmer checks in and, with Janus at his heels, drags his duffel bag from the car to the room. Inside, Janus drops, muddy, on a bed and bounces and settles and lies quiet; he seems to be thinking. Palmer makes ready to shower, but on his way to the bathroom he pauses a moment and stands with his hand on the knob of the door.

He is exhausted, cruddy, hungry, and it shows. His scrawny body bends with it, its ugliness apparent, and his beard hangs limp and dirty with its noble aspect gone.

"Well," he says quietly, "I owe you my life."

Janus glances at him from the bed.

"Buy me a beer, and we're even," he says.

"No. I'll take you."

"Where? I don't get it."

Palmer yawns and rubs his eyes, his nose, his mouth. "You climbed that hill. No sane man would've driven it or driven it and left you there. You had a ride and he came to the mountain and he saw how it was and he turned away. You got out and climbed it."

"Maybe. Maybe I was coming from the other direction. So?"

"Then you wouldn't be here. You climbed the hill. You couldn't wait. You're in a hurry to get somewhere. I'll take you."

Janus looks at him, silenced for a second; then his smooth face cracks into a grin.

"Pret-ty elementary there, Sherlock," he says. "As it so does happen, I am in a bit of a rush. I'm trying to get to New York, see; there's a sort of a bet I'd like to cash in on, and the only thing is it's like first come, first served, if you get my point. And hell, I'm broke, too. Busted flat. Pancakes. So there you are."

"Well," says Palmer; he yawns. "I owe you."

"Okay. You said it. Take me east, and call it square."

Palmer nods. "Oh, but we'll have to take Seventy," he says. "I want to hit Salt Lake and some other cities, too."

"Stopping long?"

"No. Not long."

And he goes into the bathroom, shutting the door behind him.

After peeling off his clothes, he stands naked for a moment on the tile floor. Then, shivering, he enters the shower. He turns on the water and raises his face to the nozzle to watch as the stream comes down. Mud crusts crack from him, and dirt patches fall away, and purple acne sores come out from underneath. He looks down at his body.

He is thinking of the river.

Fish styx, he's thinking.

*Aye.*

He turns off the shower, pulls a towel through the curtain, and, wrapping it around his waist, steps out and into the other room.

It's quiet, empty there, and Palmer stands still, wet and bewildered. But as he starts to look around, the door bursts in, and in bursts Janus: Janus strutting, grinning, muddy, letting loose the great laugh Palmer heard him laugh before.

"We all clean? We all prettied up? Well, look what your Uncle Janus brought you. A countergirl said I could have it if I promised to touch her on several of her more or less private parts . . . Oh, what the hell, I stole it."

Reaching into his jacket, he brings forth a loaf of bread and, flourishing it, flings it across the room.

Palmer catches it, tears the wrapping back, and eats a slice.

"Franksh," he says.

"Sure thing, good buddy. Poor we may be, but we're hungry no more. Janus Quintain has arrived."

He stomps back and forth from wall to wall, and Palmer watches carefully. There's a new look to him: a deliberate vitality, a cadence of speech like the cadence of travel, a square to the large shoulders, a life in the large man.

"Yes, sir!" he roars. "Introducing Janus Quintain: born to raise hell and the dead. Tall teller of tales. Brawler. Drinker. Poker player, liar, and a damn good running back once—All-American."

So! Palmer thinks.

Janus goes on.

"Higgs, you and me are gonna have us a time. I got lies

to tell you you won't believe and one I'm cooking up right now the likes of which the world has never known. Romance, adventure, sex—why, it might do to carry us clear to New York."

He laughs the grand laughter. His eyes shine.

"Course, with your already famous deductive powers, you're gonna be able to tear my story end from ass backwards. Aren't you, boy? Well, I dare you to. I *dare* you to. Why, I can lie on and on forever. Why, hell, I'm lying to you here right now."

Palmer, drained, walks quietly to the bed and lies down. He smiles and shuts his eyes. If Janus keeps talking, he doesn't listen, or if he listens, he will not be fooled. He's caught this lie at its beginning; he will have no trouble tracking it from here.

This will be the story of a wager.

*But how . . .*

I guessed where he was going. His pride will not allow that, so he lied about the reason. I suspect he will continue to do so.

*Lied?*

My dear Smedley, did our rambunctious comrade not inform us that he was hurrying to collect payment due him from a bet?

*Why, yes, but I don't see . . .*

A man hurrying toward a goal prepares himself for travel. The consequences of carelessness occur to him. Preparedness seems all the more important with his destination in mind. Er—dying men pray, for instance.

*So?*

But men who run from death run blindly and, blind as the hands on a rosary, make no plans.

*Yes?*

Janus didn't pack any luggage.

*Good gracious!*

Janus is running away.

*Really, Higgs, you outdo yourself.*

My blushes, Smedley.

*Quite.*

The thread's end shows. Lies like labyrinths stretch out before, and at the center waits—the bull.

*How droll.*

Bring on the tale!

## *Tuesday, December 20*

# · 7 ·

Like the eyes of mad women, deep stars shine, with a brilliant and a chilly blaze, down on a decent moment, into a time when one might pass into it all and never call it death; and then there's dawn.

The sky has no pure colors after that, only shades overlapping and turning to an alloy of muddy tan. The thought that came before, as swift as thought, is gone, and Palmer, at the wheel once more, looks sadly round the day.

He thinks of Beth and the land, his loves. He thinks of his sister, who taught him of the land that all its trees, rocks, rivers, and blooms were tombs of darlings and forms of God that grew and stood and flowered and flowed for fevered curses, desperate prayers. He thinks of his sister at the edge of his bed, peopling the earth with chased ladies in chaste barks who drank the tears that ran to Roman seas, and he thinks of dreaming, his bed a raft, and he thinks, If we could only mold a myth of mortal clay.

Beside him, in a semisilence of mutterings and huffs, Janus rears, rousing, thinking what he will.

"Hey, magumba, you ever eat?" he says. "I got the hungers."

Palmer nods, sighs, guides the car off the highway, and stops on a side road at a roadside café.

Through breakfast, Janus eats with abandon and talks. He tells tales. He talks of adventures, of fights, of women—of course—won, lost, toasted dewily, and half forgotten. He scrapes his food—eggs, toast, ham, hash—to a great pile centered on his plate, and talking, he pats it into a block and, cutting from that a good-sized square, he raises the square to his moving mouth, and pausing to let a sentence pass, he gulps it, pushing a sentence back, and drops his fork to his plate again to scrape, squash, pat, talking.

Palmer listens silently and, silently deducing, cuts an Adonis to a boy at play, knocks a battle royal down to the thump and tumble of a bully on a babe, and mixes a million bawds into a single heard-of whore.

And Janus runs on till the food runs out, and then runs down, pushes his empty plate away. He pats his stomach twice and tilts backward in his chair, lighting a cigarette.

"Well, you bout ready to hit the road?" he says. "We got good weather; we should make good time."

"Okay," Palmer says. "But if we can't reach Salt Lake before six, we'll have to stay the night."

Janus clucks, shakes his head.

"My, my. What all is in Salt Lake, I wonder."

"Mormons, I think," says Palmer. He finishes his coffee and leans back, an accidental mime.

"C'mon. You got some pretty piece holed up there. Doncha, huh?"

"No. My mail comes there."

"You can't fool me."

Palmer shrugs.

"Your mail?" says Janus. "Oh! My. Well. If Mama writes—well, then, we better just get the bill and blow this dump and roll. What say?"

He stands up, swaggers out, and Palmer, after paying the waitress, follows him to the car.

In the driver's seat Palmer turns on the ignition. Next to him Janus pats the dash.

"Awright, you hunka tin," he says. "To Salt Lake City for the mail. Not rain or sleet or gloom of night . . ."

And they are off again.

They travel by the river still, through bare forests, toward a sun all up above the eastern ridge. Janus, a butt puffed and dangling from one lip's edge, begins to talk more slowly now, his eyes on the mountains and his voice trailing backward, lazily, like smoke.

"Bet you didn't believe none of it," he says.

"Of what?" says Palmer.

"That stuff I told you back there in the restaurant. Bet you didn't believe a word."

"No," says Palmer.

"Not even that part about the frogs in Phoenix?"

"No."

"Aw, hell. That was a real good part." He arches his back, stretching. "Weel," he says. "You're prolly right. It was prolly all a pack of lies."

"Prolly," says Palmer.

"Guess you foiled me this time, good buddy. But now"—and here he turns from the mountains, his eyes dancing with that new energy, his lips in a sly smile—"now it's time for my deluxest yarn. The greatest story ever told."

Palmer glances at him.

"I'm mostly ears," he says.

"That's good."

The road and the river now divide.

Now Janus speaks in a listless drawl.

"It all began," he quietly says, "that is, if it began at all . . ."

# · 8 ·

. . . when the beer in the keg was finished, and the beer in the glasses warm. Melancholy had the men at cards. They had played for their quarters and gobbled their drinks all night, all day now, and were ready to fold. Outside, a soft spring afternoon was passing into evening. Sweet and slender women walked the grounds, more feminine for the weather, it seemed, sad, it seemed, as if the air were sad, and the giants, these heroes at their game, were as sad as the women and the winds.

Janus was winning. He always won at poker when he tried. Some called it luck and damned it, but the smart ones knew it for a talent of sorts, a constant dedication to the con that carried over to the table, that left men staring sidewise, always guessing him and always wrong.

But none who played now cared. This was their last game together, and more concerned with tradition than riches, they begrudged it nothing but their final dime.

At last, Janus, smiling through the green smoke of a thin cigar, tossed a flash of spades and numbers at the discard pile and rose.

"Aren't you suckers broke yet?" he said.

"Just about," one sucker said.

Janus shook his head and laughed. He stretched, then walked slowly across the room to the dead metal keg, stuck a mug beneath its faucet, and tried to squeeze out one last drop. There was nothing.

"Gone," he told them sadly.

The four men at the table watched him as he moved to the window.

"Is the game over?" one asked.

"Looks like it," he said, and he looked through the window at the campus.

There were hills out there, rolling to a forest, and from behind the trees there came beams of the sun, lead-heavily hung, yet glowing with a titan whiteness that spread across the grass.

Atop one hill a girl was lying. She was slim and delicate, and her hair was pink and blond. She wore a dress with flowers on it, and breezes blew the hem of it past her knees, and her white hands smoothed it down again primly. She seemed pretty to Janus. He looked at her hair and whispered a name. He was sad. A long, good time was over.

A long time ago, in the hardly-to-be-called-a-town in Illinois where he was born, he had come to the football field and won all honors. He had left, and left a girl behind, to come to this college and join its team. He had come with this team to the championship at the Rose Bowl and there conquered, and the time was done.

He looked at the girl atop the hill and whispered a name and wanted her lazily, as if to claim were somehow to recapture.

"Nice," said a voice behind him.

He turned. It was Austin, the team quarterback, a smaller man than the others in the room, and their leader.

"Hiya, Captain," said Janus. "Yeah."

"Looks like your old flame, doesn't she? What's her name?"

Janus glanced through the window again. "Yeah," he said. "A little. Her hair."

"Well . . ."

"Yeah. How you doing, Cap?"

"Well," said Austin. He shrugged and sighed. "You know."

"Yeah."

"Yeah."

They sighed together.

"Well . . ."

"Well . . ."

"We were tough," said Janus.

"Yeah."

"Yeah."

"Four good seasons and the roses," Austin said.

They sighed.

Austin was a man with the looks of a boy, good looks, and a smile for the back rows. He smiled.

"You seem to have run out of beer," he said.

"Yeah. The tap tapped out bout dawn."

"Tragic."

Janus nodded gravely, belched.

"However," said Austin, "this sad state of affairs does not exist in my refrigerator."

"It's a wonderful refrigerator."

"That is truth," Austin said.

The four big men around the table waved as their captain and their star left the room.

"Good bunch of guys," said Janus.

The two went slowly down the hall.

"Yeah."

"I hear Guy and the Lion are going pro."

Austin nodded. "Looks good for Maury, too."

"No shit."

"Yeah."

"Good. That's good. What about our famous quarterback?"

"Well . . ." Austin watched his feet, then looked up shyly. "I don't know. I'm thinking maybe I'll disappear for a while. Go back to Jersey, see the beach—get Jenny to come and meet my folks."

"Sounds serious there, buddy," said Janus.

Austin shrugged. "I'll be back. Watch the papers."

"Will do."

"How about you? You turned down a lot of good offers."

"Aw." Janus put his hands in his pockets. "I got some other things to do."

"Well." Austin laughed. "You could always go back to your strawberry blonde. What was her name?"

"Yeah," said Janus. "We could all go back to our strawberry blondes."

They came to Austin's room, Janus leading. It was a small dormitory cube, decorated sparsely, neatly kept. Jenny was there, by the window. As Janus walked in, she turned to him, and they looked at each other silently until Austin followed. Then Janus said, "Hiya, Jen."

"Hi."

"Hi, sweetheart," said Austin. He went to her and kissed her cheek. "We have come to St. Jenny of the beer cans for comfort."

"Welcome, pilgrims," said Jenny. She smiled. She was a sturdy girl, with a full figure, cap-à-pie. Her wide brown eyes were quick enough to be smart, smart enough to be sad, and they looked at everything directly. Her hair was chestnut, and light gleamed on it and flowed on it to her shoulders and lit her face. Her face had a simple, regal beauty. Austin looked regal when he stood at her side.

Now she was between the two men and between them seemed set off and alone. Her smile was frozen for a time, and in that time she stayed as still as stone.

Palmer can see her as he drives. He sees a sweet face, framed, transfixed, and sees, on either side of it, a man and—we are meant to know, he thinks, that she is with them both.

*Of course, you realize that already something . . .*

Yes, yes, but it is almost as it would be; sensed, if never really, so. For she would be standing as if not whole, not whole and unsure of her path to perfection and not unsure but tangled in and mangled by her restrained passion and her passion to restrain.

*Well, yes, but if one is to discuss intelligently the impossibility of completion in the real world, hadn't one ought to consider? . . .*

You're getting on my nerves, Smedley.

*Sorry.*

She would . . .

*Tangled and mangled was really quite good.*

Shaddup.

*Ahem.*

It's just that she *would* be caught, if only in a dream, between this Austin, good man, leader, and Janus, the fist, the heel the trampled look to from the dust, Austin's heel. It's true; she'd stand twixt arms like armor and Arthur's brow and need not both, but one to be as they both are and both as one, and both designs of her to be as one and one with all.

*Dot's wary, wary confoosing.*

Men and women meet, you see, not only in their sheets but in the very tension of the universe.

*Oh. I wasn't aware.*

And on this atom of the wide world, earth, only a kiss is cosmic, only the men at Troy know war, for we blend on battlefields as in the stars and meet, as lovers, on the field of Mars . . .

. . . thereabouts, Austin plucked the beers from the fridge, tossed one to Janus and one to Jenny, and plopped on the bed with his own, tilting a swig and farting jocosely.

"Jenny," he said. "What do you think? Jay says we should all go back to our high school sweethearts."

"Good riddance," said Jenny.

"It's a thought," he went on.

"You mean go back to the lies you told about her. She wouldn't have you."

"You jest."

"Take it from me."

Austin winked across his beer at Janus. His eyes gleamed with a tease.

"After all, woman, we're heroes," he said.

"Sure. Soon you'll be old men with bellies, hero."

Janus laughed. "She's right."

"Come, come, people," said Austin. "What blonde in her right strawberry mind would turn down a second chance at Janus Quintain here?"

Jenny returned to her window, perched on its ledge. She wasn't smiling.

"Tell her, Jay," Austin said.

"I don't know," said Janus. "Jenny is usually right."

"Rabbit! I bet she wouldn't take you back at that."

"Austin," Jenny said quietly, "shut up."

"I'll bet you she wouldn't."

Janus grinned. "You wouldn't con a master."

Austin grinned. "I wouldn't?" he said. His eyes gleamed. Jenny wasn't smiling. He nodded. "I guess you're right." He laughed. "I guess you're right," he said. He said, "I guess you're right."

They drank more beer and talked like friends. The last sun, the evening's, dropped away, and the room felt intimate in the darkness. They all grew drunk, and Austin grew thoughtful, and Jenny and Janus talked, laughing.

Austin grew thoughtful and stared at a beer, swirling the can, listening to the liquid hit the metal inside. The laughter in the room was warm. His eyes began to gleam, as with a tease.

"I'll bet she wouldn't take you back," he said suddenly.

Janus and Jenny were caught on words. There was silence.

"Who's that?" Janus said.

"Your old girl. I'll bet you."

Jenny said nothing.

"Ho there, Captain. Maintain," Janus said. "I think you got yellow fever." He smiled at Jenny. Jenny didn't smile.

Austin's eyes gleamed. "I'm saying just once. I bet she wouldn't just once."

Janus looked at him, then at the girl. There was no expression on her face. The big running back shivered.

"Fifty dollars," Austin said.

"You're drunk."

Austin laughed.

"Hell, I don't even know where she is."

"I'll give you a month. Take all summer."

Janus waved him off. "Pass out," he said.

He looked around the room nervously, and he looked at Jenny again, and again her face was blank, and again he trembled. He looked at Austin, and their eyes held; Austin's gleamed.

"How would you know?" Janus asked him.

"Word of honor."

"I haven't got one."

Austin laughed.

The door shut loudly. Jenny was gone.

Janus nodded, said: "You're on."

# · 9 ·

"You took it," says Palmer.

Janus is quiet for a moment, as if he's thinking, as if he's sad; then, pulling a cigarette off the dash, he taps it against his wrist and says, "Yeah."

"Jesus," says Palmer, "some bet."

"Yeah—I was telling the truth, though: I had no idea where my old girl was. She was a year younger'n me, and she coulda been in college, coulda been anywhere."

Palmer shakes his head and laughs. "It's a funny idea."

"Yeah."

"But why? . . ."

"What?"

"Nothing."

*. . . didn't Janus play pro ball?*

Aye.

*He said he'd better things to do.*

Yes. But observe his hands: the dirt; the skin raw, peeled as if the dirt's corrosive. As if, in fact, the dirt were acid . . .

Why didn't Janus play pro ball?

*He could no longer play perhaps.*

He could; he did. It's like battery acid, really. Like on the hands of gas station attendants. Aye. And so—with no pressing plans, with nothing else to do—why didn't Janus play pro ball? Unless he simply didn't want to. Or he was afraid. Aye, yeah, yes, or he was afraid, our Janus, with his glory gone, with his friends gone, who admired him. It's only natural. He finishes college. This abyss, this life is there, staring him in the nose, all real. So he gets a little shaky, and he tries to hold it off, to turn away, go back. Sure he does. But not for Jenny and not on a bet. Fear makes the heels go round. No, not Jenny; never a bet. He'd only need some rationale, some little thing to tell himself . . .

*Love.*

Yes. That he was in love with the pink blonde. Or . . .

*Or what?*

I don't know—Palmer scratches his beard—or what?

"You want to hear some more of this bullshit?" Janus says.

"Hm? Oh. Yeah, sure."

"Just gimme some time to make it up . . ."

Or what? thinks Palmer. Old glory, with the wind gone, limp? A smile at the end of admiring faces on a road through small-town lawns and fields beyond of wheat or corn or whatever grows wherever she is, and she in the farm where she was born, by fields of morning and fields of corn that will bend like an emerald bow, tra-la, on a crystal sea, neath an April dawn . . . And she'll stand, worth worshiping and golden-headed at the door, beside her mother sitting, rocking, reading quietly aloud above the sound of sheep at pasture, grazing.

And her mother will say, "These old eyes get so tired," or something like that. "My eyes are weak, child," or something like that. Or just: "Read awhile, Mary." Yes, and

Mary will stand, no, sit, no, stand beside her reading mother, and her mother will say, "Read awhile, Mary."

"Yes, Mama," she will say, and she will read some passage of some prophet from the book.

He, then, Palmer, will raise his eyes to survey the great country all around, a golden land of fresh-risen delights, of wheat or corn or whatever grows wherever this will be, but it will be a red-gold landscape like her hair, where a follicle can grow up straight and strong like a boy should, and Mary, too, will raise her eyes, her red-gold hair pushed gently by the Laodicean wind and whisper, say, "There's a man comin, Mama."

And the sun in Taurus, like the sun at birth, will shine on her as she were its own, as the good sheep graze on the sunlit earth, as the good girl glows where the sun has shone . . .

"Okay. Listen up. I got some more," says Janus.

"Hm?"

"Listening?"

Mary, Palmer thinks. His arms have slipped a little at the wheel.

"Well, don't you want to hear this?"

"Go ahead," he says.

They have reached the high land of Idaho, are descending now toward the Utah plains. Cold, dead trees fall back, fall away, and cold, dead deserts rise up ahead.

Palmer lifts his arms with an effort. They are heavy with driving. Janus stretches and lets go a yawn; then he sits back, and his tale goes on.

# · 10 ·

Upon the wall above his bed a painting hung, a winter scene, done by the woman he'd loved once; done in oils. It depicted a path, or the sensation of a path: an impression, in darkness, that tunneled back into the canvas. There were winds and a half-imagined star, and yellow in the window of an unseen barn, a candle glowed, solitary. There were trees, but except for the eye that traveled here, nothing moved among them.

Standing by the bed, Janus looked the scene over. The girl had given it to him when he left her, had told him it was a farm in Pennsylvania, where she was going to live with her parents. She had also given him the address, and he had written to her for a time.

Now he was going there, through the wall and into winter. He looked down at the bed where his duffel bag lay amidst a heap of clothing and, after pulling the bag's zipper back, began packing fistfuls of shirts and socks.

There was a knock at the door.

"It's open," he said.

Austin entered.

"Hey, Captain."

"How goes it, Jay?"

"All right," said Janus. He went on packing, his back to Austin. "What's up?"

"Not too much. I thought I probably won't get a chance to see you tomorrow, so, uh . . ."

"Yeah, yeah. Sit yourself."

Austin brought a chair over and sat down. He said nothing for a long time, and Janus packed more slowly.

At last, Austin shifted a little in his seat.

"Some bet," he said.

Janus snorted, grabbed clothes, stuffed them in the bag.

Austin was silent for a good while longer.

Then he said, "Forget it."

"What?"

"The bet."

"Oh. All right."

Janus was down to his last shirt. He folded it carefully.

"It's a laugh," said Austin.

"Yeah."

"I'd go pro, I think, if it weren't for Jenny."

Janus laid the folded shirt neatly on top of the bag.

"Well," he said, "you'll go pro."

"Maybe. I might. But I think it's over."

"Well," said Janus, "she's worth that, too." He zipped the bag and turned to face his friend. "She's worth that, too," he said.

Austin took a long look at him, and a longer look, and he nodded.

"Damn it," he said.

"Listen. Austin . . ."

Austin stood up and put out his hand. Janus, relieved, took it, shook it.

"Good luck, good buddy."

"Take care."

"It'll be all right."

"It's all right," Austin said. His voice was gentle. "It's all right, Jay." He turned—back straight, eyes clear—and walked from the room.

Janus slept badly all that night. He awoke many times before morning and lay staring up at the painting above his bed. Deep in the darkness, he thought of a woman; deep in the dim light of dawn, she was there, an absence between his flesh and his linen, corporeal, overwhelming . . .

When the sun crested his window, he bolted up, blinking quickly as the room grew bright. He rose and he washed and he dressed and he left.

His Chevrolet stood by itself in a nearly empty lot. He went to it, threw his bag in the back, got in, and sat as the engine warmed. He looked around him. The campus spread out in the distance, rolling to the green hills, running to the spring woods, and he did hate to leave. The sun was white and silver on the grass.

He put the car in gear and began to coast away. The road descended, lined with trees, canopied by the leaves of trees, through which the light came down in beams. He looked again to the campus and faced front just in time to see a girl step into his path.

He hit the brakes. The car screeched, skidded, stopped. The girl didn't move.

It was Jenny.

Janus got out and went to her. In the light, in the new light, and the cool spring air, she was beautiful. Her eyes were rich and wide.

"I could've run you down," he said.

"I came to tell you I love him so much."

Janus nodded. "Yeah. I know."

Then they kissed each other for a long time. Then they broke apart.

"He let it go," Janus said. "He let us off. He was tough."

Then they kissed each other, moving back and into the trees, moving down and into the grass to be lovers.

When, finally, Janus drove away, he felt miserable and he felt relieved. In the rearview mirror he could see Jenny, standing in the road and waving, and he whispered: "Good-bye," but went along, growing happier as the miles passed by, the college receded, and the girl disappeared. He patted the Chevy's flank and cooed at its old engine, for the battered car seemed to him noble in motion. The world seemed fit for adventure. Here was his charger, and here he was in the dameless days of knights in flower, in the age of the peerless men of valor and away from the blood-red gusto's pallor; in the virgin time again, the maiden hour.

Yeah, thinks Palmer, swell.

They near Utah.

# · 11 ·

Yeah, yeah, yeah, thinks Palmer. Yeah, yeah. Them in the grass, I can see it, and the trees. The sun in beams. Swell.

He props his elbow on the windowsill to keep his arm up.

But it wasn't like that.

*Your reasoning?*

I just tell you it wasn't, and I tell you it happened earlier on, when he tossed in his bed with his waking phantom, and fought temptation, and rolled on his belly, and pressed down into the deep, warm sheets . . .

*I say, let's talk of something else.*

. . . his finger, first, seducing, then flat-backed surrender to his hand . . .

*Blecch!*

And there he had her. There! While she was with Austin, the man she loved.

His stomach's sour.

Janus laughs.

"Hey, can't this crate go any faster?"

"No," says Palmer grumpily.

"Well now. Pardon me for living. Hell, we can putt through this shit till the rainy season, won't bother me."

"Uh-huh."

"I just hope we make Salt Lake before the post office closes."

"We will," says Palmer.

"Cause a fellow, he needs some home-cooked mail out here in the wilderness, with nothing for company but the tumbleweed and the call of the old coyote on the snow-capped hills." He gives Palmer a sidelong glance, throws back his head and cries, "Awooo. Awooo."

Ah, shut up, Palmer thinks.

"Awooo."

And he feels ashamed a little because, as Salt Lake City nears and as he nears his sister's letter, excitement wells in him, and his heart beats harder.

"A-wooo."

Cities come out of the desert now. The late sun's low. The Great Salt Lake appears, appears dead water on the dust, without an echo of the afternoon.

"You know," says Janus, "the state bird is a sea gull here. Look at this. Nothing but desert for miles. The Mormons say there was all these locusts, see, and the sea gulls came and et em all up. The locusts, that is. Ugly bird. Sea gulls, that is. Ugliest birds—they done swallowed the ugly stick. Why, out in San Francisco—I used to work for a fellow ran a fishing boat out there . . . You ever fish?"

"No," says Palmer. "I don't like the ocean."

"Well, the sea gulls follow you and hover at the stern—hang there with their wings out, curved like to swoop and kill. They know you got anchovy bait on board. In fact, they only follow you coming to shore, cause that's when you toss out the extras, and they know it. I'm telling you. I swear it.

"So we used . . ." He chuckles heavily. "We used to throw them the bait with the hooks still in it, see. And they'd swoop and catch it and fly real high and swallow it and hover, while the hook was catching. Then they'd drop—pow!—like a rock in the water. It was really funny."

"Mm," says Palmer.

"Yeah, yeah, see, you gotta get used to the ocean, gotta get over it, like. Like another time, when I was with the boat . . ."

But Palmer listens no longer. He peers ahead, instead, intently, sees a glint of fire at the long road's end, a touch of gold, and Salt Lake City rises from the flat land.

". . . and dive to the bottom . . . There she is," says Janus.

"Yes."

"And plenty of time for the mail, after all. I tell you what, good buddy, why don't you go on and pick up your mama's letter, and I'll stop off and have a beer somewhere, maybe catch a ball game or something?"

"All right."

"I don't want to intrude."

"All right, Janus, all right."

"Yeah, that's a good idea."

They break the city limits and head slowly for its center. Palmer keeps his eyes on the traffic. Janus watches out for bars.

"What the hell," he says.

"None?"

"No."

"I'll only be a second."

"Yeah, okay. I'll wait."

They reach the post office, and Palmer parks. He is nervous now. He cuts the engine—his hand hesitates on the keys, and then he cuts it off—and after he has listened so long to its rhythm, the silence afterward seems a sound, a sound that, with a tongue, would be a scream: a shrill note, endless. He opens the door and steps outside.

"Say hello to Mama," Janus says.

"My mother's dead," says Palmer, and he shuts the door.

He takes long strides, walking to the building. He looks directly ahead, and his face is blank and a little pale. He climbs the building's stairs—all around, in the parking lot behind him, through the doors before him, and inside, it's as quiet as a Sunday—and his heart is hammering. He enters the post office.

His footsteps, which are quick, echo in the room, which is empty, as he goes to the general delivery window and asks for his mail. He receives one letter and carries it to a counter and lays it down unopened. Tugging at the cuffs of his jacket, he unbuttons each one and rolls them both back over his forearms. He picks up his letter, opens it, and, clearing his throat, plucks a $100 money order away from the text. This he plants in his pocket like a secret. Then he lays the letter down and reads:

*December 10*

*Dearest Palmer Higgs,*

*I was so happy to get another letter from you so soon. I'm glad you write often. Your adventures around the country sound very exciting and the places you see sound beautiful and it is all very thrilling for the poor stay-at-home set.*

*I hope you are in a cold place now with lots of snow. Christmas in California is kind of silly because of the warm weather, and even though there are decorations and everything, it never seems quite right. I also hope you will be with friends for Christmas. You never tell me much about the people you meet and I hope they're not all hoboes and street people like the ones you told me about in Ann Arbor. I know you don't like me to be too concerned, but you must take a little care at least and some of these people may be dangerous, so please try to meet some nice people as well.*

*Here everything is fine. Richard is well, and his business is running along as usual. It was very sweet of you to ask about him in your last letter and he seemed very pleased. He even suggested I try again to convince you to come home for Christmas. You wouldn't have to stay and I wouldn't even nag you about it, but I do miss you, and I am not very happy. If you would only call and I could hear your voice—it's been two years! But what I really want is to sit and talk to you again. I need to talk to someone and you were always very smart and saw things I couldn't. When you were a baby, I used to imagine that you would be like that when you were older, and it made me love you more, and it's sad to not even get to see you now.*

*I am sending this letter to Salt Lake City because I have been charting your course from your letters and think this is where you will get it before Christmas. If you do, try to call so I will know. If you don't call or write before Christmas, I will know you need more time to think about it. All right? You don't have to mention it if you don't want to.*

*Take care of yourself, sweetheart. And please try to find some people who will take care of you since I can't.*

*I love you.*

*Beth*

Palmer scratches an acne sore on his cheek, and it opens, and it bleeds, and the blood trickles down his face like a tear. He folds the two pages of the letter together, stands with it in his hand, his fingers lingering busily at the paper's edge, pressing the fold flat, riffling the sheets again, folding it over again—his eyes are dreamy—and he makes a fist and the paper crumples and he hurls it at a garbage can and it hits the rim and the pages split apart and rattle to the ground.

He cashes the money order at a window, pocketing the cash with an odd, cruel smile. Then he walks through the quiet building, out and across the quiet lot to the car, and gets inside.

"So who writes?" says Janus.

Palmer turns on the engine. It rolls over, settling into a steady beat.

"My sister," he says. He lets out a long breath and puts the car in gear.

"Weel now," says Janus with a wicked grin. "Your sister. What's the little lady's name?"

Palmer doesn't answer. He steps on the gas, and the car shoots forward. He steers it hard.

"She pretty?" says Janus. "How old is she? So what's her name?"

"Janus . . . " Palmer says.

"She married? What?"

"Just—be quiet."

"Me? The man who talked the ears off corn. Why . . . "

"You."

Janus, cut off, snorts.

"All right then," he says. "Let your sister remain amnonymous. She's just your mama in disguise. Don't matter to me. Hell. Try to be friends."

Palmer stops the car at a light, waits, and pushes on more slowly. He is trembling with anger, with an urge to fight—for Janus has insulted Beth—and with fear—for if Janus is gross, he is large, too—and so with anger at himself, and he trembles; with anger, with an urge to fight—with more than that: with an echo of the shrill note under the engine, an echo splintering into demons, deities of his very own. They are gods of war as Mars was, of savageries in the prime heart and a beast rampant. And in their souls—he sees them—in their souls are phantoms on a road through corn: a farm, a woman, motionless, frozen; static images sweeter than reason, for sweeter than reason is Mary, and in her a man might be . . . A man might be . . . Then—as at night in storerooms of the Louvre, when ancient lines of marble bodies shudder, and Proserpinas pull from the abyss, and ready wings of stone begin to flutter as minds and passions meld into a kiss—the stationary phantoms start to move.

The pages of the mother's book will ripple with a breeze. The breeze will play at the hem of Mary's dress, and she, with modesty and unawares, will smooth the cloth, the rude cloth, gently, and glance up over the Illinois corn. Just so will Palmer see her first, before she knows he's near, before she stirs a hair to please or put him off, and he'll appraise her calmly from his swift albino, or his sturdy Cleveland bay or yet, yes, some black, rearing stallion, no, a wan beast fit for its lone, pale man . . .

Then will Mama pause, sigh, rub her eyes, and say, what was it?

"You read for a while, Mary."

And "Yes, Mama," she will say, and take the book and read, like a martyr, some martyr from the pages, and shift her full and precious figure slightly, modest, unawares, adjusting, modest, unawares, her white dress at the collar as a shadow from the porch roof snuffs the luster of her hair and sets her whiteness on the jet and then the crimson of the end-day, and she'll raise her eyes from some vibration in the earth and see him.

"There's a stranger comin, Mama," she will say, and there will Palmer be, looking calmly down at her and saying, "Hullo, ma'am . . . "

. . . her mother first.

And there will Palmer be, upon his charger, calmly looking down, but with profound respect, at Mary's mother, saying, "Hullo, ma'am."

And the older woman will look up, will shield her eyes, look up, will look up, shield her eyes, and say a careful "Howdy . . . "

Or perhaps look up . . .

He'll turn to her, the young girl who is faceless, who was faceless as his swift horse neared. Their eyes will click or, something soundless, blend, and he'll say, "Miss."

And she will nod back shyly, and then their eyes will blend like a mixture of creation and the world's sweet end . . .

Palmer slams on the brakes.

"Hoa!" cries Janus.

Tires screeching, the car swings full around and spurts off down the road it came by. Soon, again, Palmer stops it. He leaves the motor running when he gets out.

This time he runs up the stairs, pausing only for a moment at the door to look around.

The letter is where he left it. He runs to it, picks it up, smooths the crumpled pages on a countertop, and folds them neatly, slips them in the pocket of his shirt.

He runs back out to the car and gets back in and gets back on the road.

"Forget something?" Janus says; he laughs.

The highway slips beneath them. Salt Lake City slips away.

# · 12 ·

Wanderlust ends at the desert. Bushes pock the wasteland like the crusts of ash where cigarettes are snuffed, and dust takes up the sight of miles. All's old under the empty sky—the hidden side of the hills is bared—so the eye dies over a distance.

It is evening now. The sun, low behind the drivers, drops, from the sand of the cursed and wandering children, down toward the land of the blessed dead, until only desolation's west, and it grows dark quickly as winter will. And it grows dreary. Each stretch of road becomes as lonesome as Adam before and after Eve; each succeeding shade that spreads across the sky is like a deepening of sadness. The world seems distant from the travelers; lights in houses seem warm with supper and blood ties; melancholy comes—and just for a moment, when the day takes on its deepest violet, before the violet's eased with stars, there is even an instant without romance in which all yearnings are impossible to bear.

Then Palmer yearns for his home, for Beth; would return to the house by the ocean, would stand at the very ocean's edge and conjure ruination's angel to the shore if he could be with her.

When the wander-year is done, he thinks.

And the moon rises.

"Sure's depressing," Janus says.

"Yes," says Palmer. He wants to talk, and he tries hard to think of something to say.

"Makes you think," Janus says.

"Yes. Has it been long since you've been home?"

"Where, Illinois?"

"To see your people."

"Oh, God, yeah. Years, years and years."

Palmer grunts, then blurts, "I think of it."

"Yeah? Go back to old Sis, you mean? Well, maybe." Janus considers. "So you just travel around all the time?" he asks.

"Yes."

"Sis sends you the bucks, though, huh?"

"Yes. Well. She sends me some. I work from time to time."

"Yeah," says Janus. "I guess old Sis must be worried sick about you."

There is, there's always a slight drawl of irony to his voice. He seems, he always seems, to tease, to challenge almost. It's a small thing, anyway, hardly worth a fight, and Palmer lets it pass.

"She'd like me back," he says.

"Well . . . " Janus lights a cigarette, takes in a drag, and, while he does, takes on the faces of a Wise Old Man. "Well," he says, "I guess I've been around most everywhere, and after a while, it's all the same. Not much to see, and nothing changes, and you're always the same wherever you go.

"See, a young guy—a guy like you—comes out here

looking for experience, adventure, and like that. But that ain't real; that ain't the way things are. If you do it that way, it's all pretend."

Poof! I'm a shithead, Palmer thinks.

"Sure, kid," says Janus. "Go on home."

Sure, kid, thinks Palmer, go on home, back to your sister, and take care of her, willya, and grow up, willya, straight and strong, and always remember God loves ya and'll watch over ya and will cause you to fructify, lest de fry fruc you first. And so He giggled at your mother's funeral, He's just a kid, what does He know, and besides . . .

"A guy's young," Janus is saying, saying while Palmer drifts away, "just a kid, and everything stands still for him. Your mom and pop don't grow any older, and there's this great thing up ahead of you, and you think it's standing still, just for you, like. And then you look at your mom and pop all a sudden, and they're old, they're old people. And you break through the thing, and it's behind you all a sudden, trying to catch up. And you're outrunning it. It's . . . "

"Hm?" says Palmer.

". . . scary."

"Pardon?"

"What?"

"I just, uh . . . "

"What's that?"

"Nothing, I just . . . I just thought of something, never mind."

"Oh," says Janus.

. . . and besides, where were you when He made the world and caused Aton to rise from the formless marshes and central Baltimore to sink into them? Where were you, Jocko? Well, that's why He's creator of the universe, and you have pimples . . .

Janus shakes his head and clucks. "Sure's depressing," he says.

The stars begin to blink and glitter: one, and soon a sky of them. All are bright; each seems eternal; none seems born, or born to nova, or doomed to a lunatic fizzle and fall. They people the sky as the plains of children; they are beasts and heroes and single beacons like the lonesome wise. Around one, stationary, the rest revolve, stately. And then there is majesty over the dead land.

Palmer guides the Volvo off the road to a gas station. He steps out while the car is serviced and stands by the door and leans on the roof. Stiff and numb, he stretches and yawns. His arms feel very heavy.

Janus gets out on the car's other side and looks around. His mouth gets tight, and his lips get thin. He breathes quickly, and his breath forms quick white puffs in the air.

Palmer watches him.

"Well," Janus snorts. "Getting ready for more of my big story?"

"Yes."

"Okay. In a while, I guess." He puts his hands in his pockets, hugs his arms to his side, and shivers. "Can you wait?"

"I'll try."

"Ha. Yeah."

"It's a funny idea," says Palmer. "What was her name?"

"Which?"

"The girl you bet on."

"Oh." Janus turns to him, bouncing on his toes against the cold. He winks once wickedly.

"Mary," he says.

Palmer starts, shocked at first, and suddenly—before he has time to think: It is a common name—he is jealous. And he thinks: It is a common name, and he is jealous still, and then feels foolish, too, and then just that, and then weary, and then weary to the bone.

He pushes the car keys across the roof at Janus.

"Here," he says. "You drive awhile."

He gets back into the car and lets his body sag against the seat. His eyes slip shut. He hears the clink of keys; he hears the engine turn. The engine roars. He feels the car start moving, senses it pulling away from the station lights. He feels it travel faster, faster yet. He sleeps and dreams he feels it: moving, with a steady rhythm, into the midnight and the bleak plains.

## *Wednesday, December 21*

# · 13 ·

In sleep, Palmer curls up on the car seat. His head hangs down, his wrists cross on his belly, and his knees bend almost as high as his chest. His jaw is dropped slack, and his face looks gruesome. His body looks little and frail and weak.

He has never been very strong, in fact; he has never had any cause to be. He was always clumsy and poor at sports. He was never violent—he had no chance—and if he sometimes has known an envy of killers, it has spent itself in daydreams, and he has let it be. He has had no women to build his muscles for, because he's proud and ugly, and he can't talk well. Girls find his eyes too desperate, too greedy. So he's still a virgin.

And his body looks frail, is frail and weak, and when he stirs—for he is waking now—it is almost like an infant stirring, like an infant or an old man stirring; his thin arms stretch and he murmurs and he yawns. He opens his eyes halfway.

Things look foggy to him: yellowish brown, overlaid with a strange, pure gold. Into a dark distance two beams of light stretch like rickshaw poles, and they move, and a rhythmic, vital motion chases after, always behind.

A cold wind passes him, brings him to. He bolts up, peers through the windshield, and sees the highway rushing at him. It whips to the fender, is swallowed beneath, comes faster and faster and faster, and he turns and looks out the window, and the night's out there, flashing by in a great, cold whirl, going faster and faster and too fast now, and he turns . . .

Janus is at the wheel, leaning forward, leaning on the gas. His eyes are dreamy and bright and mad. His mouth is open, and from his mouth a steady patter dribbles, as fast as the car, lost in the patter of the engine and the wind.

Palmer is terrified, but his thoughts are very clear. He speaks in a voice that is calm and stern.

"Janus," he says. "The law."

At first, the car speeds on. Then Janus blinks, and his eyes jack open wide. He grips the wheel tightly, eases off the gas, and the Volvo slows.

Sighing, Palmer leans back against the seat.

*Ah.*

Yes.

*Brilliant, Higgs.*

So you see, Smedley, we are now not only assured that our talkative friend is, in fact, running away, we have discovered part, at least, of his motive for doing so: the police.

*BUT HOW IN THE NAME OF ALL THAT'S WONDERFUL? . . .*

Elesmedley, my dear mentry. I observed the signs. Consternation, overanxiety, panic, perturbation, eagerness, repression. Put them all together, they spell "Copper."

*BUT HOW IN THE NAME? . . .*

Oh, yank my crank. We have now only to determine why

the police are after him. Is he witness or party to the crime? Was it a precipitate instant or a cupiditous occupation? A vagary of youth or a loathsome degradation of the very name of man?

*I . . . I really . . . Could you repeat the question? Just from the part about Cupid . . .*

The question is, batter-brain, are we merely transporting a boy who has caused a bit of understandable trouble in his hometown, or? . . .

*Oh, I see! Or are we traveling with a desperate fugitive?*

Pardon?

# · 14 ·

"Pull over," says Palmer. "Pull into the diner."

Janus steers the car off the highway, up to the diner without a word. They go inside, they sit and feed, they look out the window and into their plates, at their food and into the night, all in silence.

And Palmer is thinking: Is it dangerous then?

And Janus sits sullen and quiet, smoking. He seems very tired.

And Palmer is thinking: Well, now. Well, well, well. Well now.

And after a while Janus seems to rouse a little. He starts to fidget, to drum his fingers on the table, to smoke more cigarettes more often.

And Palmer is thinking.

And Janus says, "Well, you ready to head on out?"

"No," says Palmer a little breathlessly. "Let's rest."

Janus rattles his knuckles on the table.

"There's rain coming," he says. "And it's cold enough for snow. I saw some yesterday up in the mountains."

"Really?"

"Yup."

"Mm."

"So I think we better get on the move."

"Well," says Palmer, "let's rest awhile."

Janus lights another cigarette and blows the smoke against the window, where it mushrooms out and curls away.

"So, uh . . ." Palmer says.

"What?" Janus looks at him. His broad, bare country face is haggard.

"So—what about your story?"

"Oh. Yeah. Yeah. Sure." He rubs his eyes with a massive hand. "Okay. Okay now. Let's see . . ."

Palmer relaxes, settles back. He passes a finger up over his beard, to his lips and holds it there, covering his mouth. He is watching Janus intently, and intently he listens as Janus speaks, and as Janus speaks in that lively rhythm, Palmer leans forward a little to hear. He hopes that with thought and an active ear, he'll pick the Chaucer from the Chanticleer, whom we last left, leaving, looking backward once at Jenny, and traveling off on his Mary way.

Janus drove south, from New York to Pennsylvania. The trip seemed long to him and vaguely hopeless. He listened to the radio. He sang. He whiled the time away with fantasies, silently. He imagined a rival in this wager, an adversary who raced him to his old flame's arms. He imagined the phantom's car, coming from behind him, pulling up alongside the Chevy and with a stiff jolt sending it into a skid. Then the shadow adversary shot ahead, and the race was on.

Pushing down the gas, Janus went after his nemesis, speeding. He gained ground, lost it and fell back, and, traveling faster, closed in again. At this point a real car showed in the distance. Calling it the villain, Janus pushed his heap harder, trying to catch it, trying to pass. The car, a yellow Mustang, was a good way off, and the faster Janus went, the more it seemed to pull away from him. At last, as at the first, he followed dust, gave up, and slowed the Chevy down.

"Good Chevy," he said aloud. "Good ol Chevy car." He tapped its flank, leaned back and sighed, and settled into fantasies of another kind.

He was deep in Pennsylvania now, and the land was deep in bloom. There were trees in the valleys and forests in the hills, all green, all set against an aqua distance, all lit by a white and silver sun. The colors of the world were clear and sharp. They bordered on each other without blending.

Following a map, Janus soon left the highway and traveled for a distance on a small back road. Far from the arteries of traffic, he passed by farmlands and by little towns, and far from even these, he reached a dirt road and turned onto it.

The road was rutted, and roots of trees grew up from the dust along the way. There were many trees, and they were lush and green, and their boughs intertwisted above the lane, and so the lane was dark.

As Janus crawled farther on, though, the foliage grew shabby and seemed to decay. The curving branches seemed to rot, and their barks turned gray in the dead tangle. Beneath the trees, on the dirt road, it was still dark, but the nature of the darkness changed. Jerking from a daze, Janus realized he was in the setting of the painting that had hung above his bed. He grunted and stopped the car. He stepped out, looked around.

Behind him he could still make out the path's first half, verdant, natural. But here and all before him there was no color, no movement, no life.

The big man stood, silent, and peered deeply into the eerie cluster of winter boughs ahead. His eyes strained against the dark, strained and saw: There was a wooden barn at the lane's far end, brown, like the wood and dirt around it, but lit by a single beam of sun, shining in a paneless frame.

He recognized the place, the light, stepped toward it, stopped—startled by the snap of a twig beneath his feet. But in another moment he squared his shoulders, and pitting his size against a waxing dread, started down the path.

He hurried—eldritch, preternatural seemed the dark—he hurried, and he was afraid. And sometimes, as he went, uneasiness, an aura of decadence, made him pause. But to stop, to swivel, to face, perhaps, some sudden evil, following, were more than he could think of, and the gloom, ahead, behind, threw him back, drew him on until he reached the barn.

This too, like the wood, was a ruin. Though all four walls were standing, all were sagging, atremble, fit to fall. Parts of the roof had already crumbled in, and vines, or what were once vines, had snaked up through the gaping holes, in search of light, and died.

Janus crept around the edge of the building, came to the doorway, and passed through. Once inside, he relaxed a little. He got back his swagger, and shoving his hands beneath his belt and shoving his tongue into his cheek, he began to examine the room.

There was a pale sunbeam stretched across the darkness here. There was a trough, brimful of green-black water, and there were large posts lying at weird angles on the ground. The place had been a stable once, judging by its shadows. Now little of that was left.

Janus walked through the room and came to rest beside the trough. He laid his hand on the edge of it and, as he did, considered where he might go next and, as he did, let his fingers dangle in the muck.

And—as he did—what felt like a baby's hand gently clasped his own.

For a second, Janus didn't move; couldn't. The little hand tightened its hold. Then he yelled, yanked his arm up, and jumped back, raised his hand before his eyes and groaned.

Ancient spiders and insects of decay had clutched and clustered around his fingers. It took him three hard strokes to brush them to the ground.

As he watched them scramble for hidden corners, he gagged a little, but it passed. He was a country kid and used to such things. He even began to laugh after a while, saying, "Little damn buggers! You scared me good."

And just before his laugh was done, he, laughing, turned and, turning, faced the leveled barrel of a sawed-off gun . . .

# · 15 ·

Pausing with a stagy chuckle, Janus shakes his head.

"Whooee! I near shit!" he says.

Outside, behind the clouds that have rolled on all night, the sunrise, under cover, builds, and suddenly, the vast dark span of desert sky takes on an iron shine that aches the eyes and dyes the dead land gray.

And Palmer is thinking: The bet.

*The wager?*

Aye. Let us consider it a moment. Let us look on Janus as he was. Let us construct a tale without a wager and look on Janus as he really was.

We go back to him on that morning he left college. It is done, all of it, done. He must have felt as if someone had erased his name and masked him, for in all the world, the wide world now, there was no one to salute him unexpectedly, or quote him in his absence even, or say, "That's Janus, who is this or that." I imagine it was frightening. There's no need to imagine. Is there?

*No need.*

His very manner was in the past. And he woke that morning to finally realize, to realize at last that the only woman he had wanted since . . . since . . .

*Mary.*

Yes, yes. That she, that Jenny, was beyond his reach.

*But he says not.*

But he lies.

*But how do we know?*

He told us he lies.

*But he lies.*

My point exactly.

*Still, we have no proof of this, I say.*

Trust me. I am undefeated.

*Not quite.*

Hm?

*There was the fabulous Adventure of the Empty Thigh.*

Ah. Solve that, and we're immortal.

*Aye.*

Yes, yes. Yes, yes, but at any rate, he wakes—what? Ah, he wakes to find his love is unrequited, and he soothes it in his bed alone

*Yech! Blech!*

and he's finally convinced, is convinced at last, to accomplish that which he long has planned: to return to a woman he once possessed, to a woman he might possess again, to a woman who knows his name, whose name is . . .

*Mary.*

Yes, yes. Yes, yes. Yes, yes. I put it to you, Smedley, that the only man he wagered with was the shadow on the highway: the man who has possibly outraced him to his goal and won the fair lady while he was gone.

*You're much too clever.*

You're much too kind. There was no wager, my friend. And if he says he is going east to collect on a wager, and if this is the story of a wager, and if he is going east on the run from a crime, might this not be truly the story of a crime?

*A confession.*

Yes. Of sorts. Buried in all this. And might it be that we are safe as long as we are needed for our ear? That, though I owe this man my life, I needn't pay in kind, if I will listen.

*Were I not a fabrication . . .*

"Come on. Let's hit the road."

Janus nods, slaps the table, stands.

The two leave the restaurant and run through the cold—the cold is increasing, though dawn has come—and return to the Volvo and get inside. Palmer, in the driver's seat, with shaking fingers, thrusts and twists the key in the ignition, pulls the choke, and turns the engine over. Soon they are moving along the highway, cutting through the prairie, heading toward the hills.

"All right," says Palmer. "So anyway . . ."

"Yeah, yeah. Where was I?"

"The gun."

"Yeah, yeah. A shotgun, make it. Double-barreled. Pointed straight at some of those parts of my body I consider vital to my continued entertainment."

Palmer laughs. Janus coughs. His face is pale.

On goes the tale.

The man who aimed the shotgun at him gripped its barrels almost gently in one hand while the other played dangerously with the triggers. He was an old man, small and twisted, with a square head and a face from which all ever noble had been deposed. His legs bent out unnaturally, supported him unsteadily, and even though he held the high advantage, he looked frightened and insecure in the dark.

He peered at Janus from across the gloom, and Janus put his arms up, peering back, waiting. At last, the old man spoke, his voice trembling with the rest of him.

"You—what you in here for?"

"I'm, uh—yeah, uh, I'm looking . . ." Janus swallowed without saliva. "Looking for a friend."

"Yeah?"

"Yes. Sir."

"Well, you ain't got no friends in here."

"Oh," said Janus. "Oh, well, then. Well, well, well, I'll just be going, won't I?"

He lowered his arms and made as if to move, but the man stepped toward him threateningly. Janus stopped, stood very still; the man took courage and another step. He had a pronounced swing-gimp, and Janus, seeing it, blurted out, "Mr. Williams!"

The shotgun stiffened, as if to discharge. Janus's stomach flipped. But there was no shot.

"Yeah," the man said. "I'm Williams."

"Well, hell, I'm Janus. Janus Quintain."

"Janus?"

"Yeah . . ." Then, remembering that guns and girls' fathers line the path to Heavy Bleeding, he whispered hoarsely, "Yeah."

Williams made a sad sound in the darkness; it was like a laugh.

"Well," he said. "Won't I be damned. I'll be damned, and all to hell, too."

"Are you going to kill me?" asked Janus politely.

"What? Aw. Nah. This thing ain't loaded. 'Taint loaded. Nah." There was a long pause; then Williams spoke, sounding flat and sad. "Good to see ya, boy," he said. "Come on up to the house."

Janus, his big chest collapsing with a sigh, followed the old man out of the barn.

In the comparative light, he saw Williams more clearly, and Williams seemed more pitiable seen like that. He resembled the trees around them—the twists of their limbs, their crackling motion—as he pushed through the woods.

Janus looked away. He remembered the old man as he used to be: not a giant, not ever, never strong, but never so much a wreck as now. Back in Illinois, there'd been at least a quickness in him, and a candle in the eyes, and joy in his daughter, Mary . . . Snuffed.

So Janus realized that he would not find Mary here, feared her father would not even know where she had gone. He followed the old man up a path.

The house now appeared ahead of them. Chameleonlike, it blended with its setting, gothicized by the tangle of branches curling above its roof. Something tenebrous, too, hung over it, and in fact, had Janus not recalled the object of his coming, he well might have turned, he might have gone, he might have even run.

But he went on, as children on a dare go on, conjuring up dishonor.

The old place, however, was not as bad as all that inside. It was crowded with well-kept furnishings set in an old-fashioned decor, and though the colors of generations had, with generations, faded like generations, it was good to find any color at all.

Williams moved with his awful limp into a hallway.

"Catherine." His voice was filmy and hollow. "Catherine," he said, and Janus shuddered, shuddering again when a voice returned.

"I'm here. I'm coming."

The football player turned away politely, examined the room as if with interest. He had bitten his lip over various knickknacks and was grunting at a few old photos when, hearing no footfall, some instinct made him turn around. And before he could keep himself from it, he gasped.

Mary's mother—a misnomer; nothing about her was fruitful—had entered, and she was a horrible sight. Not dark, but of the dark, she was nocturnal only as is the moon, her flesh so white it had the luminescence of naked bodies in the evening sea. Her brown eyes were sunken, and her mouth hung limp. And as she came forward, her frame seemed to crumble to a center of old and crumbling bones. She floated crazily across the room, like a bright beacon—in a night fog—with eyes.

Janus tried not to recoil. She touched him, and her touch was cold. She kissed him, and her kiss was cold.

"Janus," she said, "how good of you to come."

"Nice to see you, ma'am," he said.

"Sit down, sit down."

She lowered herself into a rocker, and Janus took a chair. Mr. Williams limped to a sofa and dropped down on it. The old woman started, back and forth, but Janus could not take his eyes from her face, that bloodless face that seemed not to rock, but to hover in a constant stream of motion, constantly away, constantly returning, without a rhythm, without a sound.

She had been lovely in her time and even past her time, had had a grace as good as beauty. Janus remembered. When he was a boy, he would see her pass with her golden girl of gold-red hair held up to her hair of yellow gold, both followed by the man with the broad swing-gimp, who had been incongruous even then. But now . . .

Laughter was coming on Janus. He could feel it, and there was nothing he could do. He pictured his vivacious Mary—"Jay, I'd like you to meet my folks. This way to the crypt"—and he coughed instead of laughing, and he smiled behind a raised fist. The old woman rocked. The old man grunted. Janus coughed again.

"I don't suppose," said Mrs. Williams, "you came here just to visit us."

"Well—harf—well, ma'am—horf. I did, huff, huff, I did sort of have in my mind to—romph—pay a call on your daughter."

"Aw, now, if that isn't a shame. Mary isn't here right now. Hasn't been for quite some time."

"We ain't heard from her in almost two years," Mr. Williams said without expression. "Two years."

His wife's eyes turned to a little window. It was very quiet.

"Dang this throat," said Janus.

"She was born out here, you know," said Mrs. Williams.

"No, ma'am, I didn't. Hoff. I thought she was born back home."

"No. Born out right by here."

"That's when we first saw this little place," said Mr. Williams.

And the woman: "Yes. That was when."

"Course it wasn't like this then."

"No, sir?"

"No, sir. Was a going concern when I first saw it. Might not seem so now . . ."

Poor Janus. Consumption, surely.

". . . but I come out here first, I remember"—Williams struggled to sit forward and clasped his hands—"it was just starting winter, and Kate here was nesting, and we figured we had time for a little trip to sorta . . . Well . . ." His voice trailed off. He shrugged. "We came out here, and sure enough, Kate says she thinks it's time. I took her to the hospital, but the doctor, he said it was gonna take quite awhile, so I, so I just went off for a bit, drove around, take a look at the country."

"He came running to me where I was lying," Mrs. Williams went on as she went on rocking, "saying, 'Kate, you should see it, you should see, just what we want, trees all over and a river by the back . . .' "

She stopped, and it was silent, and the dark grew as the sun went down in the silence, and the silence was big with her voice's cessation.

"Well, what'd you have to say to that, Mrs. Williams?" Janus asked stupidly.

She turned to him.

"I said, 'It's a girl, Seth. Baby girl.' "

Mr. Williams sat back again, and back again was his formless expression, his expressionless voice.

"Took me seventeen years to buy this place," he said. "Course—the river's dried up since then."

Janus raised his hand to his mouth, but the disease had run its course. He nodded. He stared into space. Mr. and Mrs. Williams were quiet and stared into space as well. In space were the endless valleys of the green and the endless red-haired youths of Mary; the gentle and faraway eyes—they all remembered her gentle and faraway eyes—and the child-smile, nothing like a child's, which remained then with the girl, with the hoyden, with the woman, which remained now with the mother, with the father, with the love, and watching it, each one wondered if he dreamed. They stayed just so for a long time.

Night came up to the windows like water, blotting the brown and the rot outside, making the room feel brighter and warmer. Finally, Catherine Williams stirred.

"You'll stay the night, of course," she said.

"No, ma'am, I couldn't," said Janus, standing.

"Oh, yes, yes. I'll put supper on."

Janus wavered, but there seemed no choice, and the house seemed tolerable with the fallen dark, and he did, after all, need a place to sleep, so he agreed. He went out to get his bag, striding quickly by the now black trees so as not to be afraid, and not afraid except for a moment when he thought the whisper of breeze and branch had been the whisper of his name. He paused then in the night, half expecting, fully fearing, her form to come to the hidden edges of the wood and beckon him into it, into its hand. He trembled—jealous, fair, and dangerous is the specter of a woman—but she did not come, and he went on.

Supper was served in the kitchen. It was a drab meal of a nameless meat from a beast that possibly never lived and possibly was living still. The atmosphere was oppressive, rolling back a little for conversation, but lurking at the ends of words, threatening the pauses. Even Janus, talking when he could of what he could, had fallen silent before the ordeal was over and sat, awaiting coffee, with a blank and stupid stare.

When the coffee came, he spoke again of Mary.

"So I guess you wouldn't know where I could look for your daughter," he said.

The old woman stared straight before her without speaking.

The old man said, "We ain't heard from her since she left college, Janus."

"She went to school then?"

"For a while."

"She left after a year," said Mrs. Williams. She was still staring.

"In Ohio," said the old man.

"Ohio," Janus said.

Mrs. Williams turned slowly to him, bored her grave eyes into him, and made him shiver.

"You planning to find her?" she asked.

"Yes. I'm going to find her, ma'am," he said.

She nodded. "I'd be glad of that. I'd appreciate if you'd tell her that we're still her folks. She can always come home whenever she wants."

Palmer is trembling as if touched by haunts. His hand snaps at his sister's letter. He touches the paper and clutches it tight.

•

"I'll tell her," said Janus. "I'll tell her all right. Don't you worry."

"Yes. I'd be glad of that," the woman said again.

"She was"—Mr. Williams spoke up suddenly, looking up suddenly from his coffee cup—"a funny little girl. She was. A strange one. Above things. Quiet like. Calm. I know, I know she was a bit of a tomboy later on, but as a little kid, I'm talking about, she was quiet. Like a—like—a queen." His brown eyes brightened: his bright voice dimmed. "Yeah—kinda like a queen."

"You must be tired, Janus," Mrs. Williams said quickly. "I'll make up the bed." She rose and left the room.

The old man and Janus sat alone, saying nothing. Until, with a queer stillness, Williams raised his eyes and into the silence murmured, "Like a queen. You know?"

"Yes—yes, sir," said Janus. "Yes, sir, like a queen. Yes."

It seemed a long time before the woman returned and led Janus away to his room for the night.

The room was little, a cube, indented at one corner so that all light cast upon the curve was cast again in shadows, long and angular, across the floor. The walls, painted yellow, were chipped and peeled and so revealed the bad wood underneath. And on the walls a neglected cross, a forgotten savior, and two framed pictures were all the decoration there was.

When Mrs. Williams left him, Janus fell wearily down on the bed. He felt sluggish, and he wanted to sleep. But as he lay, dozing, he sensed eyes on him, and he turned and he saw the pictures on the wall. Standing up with an effort, he went to them.

They were set together without art beneath a dull yellow light. One was a photograph, enlarged and framed, of Mary, with brilliant colors, true to hers. She was looking out at the observer, and her eyes, her green eyes, beamed and smiled, and her smile, her slight smile, was quizzical and kind.

Next to the photo was one of her paintings—Janus recognized the style right off. In the painting was a forest. In the forest was a clearing. In the clearing was a small lake, sterling and calm. The trees around the lake were spring's: regenerate; near budding; some near bloom. Their image was reflected on one side of the water. It mingled with the image of a sunlit sky, and both were marred by a small dark stain which fanned out, formless, from the calm lake's core.

Janus examined the painting well, thinking he would find its model soon.

But as he looked, his drowsiness increased. He walked, almost stumbled, back to the bed and, lying down, switched off the bedside lamp. He saw Mary's portrait, in the yellow light, shining, seeming to breathe in the light's ebb and glow.

He wanted to touch her. He could not rise. His eyes fell shut. He slept.

Perhaps he woke, perhaps he dreamed, but sometime in the night he saw the bedroom door swing slowly in. A figure or a shadow stood in Mary's lamplight, stood a moment, moved a little, entered in a while.

It came, with no sound but the drag of a limp. It came to Janus, to stand by him where he lay. Eyes wide, Janus was motionless there, and the figure silently moved on.

It went across the room, to the wall where the pictures hung. It stopped before the portrait of Mary and seemed to gaze at her for a time. At last, there was a small sound, like a small sob, and the figure wept.

Janus listened without stirring; then he shifted and grunted as if in sleep. The figure at the photo turned, and passed again, and left.

The gentle shutting of the door brought Janus up, and he shook his head to clear it, found it fully cleared, and chuckled nervously.

There was no place for him to look but one—and there he

stared—at her. His breath caught as she seemed to breathe, and now he saw it, what he had expected in the wood: a beckoning—the picture fleshed out, withered—a come-hithering, as kind, as safe, as was her smile.

And he knew he'd have to find her then, return to her in trysts, in time, come back in secret or a second life, gain her, like the summer, every spring, but some way have her back. He'd come from Jenny as from a sin; he'd come to be forgiven and recant; he'd come to let her know what he'd forgotten:

"You are my only, ever love," he said, and lay back, peacefully, upon the bed.

# · 16 ·

The long gray sky, desolate over a desolate land, lets down an even drizzle, then a steady rain. The sound of it, from a patch beyond the rearview, from a wild expanse beyond the eye, is empty and chaotic here. With a quick pull, Palmer switches on the windshield blades and sees the sheets of water burst into droplets, spatter on the glass, divide.

Janus sighs, relaxes, and leans back. Palmer stretches, pushing his hands against the steering wheel, tightening the muscles in his skinny arms. He is thinking, somberly, about the tale. There seems nothing new to gather from this part. Only the old lies, even the old lies cast away. For the wager matters no longer in it, and Janus loves her: a truer motive, if not the truth. And worse. Some sensation, some inkling of worse than this has Palmer wondering. Some inkling, some sense of an intimate theft—of his sister's letter, of Mary's name ... And worse. Some sense, some scent of even worse makes Palmer covetous, secretive, jealous, and and and, aye, worse.

*What, worse?*

The story, Smedley. The curious incident of the story.

*But nothing was wrong with the story.*

*That* was the curious incident.

*Aha! What?*

No clues, Smedley, no clues. And—

*Worse?*

Much worse, old friend. Clues forced down our gullets like worm's flesh from a mother bird.

*You mean . . .*

Exactly.

*What exactly do you mean?*

Janus has ceased to underestimate my powers and—ah, how near the truth come all great lies—has planted clues in a tale almost factual to lead us into false conjectures of our own. Deuced clever. Yes, what?

*What?*

Yes.

*Yes?*

What?

*Yes, what?*

Yes.

*What?*

Quiet, Smedley.

*Sorry, Higgs.*

Surely it must be obvious to you by now!

*What?*

Consider the clues so roguishly thrust upon us. One: a child, Mary, conceived in Illinois, but taken to a distance to be born. Two: Mr. Williams, incongruous in the days of his wife's beauty. Three—

*Green eyes!*

Precisely. The girl had green eyes when both parents

were mentioned to have brown. So you see, without conclusive evidence of his own, Janus has tried to suggest that something is not quite legitimate here.

*Namely—*

The girl herself.

*So, Janoose, you dare play patty-cakes with fate, eh?*

And worse.

*Worse, worse.*

Aye, yes, bloody worse.

*Aye worse.*

The bastard! He's insulted her!

"Yeah. Love." Janus sighs. "Love is—farting in unison."

Palmer's eyes, glistening, glare. It would be okay, it would be okay, if there weren't the constant, the grinning scam. It would just be hick philosophy then; it would be okay. . . if there weren't the baseness of it, the degradation of that—love—which, for life in genius or life in death, might be much to know of. It would just be falsehood without that, and that would be okay . . . if there weren't the arrogance, the arrogance, the arrogance which it's cruel to attack and stupid to swallow. Without that, it would just be talk, and that would be okay. If there weren't the low, mean words. Ah. Yes. There might even be some truth to it if it weren't for that. And that would be just fine.

If it weren't for Mary.

What a silence he would bring her if he could. Purity without weakness, blending without intrusion, bodies without flesh and a love to join the rended shards of God and make eternity. It would not be this helplessness, but a Viking motion of discovery in shades of blond. Unarmed but not unmanned, he'd come and across the vastness of a vision sail, to wile, to worship, and to wive the center of the liar's tale, the dream that keeps the dream alive, though he will be not our Palmer, but Greeker then. Unshirted, yes, unshirted, swinging some farm tool or other, say, an ax, say, a mallet, overhead, with a lanky Lincoln thrust to pound some country thing, some post, a fence post into the black mud.

They will have taken the drifter, Palmer, on: girl, woman, and boy too long without a man and never with such a man as this—this quiet, this taciturn, this mysterious, but the point being, man, but the point being this man, and, anyway, who will be driving in this post cause a man's got to pay his debts for the kindness shown him and just a roof and your good cooking, ma'am'll be all the wages I need, so he will be driving in some post, the fourth corner of a sheep pen blown down by the meadow winds before good spring came, and he'll fix it so no wind will ever hurt these good folks' home again.

When, out of the red and yellow of the just risen sun, her red and yellow hair will emerge, and she appear beneath it, come forward over the meadow like the bad winds, but good and carrying not havoc and destruction, but a tray of lemonade.

He will lower the mallet, pause, and, with a slapdash, man-hard hand sweep, wipe forehead sweat away and stand, watching her approach, smiling. Sadly. Full of mysterious sorrow. Yes.

"I brought you some lemonade," she'll say.

Christ! Will he be touched!

Or, "Thank you, ma'am. It's hot work," he'll say.

"Well, you just drink this and rest awhile."

"Thank you kindly."

He will drink, and she will turn her eyes to the grass demurely, searching for conversation amidst the blades.

"This is awfully kind of you, Mr. . . ."

"Higgs. Just Higgs."

"This is awfully kind of you, Higgs."

"Palmer. Just Palmer."

"This is awfully kind of you, Mr. Palmer."

"No trouble, ma'am."

"Mary."

Yes, yes.

"Mary."

Yes, yes, yes, yes.

"Mary." She will smile.

"Mary," he'll say. "A pleasure to meet you, Mary."

And she'll blush. And she'll say, "We've—we've been needing this fence a long time now, but since Papa died . . ."

Then a charming and an awkward pause. What a charming, what an awkward, God, it's charming, Lord, it's awkward . . .

"I . . . I washed yer clothes," she'll say. "I hope you don't mind."

Christ! Will he be touched!

Or, "You didn't have to do that. But I reckon they could stand for a wash."

She'll giggle. "They were powerful dirty."

"I imagine. I've come a long way."

"They're a good white now."

At this he will surely grin and, hey, let their eyes catch then in a moment of understanding and courtship, and again, then, will her eyes turn down.

"Dinner [or whatever they call lunch]'ll be ready soon," she'll say shyly. Dinner, yes. "Come on back to the house."

And suddenly she will turn, her white dress spinning into its own accordion pleats and with a half-girlish half run go from him . . .

"Hey . . ."

. . . into the grass . . .

". . . can't we . . ."

. . . through the fields . . .

". . . I mean . . ."

. . . full-bodied . . .

". . . speeding . . ."

Palmer yields.

"What? I'm sorry."

"No, hey," says Janus, grinning. "Didn't mean to intrude. It's just if we move any slower, we'll be going backwards."

"Mm."

"Not that I mind traveling like a turtle to the death house, you understand. But at this rate I coulda walked. Hell, at this rate I coulda stayed home."

Yes, yes. Yes, yes, thinks Palmer.

"I don't know. Me, if I was getting such pretty letters from my sister, I'd be doing ninety, no stops on."

Palmer doesn't answer. He grits his teeth.

"Hey," says Janus. "She married, your sister?"

"Yes."

"Yeah. What's the lucky fellow's name?"

"Uh—Richard."

"Richard, huh? She like him?"

"She's married to him."

Janus laughs. "Well, now, in my experience that doesn't always count for a whole whomping hell of a lot."

Palmer shrugs.

"I mean, some fellows, you know, they'll pick them out a nice little girl and just mess up everything, shit for beans, to lay their hands on her, get her all panting for them so they can slobber all over her. Then again, maybe this Richard's a handsome devil and . . . Yeah? Is he?"

"A beaut," Palmer says. "The single eye puts you off at first, but once you get used to it being smack in the center that way, he's just like any other dwarf."

Janus's mouth falls open, empty for a moment, and after a moment he says, "Do tell. And how'd she land a catch like that?"

"Anchovies, good buddy," says Palmer. And Janus lets loose his flat, grand laughter, the laughter without echo, filling nothing but his mouth.

"You're catching on, son," he says. "You are surely catching on."

"Am I?" says Palmer. Thinking: You don't know, boy.

*He doesn't know.*

Were I not a moral man, the lovely things that I could do.

*Virtue blushes!*

Lies? Tossed over my shoulder like stones, good buddy, blossoming into a new race of travesties, perpetrating purple evils with a smile.

*Ah, yes. These minor-league villains! Such forgivable little bores.*

Not me. I'd do it with a black flair, purely.

*No fate, no father.*

Not a grain of sand for me. I'd choose, I would—doing what I wanted, wanting what I chose, back and back to some mustache-twirling essence of universal nastiness from which I'd draw my blood. Ooh, I'd be Satan!

*Fouler than eternity!*

Were I not a moral man.

*Hem.*

"Reminds me," Janus says. "I ever tell you bout when I was working on a fishing boat out West . . . "

"Yes," says Palmer.

"What, about the gulls?"

"Yes."

"Oh, well, this is different, I was gonna tell you bout this salmon run we made . . . "

And he begins, but not for Palmer since, for Palmer, the hoisting sea lies flat, the great blue water's green, more like a pasture than the deep, and on it, billowing like a sail, no boat, but Mary's dress, as Mary seems to float, though she'll be running and he'll follow after, through the field, his stride long and the hammer in his hand held down and tapping at his thigh with each approaching step.

Sometimes she'll turn to call to him and laugh and beckon, but he'll just come on, watching the way her arms bend out and thinking nothing looks so vulnerable and such a wonder as a woman running. And he'll follow.

Soon he'll come around the bend of some-such, and he'll see the house, with warm smoke pouring from its chimney, spreading out into a broad mass, pronged and vaporous like an angel's hand and, like one, seeming to press down in benediction as it blows up and disperses, disappears.

Mary will turn again before the doorway, wave and, laughing, wave and, laughing, wave and, laughing, bend, her hands pressed to her apron, mocking, and he'll smile at her as he comes on, still striding, big and sure.

"You slowpoke," she'll call.

"Well, now, you had a head start," he will say.

Then, as the incense of the woodsmoke reaches both and as it blends with the freshness of the April grass, their smiles will fade, all laughter cease, as if all laughter on the earth had raised a finger to its lips, and he will look at her, and she will straighten, straighten, and her full breasts, bodiced and restrained, and her big or biggish hips, and her full breasts, she will straighten up, farm-woman strong, dream-woman soft, all woman and untraveled by a man, and he'll want her, no, she'll stand amidst the balsam and be lovely, but he'll want her, no, she'll straighten, and he'll want her.

No . . . this is the courtship of a queen . . .

And he'll say, "Dinner must be ready."

And she'll say, "Yes," not budging.

And he'll say, "How's about a quick one in the loft?"

No, jackass, what the fuck's wrong with you? He'll say, and his voice will be stern, why, downright parental, "The barn?"

No. "Let's go have dinner," he'll say.

And with a flicker of disappointment and a glitter of relief, she'll turn and run into the house. And he will follow.

At table. At table. At table, see, they'll sit with the mother and the little boy, observed, approved of by them, and they'll sort of, well, yearn, yes, a sort of attraction growing in their hearts, glowing in their eyes, but slowly, all must be accomplished slowly, in virtuous frustration and a virgin round, not as we murder, but as we die, proceeding to oblivion down our own trails. Slowly.

So at table, at table, Mama will tell the history of the little farm, the yarn of the, let's see, farmhand, Papa, saving enough to stake his claim or buy his claim or claim it and build his home with his own two hands, though those happy days, not told and yet suggested by the stoic mama, for the happy days are gone, for then—

The villain then. Yes, then, the villain. Let me at em. Let me at em, I say. He ain't seen the last of Palmer-just-Palmer yet, by wim-wam . . .

Or the villain's smoke. Yes. Yes. Eyeless greed and its venenation of the land and sea. The rich and their factories and their giant farms. That dried the river. That killed the trees. Till Papa-just-Papa, broken, just died.

Or something like that. He will have died. And Mary and Mama, and Mama and the boy, will need a man, this man, this taciturn and mysterious, but anyway, man, and they will take him on, and just a roof and your good cookin, ma'am, is all the wage I need, cause I'm to blame, ma'am, for this hyar tale of death, to blame, ma'am, for this yarn of greed . . .

"Can you keep from killing us?" he says.

"Say what?"

"You want to drive awhile? Just don't kill us."

"Why, sure," says Janus.

They change over at a service station and are off again, through the falling rain.

They have come to Colorado now. The wasteland's dust has hardened into stone, and before them and beneath them, mountains of the new stone rise. In the gray afternoon the gray rock glimmers, the road grows steeper, and the light behind throws long shadows unseen down the other side. The roads worsen, climb, and wind through the mounting cold of the mountain air. The Volvo's headlights bounce off rock and railing, flash over sheer deep drops to nothing and the earth. The rain begins to mix with snow, and then it is only snowing, heavily.

Janus and Palmer don't speak for a while. The night comes down, settles, and then, abruptly, out of the quiet dark, Janus begins his tale again . . .

# · 17 ·

Though the term was not yet over, the campus was quiet. Across the grounds, the busy somnolence of Dead Week—the week before final exams—had settled like a dew. Field, library, dormitory lounge—any nook where one might place a body and a binding—were occupied with students training empty eyes on open books. Talk seemed finished and, when it came, came quickly and from everywhere at once, bursting out of a bursting match, fading in a soft and vaporous murmur beneath soft, vaporous, murmuring smoke.

Since most colleges, and small colleges especially, look very much alike, and since people everywhere in every age break into much the same cliques of intellect, power, beauty, outlawry, and so on—as if a mass were but the outline of a single mind—Janus felt right at home amidst these people and in this place. He moved on the meadows and down the paths with hardly a backtracking step and was not long in finding the dorm he wanted, the dorm where the football players lived.

It was an old building, and small; there were only three stories to it. But Janus, climbing the stairs, climbed heavily, breathing heavily, hoisting heavy legs. He felt lazy because the day was fair, the air was balmy, and the sun, though bronzed with afternoon, still warm. Like gravity, the good spring pulled him down, and after every step he considered going back to bask in what was left of the light.

He was lazy, and he was tired, too. He had not slept well the night before, haunted by old man Williams and then visions of him, bothered by the revelation that he was in love, with a portrait or perhaps a girl, and taunted by the face of both, and something else he couldn't name, that scraped his fingers as it slipped his grasp, that seemed the heart of expiation for the days without Mary, for the women who were not she, for the simple time away.

He dragged his feet over every step until he reached the top.

Down the hall then, hands in pockets, eyes on open doors and other people's rooms, he wandered. The rooms were mostly empty, sloppy, the beds unmade. Books were sprawled facedown on tables littered with slanting pens, as if some shadow grind had dozed while working. But the people, the people he sought at least, were gathered in the lounge.

The scene there was also familiar to him. Hunks of men lay sidewise on soft chairs, fleshy legs hung over leather arms, chunky hands clasped over chunky heads, blank gazes fixed on walls. These were football players. They were studying.

They glanced at Janus when he walked in and knew him for one of their own. A man, clearly a commander, a quarterback, shifted in his chair.

"Yeah," he said.

"I'm looking for a broad," said Janus.

"Life's tough."

"Her name is Mary Williams. I heard she went to school here for a while."

The quarterback looked troubled, glanced at his friends.

"She's from Illinois. And then from Pennsylvania," said Janus.

"Yeah," the quarter said. He sighed. "You want to see Lee Temple."

"Temple."

"Well, you don't *want* to see Lee Temple. Nobody wants to see him. You want to see Tom Yarnell. But you gotta see Lee Temple."

"Why I gotta see Lee Temple?" said Janus. "He Yarnell's keeper?"

"No." The quarterback looked even more troubled, maybe even a little sad. "Yarnell was our quarter. Before me."

"He quit?"

"Accident."

"Like what?"

"See Lee Temple."

"See Lee Temple." Janus sighed. "Where do I go to see Lee Temple?"

"Down the hall." And the quarterback pointed with his thumb. "He's a shithead."

Janus shrugged, and the football players looked away, embarrassed.

"Thanks," said Janus, and he left in the direction of the pointed thumb.

Lee Temple's door was the only door closed on the whole hall. Janus knocked, and a stentorian baritone answered.

"Yes. Come in."

He pushed against the door a little, peered around the widening crack, and saw a portion of a messy bed.

"Come in!" the voice boomed at him.

Janus shouldered in the door. Inside, seated at a desk, was Lee Temple: something of an odd sight.

He was a very small young man, short and scrawny, his figure bent. His hair was already receding, his pale forehead already rising and already creased. On his long and beaked and broken nose sat a pair of ridiculous wire-rimmed glasses, and only in a lapse of light upon the frames could one discern the piquant eyes behind. They were the eyes of a good professor or an excellent king, of one of those Holiday Jews whose grandparents were chased from their country and whose grandchildren will be chased from this, but who nonetheless have settled in the interim, advancing.

"You are Lee Temple," said Janus with a laugh.

"I am Lee Temple," the small man's big voice said.

Janus came deeper into the room, came to rest by the edge of the bed, and sat.

"Have a seat," said Temple.

"Thanks."

The two eyed each other cautiously without speaking.

"You are not well liked," said Janus after a while.

"I am Lee Temple, and I am not well liked." He ran his finger up and down the arm of his chair. "But I am not entirely sure I couldn't have made it through the day without this information."

Janus laughed. The massive voice, the tiny man, reminded him of his father, and as he thought of it, he came to find he was not so fond of Lee Temple himself.

"Well, actually, I'm looking for Tom Yarnell," he said, "only everyone says I have to see you. Now, you got this guy locked in a cage like a monkey or . . ."

"Shut up," Temple said quietly.

Janus was jarred to hear it, jarred to find that he, in fact, shut up. With one hand he could have crushed the pip, but it seemed that if he did, the powdered bones, the mangled flesh might churn and bubble out the words "shut up"—and Janus would. It made him feel violent.

"Well, damn it, what's going on?" he said.

"Do you know Tom Yarnell?"

"No."

"Why do you want to find him?"

"None of your business, boy."

Temple shrugged.

"Well—I can find him myself," said Janus, and, standing, presented, but didn't feel, the threat of his great bulk, poised like that. He could see Temple running his tongue back and forth beneath his upper lip.

"You're right," Temple said. "It's none, that's true."

He removed his glasses, rubbed his eyes, spoke quietly, flatly, without looking up.

"Tom was a football player," he said.

"Yeah? So?"

"A very good one. Only unlike most of—you, he was intelligent as well. Very. He probably never would have gone professional. He probably would have gone on to other things, as they say. Who knows?

"Anyway, he had a girlfriend. They had a fight. The woman left. This is two years ago, I guess. After, oh, about six months, he went to find her. But he drove too fast. I guess he drove too fast and . . . "

Temple's eyes were vacant for a moment.

"Yeah?" said Janus. "He cracked up. So?"

"The doctors called him DOA. Later they called him Lazarus. He was in the hospital for a long time, and now his body's fucked up, and something happened to his head—blood vessels getting crushed or something—so he can't remember most of his life, and he can't remember yesterday. He gets a little better all the time, and by every night he's remembered more; only every morning it slips away." He paused. "And I'm his friend," he said. "I keep things quiet so he gets better faster. The school has been kind. They let him take a unit of classes every quarter. He can barely handle that. So—" Now his eyes came up at Janus, and Janus nearly turned away. "Why do you want to see Lee Temple?"

Janus stood, trying to think of words to fit the etiquette of the thing. Again he sat down on the bed.

"I'm looking for a girl named Mary Williams," he said.

Temple nodded. "That was the woman."

"Then I've come to the right place."

The little man stood and, standing, shrugged and, shrugging, said, "He won't remember."

"And you?"

"Don't know."

"I'll try him then."

"He's asleep."

"I'll wait."

"I'll wake him."

"Good."

Janus followed him down a hall and down a flight of stairs and down another hall. They came to a door directly beneath Temple's room, and Temple took out a key, switched the lock, and entered.

The room was in order, perfect order. There were many books on many shelves. They were all in their proper place. There were two beds. One was empty, neatly made; the other was a mess—the only mess in the whole room. Janus and Temple moved closer to it and saw the man beneath its rumpled sheets.

"Wake up, Yarnell," said Temple.

The sheet stirred. The man's eyes snapped open. They were brilliant blue.

Temple knelt at the bedside. He said, "Do you remember anything?"

"Mm."

"How much do you remember?"

"Nothing. A cyclone."

"And?"

"I remember a woman."

"Yes."

"A car on fire. Wind."

"The accident."

"Yes. She was strawberry blond . . . "

Then, as the eyes had opened, so the man snapped up, threw back the sheet, and sat there, naked.

"Enough!" he roared. "I goddamn well remember you, Templestein! You're a lousy Jew, and no one likes you! Stand back so I can spit!"

The two men stepped aside, and Yarnell stood up, scratched his jouncing genitals vigorously, hobbled to the sink, hawked and spat, and, spinning back, hobbled to the bed.

Sitting down, he looked at Janus, lifted a suspicious brow.

"Do I know you?"

"Uh, nope," said Janus.

"Ah! Good! Then there's hope for you. I am Tom Yarnell! Urinal to my friends! And you?"

"Quintain."

"Quintanovich! It's marvelous to meet you!"

"Thanks," he said, and taken aback by so many exclamation points, he let his hand be grasped and shook and dropped before he knew it.

"Now!" cried Yarnell. "Where was I? Ah! Sitting naked on my bed. Yes, well! Now what? Dress! Templestein, clothes! Don't make a cripple walk, man! Clothes!"

Temple walked to a dresser and brought out a shirt and a pair of pants, both carefully folded. He carried them over to Yarnell's bed and laid them by his thigh. Through all this Yarnell looked up at Janus. Through all this Janus couldn't speak.

He was staring at the man, at the figure of the man. He saw a devil's mouth surrounded by a prophet's beard and lion's hair disheveled over the sweet eyes of a saint. He saw deep white scars, covered but not hidden by the beard and hair, and a purplish patch on the throat, where some quick hero had punctured the flesh to let air in. He saw shoulders, which didn't hunch but tilted, so that the chest was lopsided, and on the chest were six small holes in two rows, three and three. And farther down, farther than it should have been, was a fish-skinned belly with a great pot. And farther still were the bowed legs. And Janus kept staring, and Yarnell watched him stare.

"Have you gandered my tits?" he barked suddenly, fingering the six holes on his chest. "Six of them! They stuck poles in me there to hold me together. Right, Templestein? "And they tell me—or do I dream?—I yanked them out and said, 'Here, these hurt. Take them away.' " He laughed loudly. His voice was as deep as Temple's. "Ah, well. I'll dress if it disturbs you."

"No," Janus muttered, wishing he would.

"Where are my jockeys, mocky?"

Temple tossed them at him. Yarnell stuffed his legs in them and pulled them up, grabbed his pants and did the same. When he'd finished dressing, he sat a moment, lost, it seemed, in wonder, lost, it seemed, behind a deep haze that had passed across his eyes. Then, suddenly, he was free of it, and his huge head jerked up at Janus.

"Are you a doctor?" he said.

"No. A football player."

"Ah! I knew . . . No, it was me, that's it. Right? Yes. Well, what do you want?"

"I, want," said Janus, speaking slowly, speaking as if to a child, "you, to, remember, something."

"Anything at all or something in particular?"

"No—I, want, you . . . "

"Stop talking like that, damn it! Templestein, you kike prick, who is this farthead?"

Janus smiled. "I'm sorry," he said. "I'm looking for a girl named Mary Williams. I heard you knew her."

Yarnell narrowed his eyes. "Mary. It strikes against metal. I remember—a woman. A strawberry blonde."

"That's it," said Janus. "Yes."

Slowly, pondering, Yarnell stood up. He hobbled across the floor to the bookshelf, leaned against it, tugging on his beard.

"Mary. The name does ring somewhere. Temple? Did I love her?"

Temple didn't answer.

"Damned Jew never helps," Yarnell said. "Mary. Maybe I loved her. Girlfriend, girlfriend, sister . . . " He laughed. "Or both. But why drag an old incest up if you can avoid it?" He stood for a second longer, but his mind seemed to wander from his thoughts to the books along the wall. He looked at them and snorted.

Then he looked at Janus, said, "You see these books? Legend has it I've read them all. I can't remember. I can't remember one. Sometimes I stand and look at them—look: Ovid, Milton, Horace, Homer. Sometimes I stand—this Homer must be Greek. Translated by an Irishman. Painstakingly, no doubt. Still Greek to me. And this one's a mystery—where is it?—this one: Keats. His work's so small he couldn't have been much—but I've thumbed it yellow, cracked the binding, tore the ribbon off . . . And over—here. This one. This one I nearly wrecked. I must've liked this Shakespeare best of all. But memory fails."

"You talk—you talk kind of like a book," Janus suggested.

"Mm. Yes. I'm told. So—" He came to. "Maybe not all of

it's forgotten. Maybe something from them—a thing of kindness maybe. Well, why not? Come on, Quintanovich! We'll find this Mary without this Jew!"

He went to the door, Janus following, but paused there and muttered to himself and turned back around to Temple.

"Mary?" he said.

Temple nodded.

Yarnell grinned and winked and snapped his fingers.

"Ah!" he said, and he and Janus went out into the hall.

With a brisk, rolling gait, Yarnell shuttled along the corridor, to stairs and down, to doors and out, and out across the lawn. He spoke to Janus as he went; to Janus or to anyone he saw. Without a pause, without a hitch, he snatched at women's breasts and rumps and shouted as they giggled, wriggled free. Outside, he laughed at the sunk orange sun, stared it down as if to see who'd go blind first, and always he kept talking.

"Football! Yes, yes! Yes, yes-yes-yes, I was a quarterback, I think, although I seem too big, but still, I think that's it. God! Days! What days! You, girl"—to a passing one—"hello! Hello? Sad creature. You can see me, though, Anus . . . "

"Janus."

"Gallant. God, you can just see me. Ha, football stars, right? We remember, Quintanovich! Right?"

"Sure," said Quintanovich. "And Mary?"

"And Mary was— Well, go slow, remember death and *déjà vu* are all the same to me, and Mary was . . . Shitseeds. But anyway, I had a pipe, and I'd read poems, and then I'd be on the field, and I was perfect. Perfect, perfect! And I can hear myself laughing—I had this big, booming laugh. Boom! I remember myself being . . . being . . . "

Janus's eyes were oddly bright; Yarnell's were dreamy.

"I wrote something," he went on. "Not a poet then. No, no, no. For the newspaper at school. And Mary was—on horseback. No, that was me. Ah! Come to the stables. That's it."

They went past the buildings to the backlands, which lay wide and sea green beneath the shadows of the afternoon.

"So!" Yarnell screamed. "Quintanovich! Anyway! What brings you here? That is the question. What are you after—do you remember?"

"Sure." But Janus shrugged unsurely. "It's just, you know, I ain't seen this girl—I mean, I wanted to see her cause . . . "

"Ah, Anus, Anus, I can see her face. Can't you?"

"Janus."

"She was very pretty, in a countryside way. Hmp, I really think I must have loved her to remember her like this. Don't you think?"

Janus shrugged again.

Before they reached the stables, which were in a small meadow beyond a hill, the head of a great roan crested, and the beast came forth, ridden by a tall young man.

Yarnell grunted and, shaking his head, began to mutter. Then he said aloud, "Cowboys."

"Hm?" said Janus.

"Cowboys, Mary said, and knights. Football players were."

Janus smiled as if he were trying not to. "Yeah, she liked her football player."

"No. Cowards, she whispered. Tristan at the gate, lance raised, passing from the white hands to the belle, gorgeous, impotent . . . "

"Wait, hold on, she said all that."

Yarnell shook his head. "No, not all that. Oh, for a man of peace, she said . . . "

"She did?"

"No. Oh, for peace, she said. Yes. She said, I just need a little peace, Tom. So that's why I . . . "

Yarnell stopped walking, and Janus went on a few steps

before he noticed. Turning then, he looked back and saw the cripple watching him intently. The dreamy eyes passed twice over Janus's figure, up and down.

"My God," Yarnell said quietly. "It's the fun house. Isn't it?"

Janus bit his lip, looked at the ground. "Yeah, sure, sure, listen, where'd she say all this? Can you remember where she said it?"

"In the water. I came upon her there. I was on the roan."

"Okay. Is there a lake nearby? A river?"

"Yes! Over this meadow and through those woods. My grandmother . . . "

"No, no. That's a song."

"Oh. Yes. Come on. Follow up." And he hobbled off, silent now.

The sun hit the ridge of the long land as they traveled, cast thick bronze beams, caused wide, soft shadows. They went past the stables and continued over a broad plain, heading north toward a distant cluster of trees.

When they reached the forest, Yarnell lifted his hand.

"Here. This. Here, there is—at least, I think there is—I'm almost sure: A lake's in there."

"Yes. There is," said Janus. "Where Mary was."

"I—can't remember."

"Well, let's go and see it."

Yarnell didn't move.

"Well?" Janus said.

Yarnell seemed to brace himself, to muster his strength, and then he stepped forth into the woods.

Past the branchless trunks of trees, the low light filtered to the forest floor. Everything was green—the startled green of a cat's eyes, the green of the new leaves that hung above the sun. The two men walked in single file down a path paved with humus, Yarnell leading, moving surely through the forks and turns as if by scent. Only once did he pause, just once to say, "We should turn back."

And Janus said, "Go on."

They came upon a clearing and, there, upon a lake. Janus knew the place on sight. Bathed in light more orange than he remembered, under leaves more full than he had seen, it was the painting in the Williams' house. He studied it. A fancy made him shudder. He glanced at Yarnell, who shuddered at his side.

Yarnell advanced to the edge of the lake, squatted on his haunches, and stared at the water. Again he looked dazed and perplexed, and he pondered.

"You know it?" asked Janus.

"Well," he said.

"And?"

"Quiet, man, can't you? I remember . . . Something. Something is there."

The sun got bloody as it neared the earth. The green wood turned a somber green. Janus, in impatience, paced. Yarnell tugged at his beard.

"Something . . . " he murmured. "My grandfather."

"That's the song," said Janus.

"No, no. My grandfather. He hunted bulls."

"Bulls? Hunted bulls?"

"I don't . . . I can't recall, Quintain. If Temple just were here. God damn. He'd know . . . "

Janus was exasperated. He threw his arms up, let them fall, and slapped his hands against his thighs.

"You came here on a horse, and there was Mary—in the water, right?"

"I met her before that. She was a painter."

"Yes!"

"I wrote something about her for the paper, here at school."

"And that's how you met."

Yarnell shook his head. The eyes that had been sky blue, as the sky grew darker, grew so, too.

"Perhaps," he said. He looked down at his fingertips.

"This hand, this mangled hand . . . " And almost tenderly he slipped one hand into the other, while Janus looked on, breathless.

Then, suddenly, Yarnell's eyes widened. Then, suddenly, he rose. He raised one arm, pointing straight ahead; one finger lifted from his hand and pointed straight ahead, at the lake, at the lake's center.

"There," he whispered, an awful look on his face. "There she is."

Janus trembled, looked; saw nothing. "Come on, Yarnell."

"She's down there. Yes. She was drowned there. Yes. She was dead there. There she died."

The sun sank completely.

# · 18 ·

Yarnell stood in his room again, by his books again, his fingers on them, sliding from a binding to a binding to another, down the line.

Janus sat gloomily on a bed. Both beds now were neatly made.

After a while Yarnell looked up, reached up, and pounded his palm on the ceiling. White plaster fell. A moment later Lee Temple came into the room.

"You knocked?" he said in his great baritone.

"The girl's dead, isn't she?" said Yarnell.

"You say so every day. Or every day you go out to the lake."

"But is she?"

"What do you remember?"

"Tell me, man."

"What do you remember?"

Yarnell was quiet for a long time. He seemed suddenly

weary. Slowly he raised his palm before his face, and again he slipped one hand into the other, gently.

Janus stood up, excited. He looked at Temple.

"That. He does that. Why does he do that?"

Temple shifted his feet. "I don't know."

"I think," said Janus. "I think—see—I think that means she's alive."

"As I said, I really don't know. He says she died. But then, he also says his grandfather hunted bulls."

"That's right," said Janus. "What's that about?"

Temple shrugged. "One of his grandfathers was a Polish tailor. A Jew."

"Dead in a sad era at the sad hands of sad men," intoned Yarnell. "Devils we missed believing in by seconds."

"As he says. But there is something else."

"What?" said Janus.

"On the wall. A painting."

Janus looked. "It's one of Mary's."

"Yes," said Temple. "Mary's. It came just before the accident. By mail."

"Where from?"

"From Indiana."

"Indiana," said Yarnell dully, winding down. "I remember a fire. A cyclone of wind. Indiana. That's where."

Janus glanced at Temple. Temple nodded. His voice was sullen.

"Yes."

"Then she is still alive," said Janus, growing more excited. "See, that's what it is—what he does with his hands—it's her hand taking his hand, like she—well, like she was at his bed when he was hurt."

"Possibly," Temple said.

"Well, she didn't drown in that lake anyhow." Janus thought about it for a moment. "All right," he said. "Let's see this painting here."

He moved in close to it. The others crowded at his back. They looked upon the scene.

It was just a picture of a room in a house. The house was ruined; the room was old. The room was dark and strung with cobwebs. The cobwebs hung from broken beams. There didn't seem much else at first. But as Janus looked on longer, the perspective of the painting changed. Through some trick of the artist the room turned into a pit, and in the pit, the beams, the cobwebs were transformed, becoming figures, almost human, human, yes, entwined, enmeshed in smoke and smiles, in carnal smiles, in swirled ice, hungry eyes—it was a portrait of a party, of a great hole filled with people, of people spouting laughter, of laughter, endless and oppressive, without delight.

Janus grunted and turned away.

"You know this place?" he asked Yarnell.

"No." Yarnell shook his head, shut his eyes. He looked very tired and very pale.

"Are you sure?" said Janus.

"I don't know." He went to the bookshelves, leaned against them. "I'm through," he said.

Pivoting swiftly, Janus paced to the wall, paused, and then returned.

"All right. All right," he said. "You had your crash in Indiana, right?"

"Mm." Yarnell yawned. "Yeah."

"Where?"

"Don't know."

"A city?"

"Six."

"What?"

"Six."

"The exit?" asked Janus. "The highway? What?"

Yarnell started moving his finger from book to book, from binding to binding, again. It came to rest this time on

Ovid's *Metamorphosis.* He looked vacantly at the volume. Something seemed to sharpen in his mind, but when he spoke, his voice was thick and sleepy.

"You see these books?" he said. "Legend—legend has it—I've read them . . . All."

"Yeah," said Janus. "Sure." And he stamped to the door, stiff-armed it back, and stepped out into the hall.

He stopped there, hands on hips, and hung his head, considering. The trail was dead. He'd lost her. He cursed. Indiana was not a big state, but a state too big to drag by inches. To search for sixes on so many roads . . .

"I can't. I can't," he muttered, like a miser to his debts. "I can't."

As he spoke, he resolved to take the nearest route to Indiana, to find an exit on it numbered six, and to check it out. He felt that he must hurry. Now, in his helplessness, he had to rush. He had to move swiftly and find that spot where the football player crashed—where she had come to him, where she had come and cared for him, where she had laid a snow hand, healing, into his. He had to move swiftly—her care, her pity, her love belonged to him, were his alone, by rights. He had to find her, swiftly. If she was underneath the lake even, even if underneath the lake were hell, he had to lie and smile and charm his way right through the gate and walk her out alive without a backward glance . .

But it was impossible. The trail was dead. He'd lost her. He cursed.

Raising his eyes, he saw Lee Temple standing beside him, looking at him strangely.

"He's asleep," said Temple.

"I'll find her," said Janus.

"I doubt it," said Temple, and started walking down the hall.

"Hey!" Janus yelled.

Temple stopped, turned around slowly.

"Yes?"

"Mary."

"Yes?"

"And Yarnell."

Temple said nothing.

"Did she love him?" Janus asked.

Temple said nothing a little longer. He seemed to wonder what to say. Then finally he smiled a bit, said, "Go to hell."

And walked away.

"Idiot."

"Hm?"

"Idiot," says Palmer.

"Yeah. Danged Jew."

"You, I mean."

"Me?" says Janus. He is driving quickly on the snowy road, taking the high cliff turns by inches.

Palmer doesn't notice.

"Sure, you," he says. "The guy knew where she was."

"Yarnell?"

"Temple. You should have asked him."

"Temple?"

"Sure. He knew the painting came from Indiana. There must've been a postmark or something, a return address."

"Why, dog my cats! I never thought of that," says Janus.

"So you lost her."

"Well, now, the story ain't done yet. You gotta wait for the next installment."

"But did . . . shit."

Palmer turns to the window. He sees the snow fall, heavy as the night, and the night is deep as snow. The white, the endless white, lit by the Volvo's headlamp, glows. The car is traveling quickly. Palmer doesn't notice still.

He is angry. He is sad. She is lost—he knows it. How, even in a lie, can Janus find her now? All that land and just that spot, that little spot where Yarnell crashed, where love seduced the beauty down to death and Mary came for him, cared for him—he sees it: sees the ivory hands on open wounds, the moaning men, too young to die. He sees the women weeping, as Ezekiel did, and sees, as he did, bones fleshed by instruction to the wind. She is lovely, Mary, lost there—perhaps remaining as the dead depart and lost forever, as Yarnell says. But Janus should have asked at least. For Temple knew. Sure, Temple knew. Sure, of course, he did. How could Janus be so stupid not to ask him?

*Ah, my friend.*

Hm?

*Don't take the liar for a fool.*

Palmer lifts a finger to his lips and puffs on it. Janus did ask him? Sure he did. Of course he did. Me, I'm dumb. It's just some new diversion. But it's a sloppy one. Why? Because he threw it in without thinking. Why? Because he was in a hurry. Why? To divert me. Why? Because . . . Because . . . Because he slipped, that's why. Not slipped but put in some portion of the true story he didn't fully understand. Then, sensing it was dangerous, he tried this gambit.

*You scintillate, my good fellow.*

And the only part, the only part he couldn't understand was:

The bull. The grandfather who killed a bull. Obviously not a true story. Obviously something half remembered, culled from the pages of his books and half remembered. And that's what Yarnell was looking for, with his finger moving from book to book and coming to rest, at last, at last on . . .

*Ovid.*

Aaaah! He truly slipped then. That's my clue. So let's

see: Theseus slew a bull. And had a son. But was the son a sire?

*And did son sire son?*

And then there's Hercules . . . Burned, though, wasn't he? Heaven-taken, saintlike. Yes. But godlike left a mortal son who manlike may have had a son who sunlike may have run the gamut of the winter months to grapple with a Taurus in the May sky . . . Christ! Who can keep an Attic lineage straight? Gods fucking gods. Men fucking men. Gods, men; men, girls; girls, gods . . .

*Hey, wait.*

Fuck, fuck, fuck.

*And he didn't say his grandfather killed a bull . . .*

Hey, wait . . .

The car's rhythm ceases. It is not on the ground. It is raised in full, in silence, in a deadly skid. The tires turn on nothing. One flies out over the edge of the cliff, and the whole body tilts with it and tips.

But the spin keeps on, and the wheel rides back, and the car is on the road again, still turning. It comes full around. Still turning, it starts sliding, backward, down the highway's slope.

The lights of Denver are down there, hidden by the snow, shown in the snow as a peaceful gleam, not far away.

The car flies out across the lane and slams into the mountainside. A window in the rear collapses, shatters, glass hunks chinking down.

Palmer is thrown against the dash. His nose hits first and breaks. His body slumps, falls halfway to the floor, remains as in suspension, curled. A drop of blood appears upon his forehead, rises and begins to drip, runs in a trickle down his cheek, and disappears inside his beard.

The car, stopped for a moment by the blow, begins to drift again, backward, down the hill, along the mountainside, toward the cliff.

# · 19 ·

Palmer raises his head and sneezes. Blood bursts from his nose and mouth, spattering on the dashboard and his face. His head sinks down again.

Somewhere, at some distance, in some place indifferent and beside himself, he hears a voice, a whisper or a shriek, say, "God damn . . . God damn . . . God damn . . ."

But the sounds are nothing in the dark he is, in the violet dark around him which he also is, which is deep as the night is deep, black as the snow is white, peaceful as a plain of hands, healing . . .

"God damn . . . fucking God . . ."

And he wants to know the deeper darkness he is not, for it's warm here, wet, so wet, so warm, too wet almost, too wet, too warm . . .

Palmer lifts his head once more. The blackness mellows to a dull sea green. The blackness disperses, or changes really, in kaleidoscopic fashion, around a central point of light. He sees.

He sees, a little fuzzily at first, the windshield, thickening with snow. He turns. He sees the steering wheel. He turns. He sees Janus as through a fog, making funny gestures, making funny faces, and he hears "God damn ... Fucking car, fucking God ..."

And the funny gestures seem more like panic; the silly faces look like fear.

"Hel-lo," says Palmer thickly. "What's ... wrong?" Someone's teeth are chattering, he thinks; not mine.

"The car's dead; brakes don't work. We're starting to drift," says Janus.

Palmer laughs; it sounds like a child being dropped down a well.

"Man, take hold!" Janus yells.

"Wha?"

"Take hold."

"My ears ring."

"God."

Hmmm. Palmer whiffs hysteria, blood, vinyl, and the bright cold air coming in through the broken window. It's kind of like a sound, he thinks, but soft, no?

*No.*

Like a nightingale.

*No. It is the lark.*

The night. The nightingale. A sweet name.

*Swell. But it's the lark, I'm telling you.*

Nightingale.

*Lark.*

Oh, all right, motherfucker: lark.

He sits erect and lifts his head yet more.

"Okay," he says. "Okay. What's wrong here?"

"We're drifting backwards," Janus screams. "We're heading for the edge."

Palmer nods, smiling.

"I just can't get the brakes ..." says Janus.

Palmer feels it now: The car is sliding, speeding up, then

scraping against the mountain rock and slowing, slipping then again. He sees the mountain pressed against his window, sees it passing by, and thinks: Ah, then we will be killed. I see. And nods to himself.

He wraps his fingers around the door latch and pulls it back. He shoves the door. It springs out and bounces off the mountainside. He leans on it, wedging it against a jutting rock. The car stops drifting.

"Now get out," he says to Janus.

"It stopped."

"Get out. Give me the wheel."

Janus pushes his door out, jumps into the snow, and disappears. Moving his bruised limbs stiffly, Palmer crawls across the seat and climbs out after him.

"Where are you?" he calls.

"It's slippery," says Janus, rising to his knees.

Palmer stretches a hand to him and slips as well, thudding on his rump and sliding down past the car. He lies there flat a moment, then skitters to his feet.

"The tires," he says groggily.

"What?"

"No tread. Look. They're worn flat. We've got no traction."

"Shit."

With difficulty, Janus stands.

"I don't think we can get down," Palmer says. "If we can get her to the shoulder . . ."

"No."

"What?"

"We can't," Janus says, and again: "We can't."

They look at each other. Palmer's eyes are dull; his hair is white with snow. He nods.

"All right then. I'll bring it down."

"The brakes . . ."

"I'll bring it down," says Palmer. "Just get in."

Quickly Janus pulls the door out, gets inside, and climbs across the seat. Palmer follows, sits behind the wheel.

The car's as cold as the weather, the weather coming through the door wedged open and the busted pane. There's snow and water on all the seats.

"Close your side," says Palmer.

Janus yanks his door free, shuts it. The car begins to slide again. Pushing it into low gear, Palmer turns the wheel around and waits. The car does not respond, heads down the mountain, toward the edge of the road. Palmer guns the engine, hears the tires spin, then feels them start to catch and turn. In a frightening, silent skid, the Volvo rights itself and gains its lane. It makes the turn, still sliding, forward now and toward the city lights.

"Jesus," Janus says.

Ahead the air's gray, thick with snow. Small patches of it are aglow with the headlamps, but the road's hidden, and every yard's a distance to be reckoned in inches. Palmer steers gently, his fingers hesitant, his touch light. They pick up speed. Palmer taps the brake. The car skids halfway around and stops, flung out across both lanes.

"Jesus," Palmer whispers. "It's very bad."

He brings the car around. He tries to think of nothing but the road, the tiny stretch of road that can be seen beneath the lights, beneath the snow. He tries to look at nothing but the road. Sweat puddles on his neck, runs down behind his collar. New blood breaks from his nose and trickles down. He thinks about the road. The sole of his left foot itches. The road. The road, invisible, winding, deadly, snowy, how I bleed, I bleed, and if I lift my eyes, I'll die, God, God, hollow, bloodless, ignorant, a man might be, a man might be . . .

A horn blasts at their rear.

"Sons of bitches!" someone screams.

A car pulls out to pass before a curve, and Palmer, startled, hits the brakes. They skid. The other car goes by at speed. The Volvo spins in toward it. Palmer leans upon the wheel, turns to the skid. Their front end scrapes the other's rear. They spin on, backward, then around, to where they were before.

Janus says, "Close."

Palmer says, "Yes."

He moves the car slowly. He watches the road. He thinks of the road, of the road alone. Cold air from the broken window hits his shirt. His shirt is soaked with sweat. He shivers. Only the road, he thinks, but the end is distant, distant, distant, only half desired, as it is half desired to have not begun.

Some distance behind, a car is coming, visible at moments as a flash of light.

Janus sees it.

"One's coming," he says.

Palmer grips the wheel. Blood tickles hair inside his nose and makes him want to sneeze. Headlights come behind him from around the bend.

"See it?"

"Yeah," he says.

"Here goes."

The car approaches swiftly. Palmer's foot hovers, trembling, over the brake. Lights flash in the rearview, and the car pulls out, pulls parallel with the Volvo.

Palmer lets his foot down, very lightly, on the brake. The Volvo tugs toward the other lane. He turns the wheel against the tug, and the car goes out of control.

From the night beside his window Palmer hears soft and wicked, sexy laughter. Then the two cars collide.

There is a terrible shatter of glass. A woman screams. There's a moment that's only a second that seems to go on too long, as if it were happening over and over.

And Palmer thinks: Just a minute ago there was none of this . . .

The Volvo has stopped. The other car slows and stops. A young man gets out of it and looks out his rear door closely. He turns to Palmer.

"Sons of bitches!" he yells.

He gets in his car and drives away.

"Janus?" Palmer says.

"Yeah, yeah."

"Okay?"

"Yeah. You?"

"Yeah."

"What broke?"

"I don't know." Palmer looks out. "Headlight."

"Fuck, there's another."

Palmer hits the gas. The wheels spin, kicking snow, but nothing grips, and they don't move at all. The new car comes around the bend, comes for them fast.

Pulling his foot back quickly, Palmer throws the car into reverse. This time he softly eases the accelerator down. The car backs up, and Palmer rights it. The car behind them swerves, goes by.

"Sons of bitches!"

Palmer starts the car forward again.

"Seems we're sons of bitches," he says. He giggles.

"Seems so," says Janus. He laughs.

"Can't see a thing," says Palmer, laughing.

"Just one light, that's why." Janus roars.

"There's not much left of us."

"Enough for me."

"You shouldn't laugh, you know. We're going to die," says Palmer.

"Nah."

"Yes, yes. We're going to die."

"Come on here. We can't die. We're us."

Palmer whoops with laughter.

"You're right," says Janus. "We're gonna die."

He laughs. Palmer laughs. They stop laughing.

"Whew," says Janus.

"Shit," says Palmer.

"Yeah," says Janus. "Shit."

The car pushes forward precariously. Janus looks at Palmer, asks, "Can you see with all that blood on you?"

"Is it awful?"

"Nah, it's mostly from your nose, when you sneezed."

"God bless me."

"Yeah. Here, wait."

He pulls his shirtfront out and uses it to dab at Palmer's cheek and then beneath his nose.

"That better?"

"Yeah, thanks."

"Yeah."

In silence, they travel for an hour more—for five miles more—and no cars pass them. The snow comes through the broken window, makes them wet. Like sweat, it cools them, mingling with their sweat. More time, more miles go by, in the dark. The curves of road grow longer, and the angle of the drop less sharp. Breath like wind and breathlike wind beat against each other till they blend and blend until they seem to fade, leaving the car to travel for an hour more, for five miles more, in silence.

Another car appears behind them then, moves outside, and starts to pass. Palmer doesn't touch the brake until the car's rear wheels spit slush into the Volvo's windshield, blinding him. He drops his foot at that point and feels the skid, but only for a moment. There's a hard jolt, and the Volvo bounces back on course.

"What we hit?" Palmer asks.

Janus looks behind. "I think—a dry spot."

The car jolts again.

"Another one. I saw it," Palmer says.

"Are we down? We're down. Are we down?" says Janus.

They are down. The road's snow parts before them, shoveled away by a city machine.

Janus whoops. "You did it, double-ugly! You did it. You brought the damn thing down."

Palmer's nose is swelling. He is bloody. He laughs.

"I guess . . ." says Janus. The smile on his broad face drops. "I guess we're even all."

Palmer stops laughing.

"No, hell," he says. "You saved my life. All I saved was yours."

# · 20 ·

There's a blizzard. Through the black hours that lead to the dawn, and into the dawn, snow falls thickly. It covers the Denver streets and sidewalks, rises on them, mounts upon itself, gray all night, bronze in the early morning, swirling.

On the windows of a hotel room, flakes fall, stick, describing each a vast and intricate pattern before dissolving and dribbling away. Inside the room Palmer and Janus are sleeping, lying atop the made-up beds, fully clothed, freshly washed, snoring quietly. At intervals one or the other rises, watches television, stands beside the window looking out at the storm or through it to the outline of the diner across the street, or merely lies, staring upward, until he falls asleep again. At dawn both wake together. Janus lifts himself up on his elbows.

"Are the roads still closed?" he asks.

The television's on. A TV newsman says the roads are

closed. Janus sighs and lies back down, his hands behind his head.

"Are you going back to sleep?" asks Palmer.

"Nah."

"So tell me what happened"—not wanting to speak the name aloud—"about Mary."

"Hm? Oh. You wanna hear more?"

"Sure."

"You probably won't even stick around to hear the ending now."

"Well—anyway."

"Well," says Janus, looking up at the ceiling. "I just started making for Indiana, figuring to find the exit where Yarnell cracked up. Now you'd think there was hardly a chance of that. But then that's the difference between a story and a lie." He sniffs and stalls. "I was thinking—I remember I was thinking about my daddy. I ever tell you about my daddy?" One hand comes from behind his head and hangs before his eyes. Slowly it begins to move, describing an ellipse, as if it polished a mirror's face, as if it smoothed a page—and then stands still and stiffened, held before him, like a shield where his image—or a hero's—is reflected and revealed.

He thought of his father as he drove the road to Indiana, conjured him on the windshield in his prime. Most of what he knew about him had been muttered by the man himself, implied by him, and fleshed out at night in whispers passed from brother to brother, lies held low against sleep and the strap. Janus constructed for his father a childhood of weak siblings and mean dogs, ended early and on the lam, as kid Dad, depressed, skipped out into the Great Depression, hoboed, hopped ship, jumped ship in the Orient, wherever that was, and came back home in uniform just long enough to wave and go to war.

And what a war it was, that war. That good war, what a war it was. Hero Daddy did the gritty: hit the beach in short sentences, crawled over tapestries of the dead that carpeted the earth like grass, the grass like earth, dust and buddies strewn beneath skies of blossoming shellfire and rose blood. He caught his shrapnel somewhere—Normandy or his leg—and, adventure on adventure, met the nurse who would become his wife while lying prostrate, one of the best possible ways to lie, in a military hospital with his military wound.

And so forth, until the end of the war, when he became a policeman somewhere and then a sheriff somewhere else and then a security guard in Illinois and then an old man, stiff where his bones had broken—there were many places—and a hard youth bereaving him of an easy old age.

Belay that, though. Janus saw him as he must have been: light of all his fathers as they must have been, each with a war of his own, each war with an instant of perfect courage bringing in its wake a perfect peace.

And here was Janus. All dressed up and no war to go. No good war. No war worth his arm or his leg, as the old wars were. The villains were pitied; the good corrupt; the Fields Terrific, where men are made, just parks and gardens now. He could not be sure he was happy with that. He could not be sure his father was proud.

Belay that, though. His life was crammed with adventure end to end. The violence of football and the romance of his lost love, and the time he was the captain of a fishing boat somewhere, and that time he saw a dead guy on a New Orleans street, and the time he maybe killed a man in a Paris whorehouse . . . It was all in the way you told it, after all.

He was driving quickly, and the flat farmland, the heave of hills, the sometime lines of trees were blurred and blending all their seasonal mutations—this green, an autumn red, a dead white—in the floored-pedal passage of the Chevrolet.

He crossed the border into Indiana and came off the interstate at the sixth exit, as he had planned. He drove, more slowly, down a shiny line of shopping centers and bad restaurants, to a gas station, where he stopped, got out, and waited for a round-faced, pale-faced, pimple-faced boy to serve him.

The boy looked at the car and the license and Janus suspiciously and started to fill the Chevy with gas.

"New York, huh?" he said.

"Yeah."

"Big City."

"Not upstate. Country there."

"Really."

"Yeah."

"Just passing through?"

Janus shrugged.

"I might stay awhile."

"You been here before. Oil?"

"Yeah, I think it's low. No, never was. Seems like a quiet place."

"Boy, that's for sure. You're down a quart."

"Okay."

"Thirty?"

"Yeah."

The boy went inside, and Janus leaned against the car. He cursed. The boy returned with an oil can and a funnel, jammed the funnel in the can, the can in the car, and let it run.

"Wasn't there some kind of accident here awhile back?" Janus asked him. "Big blowup on the interstate? Bout a year and a half ago?"

"That right?"

"I heard it killed some kid."

"Gee. Too bad."

"No. wait. I heard they thought he was dead, but they saved him. Something like that?"

The boy looked at him, open-eyed, earnest.

"You never can tell," he said firmly. "The things they can do these days. Cash or charge?"

Janus bit his lip and gave the boy some money. The boy went back inside to make the change.

This time Janus cursed louder than before. This time he frowned and stared at his shoes. His last lead, his last chance, blown mile high as it settled in his hand. Like a bubble, just like bubbles burst. He kicked at the gravel. Bubbles burst anyway.

"Course if you mean the Yarnell crackup, there was a girl there probably did more for him than any doctor could've," said the boy, coming back with Janus's change.

"What?"

"Caused a lot of talk, that one. Real mystery woman. Sewed him up better than any doctor could've. Little Pete, he puffed up just like one of those frogs he catches cause he knew her. Even the doctors didn't know where she came from."

"Yeah?"

"Yeah, and you know Pete. He wouldn't tell."

"Sure," said Janus. "Good old Pete."

"Is that the accident you mean?"

"Yeah, sure. I bet it is."

"Well, I'd tell you to ask Pete about it, but he won't tell."

"Well, you know Pete."

"Yeah."

"Where do you think he'd be around now?"

"Who?"

"Pete."

"Oh." The boy laughed with a huffing sound. "He's supposed to be in school, ain't he? And that means for sure he's catching frogs."

"Yeah," said Janus. "Well, so long."

"Quite a thing," the boy said.

Janus nodded. "Well, so long."

He jumped in his car and drove off quickly. His eyes were bright. He hummed. He'd done it.

Well, well, well—was all he kept thinking—that's what it means to be a Quintain.

He knew where to find a little boy who liked to catch frogs when school was on, and he knew how to find a hooky crik, too: He would just follow the trees till they hid the water and follow the water till the water pooled.

He drove in toward the center of town and cruised until he found a bridge. He parked nearby and walked out on it, looked over the railing and down below. Clear water ran there, in a shallow stream, swift over the rocks, bright; ferric; sparkling in the midday. It rushed beneath the bridge and gathered, and widened, and deepened, and slowed, and pushed on, running beside the road and curving as the road curved, out of sight. Upstream, beyond, it came through trees to appear, murky and green, with white flashes of speed and rock and sun.

Walking around the bridge, Janus half climbed, half slid down a hill and, reaching the brook's banks, began to travel against the flow.

The mud squished, rose, around his shoes as he walked beside the water and under the trees. The leaves, the grass were lush, were in full blow here and were very green. Now and then Janus would pause. He'd listen, and what, for an instant, had seemed like silence would seem like the din of a city of small-life, trafficking in the river and its rich soil. He would listen to the water as it wound back and out of sight, as it glugged and burbled, swashed stones and passed, by and beneath the bridge, and he'd go on again.

The boy, Pete, was sitting—in the deep of the wood, where the creek collected in a flat pool broken by the tips of rocks—with his back on the bottom of a giant tree and his legs sprawled out in the mud. He was holding a small stick to which was tied a piece of twine which dangled in the gathered water, motionless. A quiet intensity marked him as he gazed steadily at the little rings spread from the water where it met the twine. To Janus, who stopped at a distance to watch, he seemed for just a moment more than just a boy; he seemed a thing of a Beltane solitude, profound, remembered, wished for, once possessed. Janus felt, somehow, he knew the child, though he saw him now for the first time.

He approached. The boy heard him coming and jumped up. Janus raised his hand.

"Whoa. I ain't from the school," he said.

The boy hesitated.

"Just walkin," said Janus. "Just walkin the stream."

They boy considered this, rather absently, and sat down again in his old position.

Janus came nearer, looking down at the pool.

"Fish?" he said.

"Yeah," said the boy.

Janus squatted beside him, picked up two stones, and began to rattle them in his fist.

"Any luck?" he asked.

"Naw."

"Too bad."

The boy shrugged. "Hardly even any fish in there," he said.

"Frogs, I bet, though."

"Yeah. Some frogs."

"Big ones?"

"Not mostly. Mostly little ones. Not good for nothing cept foolin."

"Oh."

The boy had neither raised his voice nor raised his eyes from the dangling twine. He was like a man with a book attacked by a boor, trying vainly to mumble back to solitude.

"I heard," said Janus, taking up the frog issue again, "that if you feed a little one to a dog, it'll stop him barking."

The boy shook his head. "Don't work," he said.

"Don't."

He shook his head again.

"Well," said Janus, "you can't believe everything you hear, I guess."

"Just makes em throw up."

"Does."

"Yep."

"Oh. Yeah," Janus said. "Bet that stops em barking, though."

He laughed, and the boy almost smiled, trying not to. Janus took a stone from his hand and skimmed it masterfully across the pool. It bounced seven times before it leveled to a patter that carried it out to the faster water.

"Course," he said, "if you could maybe get onto one of them rocks out there, maybe you could get in under the deep banks at some of the bigger fellahs."

"Can't," said the boy. "I'm too small. I'd drowned."

"Can't you swim?"

"Sure I can swim." He pointed at the pool. "There's mud on the bottom. Kids get stuck in it and drowned all the time."

"Oh," said Janus. "Damn." He shifted his position slightly and, looking out at the water, seemed to consider the matter deeply.

"I used to know this girl," he said after a while. "She could pull in more frogs in a day than you could count all night." He paused. Another boy would have protested: Can a girl catch frogs? Yet Pete was quiet, thoughtful, as if he'd had his faith in the rightful order of such things shaken. Janus went on. "Man, what she'd do—she'd go climbing out on a rock like that one there, no more of it showing than that, just the tip, and lie on it like a seesaw like, with her toes touching water, and then she'd drop in a pebble, see, and a big old frog'd come out from under the bark, and you know what she'd do . . ."

"Catch it right in her hand," said the boy quietly. "It would almost just swim into her hand and lay there."

"Hey, that's right," said Janus.

"She'd even pet it. And she didn't squeal about it neither."

"Yeah. Yeah."

The boy looked wistfully across the water at the rock. Janus looked wistfully at the boy. He didn't want to fool this kid anymore.

"I grew up with her," he told him. "I was her friend—you know."

The boy nodded.

"I know," he said. "The football player."

Janus snorted. "Yeah, yeah. That's right."

"You still play?"

"Some."

"You're good, she said."

"I have my days," said Janus.

The boy studied his fishing pole thoughtfully, then looked up to check the measure of the sun.

"You looking for her?" he asked.

Janus nodded. "She say I would?"

"No."

"Well, I am."

Now the little boy seemed sad, sad in a strange way, not a little boy's. Janus watched and wanted to touch him, to somehow make the connection between them graphic and complete. But he didn't. It would have been like passing a law against the damned—futile, reassuring, selfish—so he did not.

"She's gone now," said Pete finally. "She used to come here from Eddy's. She could catch frogs, just like you said, whole loads of em outta there. We let most of em go, just one or two we kept for racing, real fast ones."

"Is she okay and everything?" Janus asked.

The boy shook his head. "I think she was real sad mosta the time."

"Sad? Like what? She sick?"

"Sorta. I don't know. She liked it here"—this proudly—"she didn't like Eddy's. She was just kinda thinking a lot, I think."

"Yeah," said Janus. "Yeah. Well, listen, she talked about me, huh?"

Pete shrugged. "Sometimes."

"Yeah. Well, was she mad or anything?"

"Naw."

"I mean . . ."

"Naw. She didn't say that much about you."

"Oh," said Janus, crestfallen. "I mean, like, she mention that I stopped writing, like?"

"Naw." The boy thought about this for a while. Then he turned to Janus and said earnestly, "That was real dumb."

"Yeah, well," said Janus. "Yeah. Well, you make mistakes, kid. You can make mistakes for your whole lifetime in a second."

"Yeah," said the boy.

They both were silent for a moment.

"She ain't like other girls," Pete said.

"No."

"She's . . ."

But he stopped, and Janus let him. He knew about all that. She sang sometimes to you and held you to her blouse where nothing worried you but what she thought, and she'd be staring off so you couldn't tell, and it was all right. Not like other girls.

"Yeah," said Janus. "Listen. Where'd she go to? Do you know?"

"Not so much. She told me . . . she said she had to go and help the accident man. She never came back from there."

"Okay. What about Eddy's? Where's that?"

"Right on Center and Main."

Janus stood up. "Well, listen, if I find her . . ."

But the boy, though he said nothing, seemed to listen no longer, to no longer care. If he'd lost, if here in the wood he'd lost his heart to her, and her then, maybe he did not want her back on any but the wood's old terms: walking up the river as she had before, her white dress set against the trees, gold head bowing by the golden boughs; his own. At any rate, he turned his eyes back to the water, gazing as he had when Janus came upon him, when Janus first saw him and felt he'd seen him once before.

And as Janus walked away now, he felt the boy receding at his back, fading in a remembered way to a remembered point of distance in the lost woods.

# · 21 ·

Two rounded hills converged, or so it seemed to the eye, and at their juncture, a house stood, black, like a hole dug through the bright day to the universe. Janus drove toward it slowly, watching it, knowing that inside it was the haunted room Mary had painted. And as the road he traveled climbed, and as he closed upon the building, its features stood out in detail, revealing, in detail, their story.

Upon this site—this structure seemed to say—myriad dwellings once were wrought and raised, wrecked and ruined, their myriad histories leaving the myriad souvenirs that built the place in layers to its present state. The façade was small, the façade of a shanty, but before it, what once was a fine perron, blackened as if by fire, stood between the remnants of two Ionic columns, blackened, too. Behind, jutting at odd angles, was the bulk of a pink prefabricated house, plopped down, it seemed mistakenly, upon the rest, completing an impression at once lopsided and majestic, like a cretin's head.

The sun was now a late sun. It had taken Janus all the afternoon to come this far. He had gone to Eddy's first, a dark, empty cocktail lounge, very red: electric candles, cheap rug, red—red plastic seats with fake brass studs—a forty-year-old waitress in a short barmaid's suit, her eyes red. Janus ordered a beer from her.

"Whatever happened to the strawberry blonde?" he said.

She gave him his glass. "Don't you like the new help?"

"Nah, I like you. Whatever happened to the strawberry blonde?"

"Guess you're not around much."

"Just passing through. Whatever happened to her?"

"Melissa."

"Pug little nose. Good figure. Young girl," said Janus.

"Melissa."

"Yeah. Sure."

"Everybody knows she's gone. Been gone more'n a year."

"I don't come by much."

"I guess not." The waitress leaned against his table. "Anyway, she quit. Her beau got in some smashup, damned near killed himself; that was the last we saw of her."

"Too bad. Nice girl."

She shrugged. "Nice enough. Didn't talk much, did her job. Like she was too good for the help, you know." Then conspiratorily: "But you know what I think?"

Janus said he had no idea.

"I think she was running away from something."

"Probably the guy."

"Which?"

"In the smashup."

"Hey, that's what I think," said the waitress, as if surprised by a kindred, uncommon thought. "But she went to him fast enough he was hurt. We women are fools that way. She called once to say she wouldn't be coming to work anymore, so we figured this fellah was supporting her or something till Harve Perkins comes in and says he had to give her the rush."

Janus's eyes opened wide. "*The* Harve Perkins?"

"Only one I know. Runs the place on Fulton Street."

"Sure. Fulton and Sixteenth."

"Fulton off Maple."

"Oh. Nope, that's not him." Janus raised his glass to his lips and was about to polish it when he paused. "Know why I remember her?" he said.

The waitress lifted her chin by way of asking.

Janus looked at her closely. "I must've talked with her—Melissa—maybe all of five minutes. And I think I told her the whole lousy story of my life."

The waitress lifted her chin even higher, and when she spoke, Janus was sure he heard strains of envy and embarrassment running through her voice. "Yeah," she huffed. "Lot of em say that. But too good for the help's what I say."

"Well, thanks." He killed the beer and threw down some money. "See ya."

*" 'Rivederci."*

"Yeah."

So Janus went to Harve Perkins—the one and only Harve, truth told—who ran a shabby little boardinghouse not far from the center of town. The Harve was an obese gentleman with a face pale and pink by turns. He sat in his landlord's apartment, rooted, it seemed, to a cushioned chair, still as a frog in waiting, expending energy in nothing but his slow, laborious breath.

"Ah gave. Melissa. The rush," he said, in three separate exhalations. "She couldn't pay no rent. No more."

This seemed petty and unfair to Janus, but he hid his annoyance, shuffling his feet.

"Too bad. I wanted to see her," he said. "Know where she went?"

The Harve started blinking his small eyes rapidly. It looked as if he were blinking away tears, but he wasn't. No. It was just another facet of his ever-new personality; it meant he was going to speak at length.

"They built this shack. Up yonder there?" He kept on blinking. "Some years back. They built. It and it burned up. Father died, and the son he got some money. Built the house up better with it. Then he." Much blinking and a great long breath. "Went crazy. Shot his ma. Then hisself after. Nice folks bought. The place, built it up nice. Second fire gutted the whole inside."

The blinking stopped, and for a long while there was no sound but the heave and ho of Harve and air.

"You trying to tell me something, pal?" Janus said.

"Bums use it now," said Harve with one long wink. "Bums and the hoboes. I told her she. Could go there when I gives her. The rush."

"Where? Where is it, you—Harve?" said Janus, himself taking a breath to control his anger.

"Jest. Follow the river. Up top the hill. Can't miss it."

And Janus came to this house in this late afternoon.

There was a green slope in front of the place. He pulled the Chevy off the road, parked, and covered the final yards on foot.

He climbed up the perron, stood at the door for a moment, and knocked. The door, a very small door, part of the original shack, was soft and rotten to the touch. Janus pushed it, and it budged. He pushed it again, and it opened, and he entered.

First, inside, there was peace; first, he was sensible of an ancient, civilized peace in the place's atmosphere, as if the room, the ruined room, the room so full, it felt, of death, the room he came upon, had been most recently inhabited by self-sufficient, self-made men who'd sat at brandy, discussing cards, and left self-satisfied, and left their mark. It seemed so odd an image compared to the sight of it: No candle burned, no light but what came in the open windows shone on the fallen beams or the cobwebs on the beams or the charred walls—but still and first, there was that air of peace.

Then a stench—it took a moment—but then a stench blew up his nostrils in a draft and almost made him gag, and did make him gag, it was so awful. His instinct was to turn and get back to the open air, but he did not—it was, he found, a human stench, and so not overpowering, and not, in fact, incongruous to the peace which it befouled. But realizing this, Janus paused. And then he knew he was not alone.

For that's when the sounds came, or the single sound, for it was a single sound composed of many, as one might say the wail of hell and mean the tortures of a multitude; it was a sound like that. It was a moan, it was a million moans, a sigh, a thousand sighs, a shriek, one shriek that shattered, like the light on diamonds, met in something like the sun at diamond's core; a sound like that. It came from all around the room; it came, it seemed, upon the stench, upon the draft the stench was on—and that, too, was a thousand drafts, a thousand smells—and all combined at Janus and his senses, into one.

He saw the inhabitants of the house.

They were young, most of them. Most of them were men. They were languid outcasts, lower than despair; hoboes, as the Harve had said, so black from grime they blended with the walls.

Some sat, some lay, upon the floor. Some were silent, some were mumbling lowly to themselves, and others moaned. Sometimes two would turn, each to the other, stiffly, as if under a silent command, and they would bring their bodies together, men on men, men on women, women on women, and begin the motions of sex and the groans of it, deep groans, pleasureless, rising to a pleasureless peak.

All of Janus's flesh sensed illness, passed round the room like a warm coal.

By now he was used to the stench, and the nausea it had caused him had passed a little. He moved to the center of the room and stood. The hoboes took no notice of him, though for his part he examined each of them, looked from face to face to face, slowly, steadily, even as he dreaded one face rising, one pair of empty eyes pale green, one mop of matted hair, once red, once blond.

When he was satisfied she was not among them, he selected a young man seated by the wall and picked his way over the bodies of the others. The young man, his dirt-blackened head bent over, was engaged in rolling a cigarette, his fingers accomplishing it with great precision and purpose. Janus stopped to watch him.

There is an economy of movement in a vagabond. He has only two goals, after all: the creature needs—food, sleep, the working of the bowels—and, these achieved, the creature comforts—shelter, cigarettes, relief from fever (there is no relief), and traffic with his fellow. To this last end, the young man, finished with the butt, lifted and lit it, and, seeing Janus, offered him a drag.

Janus took the cigarette and sucked it greedily. He had never smoked a cigarette before. He handed it back.

"Thanks," he said.

With great difficulty, his eyes tearing, queasy, he knelt down on the stained floor. A boy, not far away from him, sitting in a pile of tattered clothing, began laughing and talking to himself.

"Uh—listen," said Janus to the smoking man.

The man's lips parted. He had six teeth. His voice rasped. "Eh?"

"Uh—yeah. Well. Listen. A girl—they tell me a girl was here."

"Girl?"

Janus choked. "A beautiful—a beautiful girl. She had real nice hair, green eyes—can I have another, another hit?"

The young man gave the cigarette readily, but Janus tugged at it so hard and long that he began to look nervous. Janus gave it back.

As it had in the woods, as it had with Pete, a sense of having seen all this before began to oppress him. The moaning in the room grew louder, lulled then. Janus felt very bad.

"More than a year ago," he said absently.

The young man nodded a few times, wisely, lowered his head finally, and remained like that, smoking.

Confused, Janus looked away. The boy who had been laughing and talking to himself had stopped. He was staring at Janus now.

"Hi," he said. "I'm Jimmy."

"Hi," said Janus.

The boy's face was very dirty, but he had blue, clear, innocent eyes, and his voice was high-pitched and young. Janus judged him to be no more than sixteen.

"They all go," Jimmy said, seeming to mean everyone, everywhere. "In the winter, they all go to New Orleans. Because—because it's warm." The boy spoke as if reciting a lesson. He ticked each city off on his fingers. "Then—when spring comes—they go, they go to Tempe. That's in Arizona. To Berkeley. In California. Then to—to A—a—Aspen. Co-lo-ra-do. Because it's cool. Then Ann Arbor, last of all. And they stop here—because—well, because the house is here. And—to see me!" And here Jimmy laughed again and clapped his hands happily.

"Crazy," said the smoking man to his cigarette.

Janus ignored him and moved closer to Jimmy.

"So you're here all the time?" he asked.

"I'm here aaallll the time," Jimmy said. "That's why I knew her. No one else is here anymore."

"No one else who knew Melissa?"

Jimmy looked hurt. He frowned. "No Melissa. Mary," he whined.

"Yeah, yeah. I meant that. Mary."

"Mary," said Jimmy, and then he stopped, evidently thinking very hard—and finally: "She was good."

"Sure. Sure she was," said Janus. He looked around him at the ragged vags. Two boys across the room were fumbling silently at each other's clothing. Soon they were moaning, too.

"What was she doing here?" Janus asked, half to himself, half to the poor young idiot, who was now sucking at the tip of his filthy shirt's collar. "What'd, she just stay here?"

"Oh, no! She did the most important things! Every day." Jimmy nodded portentously, sucking the tip. "She went to the Man, every day, the Very Important Man. She went right to Him and helped. Everyone said."

"Yeah," said Janus. "Yeah." His gaze kept returning behind him to the two boys, who were screeching with a furious stillness which reverberated in the deadness of their eyes. "But what'd she do here?" he said. "What was she doing here?" He turned back to Jimmy. Jimmy stared at him, a little frightened. Janus felt sick.

"She was good," Jimmy said again, as if this were all the explanation anyone could want.

"Sure," said Janus. His chest was heaving. "Sure. I mean, I'm just, I'm just kind of wondering, like. Like did she, did she do any of that?" He shoved his thumb in the direction of the two boys.

Jimmy did not even look. His eyes were wide, as if he did

not understand what Janus was saying. Obviously he had lived in this shack-mansion long enough to know what to ignore.

Janus, his anger and curiosity aroused now, decided to be subtle. He spoke to the boy quietly, coaxingly. "Listen, Jimmy, tell me, buddy. She do that? What they're doing there? She do any of that? Huh, Jim-boy?"

Poor Jimmy just went on staring, apparently trying to guess what answer would please his catechist most. He only wanted to be friends.

"Huh, Jimmy-Jim? She do a little of that?" said Janus. He could not stop.

Jimmy ventured a small negative shake of the head.

And suddenly, Janus, without knowing himself what he was doing, reached out and, grabbing the boy's soggy lapel, dragged him halfway across the room.

"Is that what she was doing?" he screamed, pointing at the two boys. "Huh, Jim, is that it?"

His first attempt at friendship having failed so miserably, Jimmy shook his head yes in a pitiful effort to appease, then, terrified, pulled loose and scrambled back to his corner and his little pile of clothes.

For a long moment the whole room fell silent, but for a small, high-pitched choking sound coming from Janus. The football player pressed his palm to his forehead. Hadn't this happened before, before and before?

Yes, yes and yes.

The sounds of the room began again, and Janus lifted his eyes. He saw Jimmy digging furtively in his clothing pile, casting glances over his shoulder to make sure nobody could see him (anyone could see him) until he pulled something out and hugged it to his chest for comfort. He rocked with it back and forth for a few minutes and then glanced down at it lovingly. When he did so, his eyes widened, and he looked from the object to Janus and back again. Finally, with a little, conciliatory smile, he lifted the thing into the air.

Janus looked. It seemed like a mirror. But as he turned from it determined to leave this hideous place, he noticed, from the corner of his eye, that his reflection did not respond. He took a step, looked closer. It was not a mirror. It was a painting. Of himself.

Staring at it, Janus felt the strange nostalgia, the haunting *déjà vu,* even more strongly than he had before, if, in fact, he had before at all—he might only think so now.

The sounds of the room increased. Thunderingly the people moaned. The smells grew stronger. Janus took another step and looked at the picture the boy held up.

It was not in Mary's style, but she was not hidden in it, and it was hers. Done with a ragged, slashing violence, it was like a death throe, like a final and defining cry when all articulation failed, with its passion given from a dying race to this one dying. And it made him fear for her. And it made him fear as now he saw: It wasn't of him as he was, but as a sculptor might have carved him, with the pallor of stone, the immortality of death and monument; a memory, not a man.

Then he choked, and he saw the last touch, saw the sculptor's hands still on the marble flesh, and he staggered, and he staggered from the room and from the house and fell, on the lawn before it, to his knees.

"She's dying, Papa," he said aloud, feeling it had all been said before, been done and done and done and done right here. *Déjà vu* had him fully now: a whole spring of it, this whole town, all land. As if he'd lived before, like a memory in the blood, as if fathers on fathers on fathers were at his eyes, back beyond his parentage, till Adam carved these visions in him as if he were a tree, a deep, a jagged and prime reminder that all blood runs like a river and all rivers run to the sea.

•

"Then you'd lost her," says Palmer.

"Nah, I knew where she was."

"Yeah? How?"

"Later. I'll tell you later."

He stands up and paces back and forth, and Palmer watches calmly, deep in thought. He picks his questions carefully.

"But she was alive, right?"

Janus paces faster. "I didn't know. I began to figure not."

"Oh," says Palmer. Something flicks across his face. An ache. "Did you ask the guy any more questions?"

"No. I'll tell you later anyway. Forget it now."

Palmer nods sympathetically. "Yes. Sure. Sounds like some place."

"Jesus! Wow."

"Really got you sick, huh?"

"Man, you just had to be there. All that damn hambangering going on. Jesus! Couldn't think, and all that shit."

"Yes." Palmer nods again. "I'd guess," he says.

"This room," says Janus, "this room gets me. This room gets me." Pacing faster.

"Hey, forget it," Palmer says.

"Naw, man, I mean it. This room gets me. I'm going out."

"Uh—it's snowing there, fellah."

"I'm going out. I'm going to that diner. Are the roads still closed?"

"Yeah," Palmer says.

"I'm going to that diner."

Janus grabs his coat and puts it on, stands still a moment, agitated, indecisive, walks unsurely to the door. There, again, he pauses.

Then he sighs, says, "Tell me if the roads clear, Higgs," and goes out into the morning snow.

The door clicks shut. Palmer's alone. He's lying on the

bed, his clothes, his thoughts, in jumbles. He starts to cry . . .

. . . not cry, but tears well in his eyes, his lips begin to tremble. He would like to cry; he tries to; it would help relieve him—he feels miserable . . .

. . . not miserable, but demeaned, inferior—to Janus.

*Quite a father he had.*

Aye.

*And quite a war.*

Aye, we're all sorry we missed that one.

*Aye.*

But let's be reasonable; it's foolishness at its heart, really, at its real heart. Fighting over what? Just another passing empire on the earth of ages, born but in some bloody years to die. Why, one era they will strike it like a set, and we will all go home.

*Uh, Professor, may I ask a question, sir?*

What is it, Mr. Smedley?

*Do you want to go home, sir?*

I'd like to go home, triumphant from such a war, banner on my rifle, rifle on my arm . . .

*Uh, Professor.*

Now, if I'd had a father like Janus had . . .

*Don't get too close, Professor.*

I too would be really . . . really very . . . fucked up . . .

*Don't get too close; you might forgive him.*

Poor bastard—the orphan thinks.

*But, uh, Professor.*

Yes, yes, what is it now, Mr. Smedley?

*But do you want to go home, sir?*

I want to go home.

*Do you want to go home to Beth?*

I want Beth.

Palmer rolls his head on the pillow, wet cheek to wet linen, and sees the telephone. Marvelous invention. Funny little thing. It would be ten o'clock in California now. Where winter comes with rain. It would be raining there, the windows washed in that soothing gray patter that blurs the debts and obligations of a day and makes the eyes pass slyly to the bookshelf, to the thickest binding, then to the softest chair. She, Beth, she, already shamelessly succumbed, she would be sitting in the study, with a sherry on the table and a Dickens in her lap, she would be sitting in the tan recliner, right beside the phone—it wouldn't even make her stand. Such a marvelous invention. Such a funny thing.

He raises himself on one elbow, draws a hand across his eyes, and reaches out . . . But pauses—pride, ceaseless, on the face of his good-byes to her, catches him, and he pauses. Is this *our* hero? No. Just his sister's son, a baby wanderer from word to word, from mail to mail, from her arms to her comfort—arms, comfort, embraced now by the arms, the comfort of the tan recliner; eyes that shed the last tears ever for him engrossed by gross Victorians with hats and troubles . . .

He picks the phone receiver up. He dials the hotel operator, asks her for an outside line, and, very slowly, dials again.

He breathes fast. He can hear the lines connecting. And the bell in his brother-in-law's house rings.

He can see her, through the nation-length cable, see her skirt collapsing smoothly over her lap as she lays the book down on it. He can see now it's no Dickens but their father's volume of her favorite, and her eyes are lost in his own old bedtime stories, and her lips are moving silently, pretending to recite again, to the baby boy again, gone . . .

The bell rings a second time.

Or perhaps in that study with its window on the sea, with the rainwater graying the seawater and the grass, her mind is fully engaged in those sayings, metered and lost, on that sweet turf of time-forgotten towns, and she is with the gods . . .

And thus, the bell again.

. . . and she is captured by the phrases, for they cling, returning to the blank heart's places to flesh the shadows out, revive the view. They become, those words, for those who seek the universe in order, a truer version of life itself, so that one might stand before his mother's coffin . . .

And again: the bell.

. . . at the edge of grief, some green grove lover-empty, and, while not remembering, recite and, unable to recall a passion, speak a rhyme, until even the deepest moment becomes metamorphosized into the sun of Phaeton or the father of Jove or grandfather Cadmus who hunted the bull that raped Europa . . .

Palmer holds the phone away from his ear and hears the next bell from a distance. His teeth click loudly together.

Gods fucking women and a grandpa hunting bulls. Cadmus, his daughter, and his grandson . . .

There's a faraway click, a faraway "Hello?"

Actaeon. Right! Who came upon Diana in a lake—the virgin. And the painting—wait, I've got it—Jesus—Mary's painting . . .

"Hello?"

"Who's that?" says Palmer. He looks at the telephone, remembers, pulls it to his ear. His breath gets short again. "Beth?" he whispers. "Beth."

"I'm sorry. Mrs. Hayden is not at home right now. Who's calling?"

Palmer's short breath breaks into a long sigh. "Oh. No. No, just tell her—I asked for her."

"Would you like to leave a message?"

Palmer shakes his head. "No. Just tell her I asked for her—tell her I asked for Beth," he says, and hangs up.

There's a moment of emptiness, of relief, of confusion, and still, he cannot help returning to the thought that is battering inside his brain like the headboard of a bed. He sees it all clearly now, as it must have been: roan and rider in the high spring grass; Yarnell, tall in the saddle, a noble, brown-bearded giant, unscarred then, riding fast, full of fire, full of haughty humor and, aye, yes, love. He is galloping for the wood ahead, in which have disappeared, only a moment since, the woman and the bay, the woman's red-gold hair, the horse's mane, the woman's white dress, motion-blown and flowing, going deeper, deeper, into the trees until they're just a flash of gold amidst the foliage, and Yarnell spurs his horse on even faster and in an instant the woods are on him, too, flying past him as he flies on to an assignation by the water buried at their core.

And when he came upon her, like Actaeon, she was, like Diana, naked in the lake, or no, he was too close upon her heels, too eager chasing her across the fields, so came upon her as she undressed. He dismounted, watching, his broad shoulders, his great legs swinging gracefully from the horse, watching as she loosed her bodice and her bra and her breasts flowed, naked, free, and as she pushed her dress down past her hips and down, to where she let it go and let it slide to her ankles and stepped from it and dove, white, into the water, stroking slowly to its middle, where she paused and turned and pried her damp hair from her face to look at him and call him after.

And after her he came, parting his shirt before his broad chest and undressing with a flourish, running lightly, like the quarterback he was, into the lake, until he flattened and swam toward her, to her, to her embrace. While the still blue sent out circular ripples from them, he kissed that hair, that flesh, that reminiscent softness just below the surface, rose up splashing, kissed her, joined her as in the old dark books, running his tongue across her moist and slightly parted lips as she slid her luxuriant fingers down his quivering thigh and over his stiffening rod of Aaron and he moves his hand to her pulsating mound of delight and toys with her knob of moral turpitude while thrusting his tongue against the soft, pungent flesh of her orbs of prurience making her gasp as he enters her as her skirt collapses smoothly over her lap as she lays him upon, across it nodont and her brother gone to church and he across her naughty nodont burst in I am bareass and across her lap sweet punished red she'll say red-gold hand-raised on top and purring ssh naughty Palmer entering wet as just as wet as Austin Bowie Corpus Christi Dallas ssh naughty Mary spank not Austin Bowie ifhe Burstin Bareass eating gagging bareass flesh damn it naughty damn it Mary punish purring now naughty Palmer now Palmer now and . . .

Then!

he thinks, gasping,

Then it happened! Shockingly, for she would show no pain, the still blue water choked up scarlet. The ripples thickened and stopped—with blood.

That was the stain upon the water in Mary's painting of the lake. That was what Yarnell mistook for death: the blood, the maidenhead, the blood. For like a true Actaeon, he had come upon a true Diana. Janus—no man and not Janus—had ever entered her before. And that—

That was why Janus had to reclaim her. Not for Jenny and not on a bet. And not for love. But for an unfinished fantasy, running through his head like one of those dull musics until he loved her for his image of her and for his pride. And he didn't know that his whole damned search had ended at that lake, that he was now pursuing a faulty passion, was now consumed not by Jenny, and not by a bet, and surely not by love, but by a vision of a virgin and his own dogs.

*Uh, Professor.*

You rang.

*That vision? That virgin?*

A trifle. Vanity. Something insecure. Virginity's a thing maintained through whoredoms, lost to love.

*To love.*

Right. Now, where was I?

*She was just getting boffed.*

Shut your filthy mouth!

*Ahem.*

Now—

Now that explains the rest.

Done with it, they swam to shore. She would not cry. He would be silent, out of respect. The water cleansed her, and when she climbed out onto the bank and lay down in the grass, she was white again, and her skin, which seemed delicate and ephemeral, seemed impenetrable, too, having endured him unmarked.

Yarnell splashed up slowly behind her, his eyes, the consciously soulful eyes of a romantic, covering her again and again, breathless at the places where her body, full and fleshy, parted from itself. He was prepared already to take her once more; everything of him physical asserted that if he strained into her deeply enough, she, the essence of her, could be had this time. And he knew he could feel like that forever and be always mistaken.

He sat down next to her, and she looked at him, gave him a smile.

"You're all right?" he asked.

"I'm fine. Are you?"

"Yes, sure, but you, are you all right?"

"Of course I am. Don't look so—hairy and concerned."

"Well, I can be hairy and indifferent, but that's about the best I can do." He relaxed a little, reached out with his big hand, and laid it on her as gently as he could, afraid of the strength in it, and the life in it, because like all romantics, he knew he was doomed but never believed he was. She shifted comfortably under his grip.

"Mary." That's what he would say, just her name. "That's a nice name. I like that name."

And she smiled again, but her green eyes were unfocused, and he sensed with a sort of urgency, his distance from her.

And maybe also the thing was that Yarnell was a simple man, basic and sensual even among his poems and at the bottom of his mind. So maybe when he saw this girl, complex only in her femininity, simple in herself, with whom he could spend a lifetime on the threshold of possession, he lost all art and every wile and said:

"I love you."

That would be it. And something would pull across her face—the mystery, the thing that can't be guessed as yet, something—so that when he said:

"I love you,"

she paused, and when he said:

"I love you, Mary Williams,"

she paused, and suddenly sat up and hugged him, her face next to his, hidden from him, and said, "My Tom. My sweet Tom, you're so good. All my life . . ." But then fell back a little, looked with a bright frankness into his eyes and said, "But I need . . . Tom, I need a little—peace. Just for a while. I need some peace, some time. To think things over. Okay?"

It would take a better sort of man even to only nod. Yarnell nodded.

Palmer slides to his feet and fumbles clumsily into the bathroom, jangling.

So she went away. It's hard to know why she picked that town in Indiana. It could have reminded her of home or been as far as what money she had would take her. But she must have wanted in some way to be able to think herself outside herself, to be in a place and absent from it at the same time so that her life might stop and allow her to catch up to it again, to start it fresh when whatever, whatever it was that bothered her, that kept her from loving Yarnell, was sorted out. She changed her name, took a job that could not, she thought, have to do with her, and walked along the town's river, back and back, she thought, to a time when her life, she thought, was simple.

That such an enterprise was bound to fail, that the manner of the world with her and hers with it were fixed in her beginnings, that strait is the way and narrow is the gate we are condemned to must have been obvious and unfathomable to her.

She walked along the river, back and back, and was deluded further by finding there exactly what she'd hoped to find. The little boy, Pete, let her play in stopped time with him, not young again, but not advancing either, until she imagined that there in the woods she was thinking clearly about her life. The little boy, Pete, was the meat of the illusion, feeding it until she believed she had escaped whatever it was, whatever past, until she felt free to love Tom Yarnell. And she beckoned him.

"Tom?" Over the cable.

"Yes. Mary!"

"Would you come for me? Would you come and get me?"

"Is it all right?"

"Yes. It's going to be, I think. Do you still . . . is it all right, too?"

"Yes, yes. I love you, Mary."

"Yes."

And Yarnell came quickly. He came too fast. In a screech and shatter of rubber and glass, the world returned to her forever.

Aw, Mary. Poor, guiltless, guilt-ridden girl knelt at his bedside, thinking: I've done this.

Giving up her job, and so losing her room, giving up her false name and losing hope, she took refuge in the hoboes' home, maybe even, yeah, yes, sure, aye, in the dull-witted sex of it, yes, yes, trying to make the horror of this thing, this horror she knelt by every day just—just stop.

Stop.

Palmer looks in the bathroom mirror, sees something awful and ludicrous in its face. With the broken, swollen nose and the acne and the tears, something so ugly. Aw, Mary.

*Uh, Prof.*

Aw, Mary.

*Uh, Prof, Prof, Prof.*

Aw, pretty, simple, kind girl.

*Uh, Proffity-prof.*

Gee, hell.

*Yo! Doc!*

What?

*Uh, excuse me, sir, but isn't something . . .*

Palmer's eyes brighten, and he walks out into the room, pacing, fast, in a fury.

Something is

*Strange*

about all this.

*Janus.*

Yes. Janus. He still doesn't know.

*I'll be buggered.*

It is, Janus feels, to his shame that he had never slept with her. It's the shame he went back to erase. If he'd known that her virgin blood was in the tale, was in the clues, was in the lake, he would have held it back or changed it. And that means . . .

*Hmmm?*

He never found her. Or she never told him.

*Or, in fact, she's dead.*

And that means . . .

*Hmmm?*

I can find her.

*Pardon?*

I can if I can hear the ending of the tale.

If I can hear the end, yes, I can find her. She must be found. If my sister hadn't saved me from that town in Illinois, she might be found already. And if I hear this tale, I'll find her yet, because I . . .

*Gee, what if he's made it all up, and there is no Mary?*

Quiet, Smedley.

*Sorry, Higgs.*

Canaan or Canens, I will find her yet. This is why I've wandered, and I'll find her. Dead of waiting for me, waiting for me in the grave, I'll find her because I . . .

*Ya love her, dontcha, ya big galoot?*

I love her so. Aw, man, aw, Mary, I do, I swear.

He pauses on the hotel floor, and pauses with a murmured purr and pauses, and can do no more than close his eyes and picture her . . .

# · 22 ·

Janus shivers in the small café, though the lights are bright here and the air is warm. Perhaps the trek across the street has chilled him. The snow was very deep. The wind, at first refreshing, cool, felt bitter and wicked soon enough. Perhaps that's why he shivers now, though it's warm here.

Cigarette after cigarette, and he huddles over coffee. His shoulders are hunched. Beneath his eyes, deep circles seem to deepen; it's the light that does it. It casts dark shadows. He smokes cigarette after cigarette.

The diner is a long room and seems longer because it is very thin. There are no tables, just the counter and stools. There is a mirror behind the counter, on the wall, and the counterman is swiping at it with a cloth. There is also a woman, seated at one of the stools. And there is Janus.

The woman is seated at the far end of the room from Janus. She is smoking, too, but her coffee cup's empty. She is pale and overweight and either younger than her looks or older than her age. One or the other. She is too heavily made up, and the problem is that it all shows in this light and makes her look worse than she would barefaced. Or maybe not.

And there's a strange trick the snow does here. It's so heavy and it so completely curtains the windows and captures the glow of the diner's lights that it makes the room inside seem closer, warmer, makes it seem secluded, out of space, as it were, out of time, as it were, or more exactly, as it were itself a tiny bit of space, a tiny bit of time, set alone in the vast whole of both, dealing with minutes to the great amusement of the rest. As it were. One might believe eternity were outside . . . But be that as it may.

Janus shivers, stretches, looks around. He glances at the woman, secretly, and glances at the door so as to seem he wasn't only glancing at the woman. He folds again, into the same position he was in before, the same hunch-shouldered, smoking business, starting into his coffee as it grows cold. He appears very tired, and maybe he is. Maybe he sighs. He purses his lips when he lets his breath out, as if waiting or as if anxious or as if annoyed. He puffs on a cigarette and crushes it hard into the ashtray. That could mean anything. He lights another, lets it burn.

The woman opens the handbag that is in her lap and rummages through it with an air of importance. She lifts a circular compact from it and snaps it open. There is a small, round mirror on the underside of the top, and she looks into it, touching the corners of her mouth delicately with her index finger. She flicks her eyes sideways and looks at Janus. They are large, almond-shaped, almond-colored eyes, and they are the nicest thing about her. Looking at the mirror again, she shifts it in her hand as if with some secret feminine purpose. She is trying to get a better look at Janus really, but the mirror catches the light and flashes, and she snaps it closed—puckering her lips—and puts it back in the handbag.

Janus suddenly groans, and both the counterman and the woman look at him. Self-consciously he jerks a cigarette out of the pack and into his teeth, then jabs the pack back onto the counter. It slides a way, stopping against a napkin box. Janus looks at it as he lights his cigarette. He swivels in his seat and stands.

He paces. He looks serious and thoughtful because he knows he's being watched, and the effort keeps him from thinking, and since that is why he started pacing, the pacing's useless, but he paces faster.

He walks the length of the diner and comes to rest before the window, smoking. He looks out. There's nothing but the snow: large fast-falling flakes close up, but at a distance just a blanket white and gray, seeming to put pressure on the window. Janus turns, walks back and puts his cigarette out, lights another one, and walks to the window at the front of the place. The diner lights cut farther here. He can see individual flakes farther off, but beyond that are still the pressure and the snow.

He moves closer to the pane, and he looks—feels maybe—as if his whole body were in his eyes. They are that intent; he stares that hard. He leans, and his breath clouds the glass, a white against the white outside. The cigarette slips from his fingers to the floor, and he grinds it out without looking down. He lifts his hand and wipes the breath from the window, and he breathes, and it comes back again. He lifts his hand, extends a finger, and starts to carve a circle in the mist, but he doesn't complete the line, and he makes it a spiral instead, circling until it is just a dot, representing what his finger is too thick to draw. He breathes again, and the spiral fades. This time neither the counterman nor the woman hears him groan. They watch him, though, because he paces now more quickly, with the muscular spring of an ape or lion caged. Maybe he is muttering a name.

He walks back to the far window and does the trick with his breath again. He draws only straight lines this time, vertically, one right next to another. He does it even past the patch of mist. He does it intently, carving, with purpose, purposeless lines in his own breath.

He shivers, grunts. His eyes get wet a moment; just a moment. He doesn't even have to wipe them; they just dry; the water just sort of recedes. He turns from the window, almost spins around, almost as if in challenge, to face the other two. The counterman seems a little worried. The woman looks at Janus tenderly. Janus walks, in long, steady strides, to his seat and gets a new cigarette. He lights it firmly and walks to the counter flap. He lifts it and strides past the counterman to the back door. He enters a hall of mops and closets—a dark hall—and he goes through one door, into a bathroom, and shuts the door behind him.

He looks at himself in the sink's dirty mirror and curses. His face crinkles up, and he looks up at the ceiling and whispers things and shakes his head. Finally, he looks back at the mirror and drags his sleeve across his eyes. He flicks his cigarette into the toilet and, pretending it is an enemy boat, pisses on it, trying to make it shatter and sink. He manages to piss the black tip off, and the tobacco starts to leak out. Then, just before the piss stream flags, the whole cigarette comes apart in a satisfying burst. Janus thinks a message back to headquarters that the mission's accomplished, shakes himself off, and flushes the wreckage away. He washes his face carefully before leaving the room.

When he comes back out behind the counter, he stands for a second, legs spread, turning his head in a cool survey of the room. His eyes come to rest on the woman. She looks at him, defiant and frightened, waiting. The air is like a light bulb before the switch is put on. Then Janus looks away . . .

# · 23 ·

Twilight, yes, there will be that, a long, sweet dusk without a sun. The sun will have fallen behind the house, and they, they, Mary and he—and Mama, that sweet old dear, that sweet, that sweet old dear—will be on the porch, rocking and watching the broad darkling of the fair day with Palmer, just Palmer, sitting close behind her, Mary, close enough to sniff her fragrance—she will have perfumed herself in a clumsy feminine wile, endearing to one who's seen such tricks done so cruelly and too well. He will be really—charmed. Charmed, charmed, charmed. But—the broad darkling of the fair day when the big and soft white clouds turn dark and powerful, as if with rain and yet with sunset only, and stretch back and far across the sky to the hills and the horizon; all eyes will be on those clouds and that sky, waiting for darkness, the moon and the first stars . . .

Ah, country girl. You'll know all this already. Fresh as

dawn each dawn, the stars, the key, will be as yours, as you were born to them, as they are in you.

He will wait, but she will inhabit the changing day and die with it and so never die. The end will cling to her, just as the star to wish on will hold back and the violet whence Vesper comes will linger.

They'll speak. No, they'll be quiet. Could there be a silence like a word? It will be that.

And might there be a moment when she'll turn and he will see her eyes and plunge into the deep green and nestle there as if embraced?

Palmer?

Aye, just Palmer.

And they'll both turn back to see the dazzle of the first true star, and the word, nay, wishes, nay, they are but words, and the words that are for stars alone will issue from their minds and eyes, tender and unsaid, and might there be a moment when she'll turn and wish upon his countenance as on the distant dazzle, might there be, and might there be a moment, might we dream strange sympathies for just a one, when he will hear it clearly, hear her never whisper but pray still: Let my children bear this stranger's name, let the infants of the hearth be his and mine, this roaming boy's and mine? . . .

Too soon, build tension, roaming boy.

Won't they? They will—turn to see the dazzle of the first true star, and the first star they will see will fall, sweeping down the distance like to plow its way to hell, hell's bride, and the days will not grow longer anymore, aw, Mary, too soon and too soon.

She will rise. She'll stand, perhaps with mystic, hallelujah eyes, no innocent, she'll rise, she'll stand, a mystic silence on her, just the quiet of a country girl who knows, who knows where stars fall and how to deep-six pebbles to call up frogs and why lilies grow on illusion fields, but we digress, and she will rise and glide along the porch and off and off into the pasture where the star might lie.

Palmer and Mama will watch her go, and the little boy, her little brother, Mary's, already imitating Palmer's way of moving, walking, talking. They will watch her go.

"She's always been a strange one," Mama will mutter.

Palmer will smile with knowledge, will say, say softly, surely, "Aw, shut up, fartbag."

Will say, "Yes, she's like a queen."

Mama will nod. "Yes. I do worry for her sometimes."

Palmer will stand, as well, as casually as he can and, under the unfooled eyes of Mama, will say, "I reckon I'll just take a walk."

"You do that," she will say, unfooled; wise old child of sod and clay. Basically, a fartbag.

He'll swagger off the porch end, toward the far white figure in the fallen night. Her shape will lessen, dim; the dark will gather on it as it did the day, ragged its edges, blur them, blur the rest until he walks on toward an empty stretch of blue, seeking the pit to which she seems to've gone. His step will quicken into a virile trot, a manly run, a virile manly, deeper toward her, and, and as he seeks her now, he'll seek her then, in this, a dream, might find her where . . .

Where?

He'll swagger off the porch, see her; she will fade, and he'll begin to run and find her, find her—swagger, fade, run, feel the grass brush on his calves, the mud sink under his cowboy boots (he'll have bought a pair of cowboy boots) and find her by a river with a boy or by a star rock like a wish. No . . .

He will swagger, she will fade, he'll run, and, yes, she would, will disappear—some damnable season will have begun that takes her hence, that leaves him here, that bids him wish her in the sky and makes him seek her on the ground, that cruelly brings her godship by: the thing that comes but can't be found and he steps to the door—his face unscrewing, his pulse slowing, his breath easing off—and puts the chain lock on. He swivels, decisive, and walks to a writing desk by the wall, sits at it, riffles through the drawer, past Bible and phone book, to stationery and pen. Stacking the paper and laying it before him, he begins to write:

*Janus Quintain . . .*

He crosses that out furiously and begins again beneath it:

*Dearest Beth,*
*Janus Quintain . . .*

He curses, seizes the paper, crumples it, tosses it aside, and is about to start on the next but pauses. He takes up the ball of paper and carries it quickly into the bathroom. He watches, impatiently, to see it fully flushed away and then returns to begin again. Huddled over the page like some student scared of cheaters, he writes, swiftly.

*Dearest Beth,*
*We are stuck in a blizzard in Denver, Colorado, and all the roads are closed. We were almost killed trying to get out of the mountains and into town. The car is pretty well battered up, but it will serve, and so, I hope, will we. Now we are safe in a Denver motel—me and my present traveling companion, one Janus Quintain. He is a young man, about twenty-five, from somewhere in Illinois, and he helps pass the time telling stories about playing football for a college in New York and other things. I don't much like him, but I have promised to take him to New York because he*

*saved my life in Montana—another thrilling story which I will tell you later.*

*Beth, I am coming home. If you'll let me. I love you so much, and I miss you. I don't think I'll get back for Christmas or maybe even for a month or so, but I'll call you and let you know. Beth, I love you. How can you stand me? I am such a stupid brother, and you are such a good sister. I thought, coming out of those treacherous mountains, how I always really planned to come back to you, proud and terrible, hoping you'd learned your lesson. I'm an awful brother. I can't stand it. And about how I was going to get killed in the mountains and never see you again. It was terrible.*

The words are crowding into each other, none the one he wants, none the thing he means to say. He's forgotten his pride and his wanderlust; that hunger to have mystery—that mystery without which his childish sullenness seemed hardly worth the keeping—seems hardly worth the keeping now.

He writes again:

*I love you*

and would write it again, but then the door latch clicks, and the door crashes in, and horrified, Palmer jumps up with the letter. The door hits on, bounces off, the chain and is held to just a chink between the jambs.

"This is a raid!" yells Janus, sticking his nose in at the crack.

"Just a—just—nabshit," Palmer yells back, trying to fold the letter in half.

Janus pounds on the door.

"Police! Police!" he screams.

Palmer is jamming the letter in his pocket and looking guiltily at the unmade bed.

"Everybody up against the wall!"

With a final survey of the room, Palmer nods and says "Okay," and goes to the door.

"Fire the gas, Sergeant!"

"Aw, shut up," says Palmer. He pushes the door in on Janus's face, removes the chain, and steps back. Janus enters, erect, composed, and glances around.

He lifts his shoulders, pretending to write.

"Okay," he says. "Let's have some names."

Palmer waves an arm at him and turns away.

"Hey," says Janus, "you bucking for a trip downtown? Don't think I don't know what's going on here." He walks over to the rumpled bed and leans his face into it, sniffing. Palmer feels his cheeks getting hot.

"Still warm," says Janus. "Smells like shit. We'll have to do a bedtopsy. You been touching yourself in any unnatural places, boy?"

"Only in bed," Palmer mutters, trying to smile.

Janus shakes his head and clucks tragically. "Boy, I'm shocked. I am shocked. Don't you know the consequentials of your actions? Why, one of these days you're gonna get laid and your right hand is gonna beat you to death out of jealousy. Happens all the time."

As if facing a real reprimand, Palmer has nothing to say. Uncomfortable, he shuffles off, to the bed first, then, seeing it all undone, to the chair before the TV set.

"You wanna wake up one morning with a green-eyed hand at your throat," says Janus.

Palmer snorts distractedly. He doesn't feel like this at all.

"Sure. You can laugh all right," Janus goes on, "but I'm gonna go into that bathroom there and take a dump, and when I return, I expect to find you ready to go."

"Go where?" Palmer waves his hand at the window. "The snow."

Janus is emptying his pockets, throwing his keys and change and wallet on the bed. "That flurry? Those couple of flakes? Highway patrolman in the diner says the east road's clear, so I say we blow this town."

"He did? Great, sure."

"Sure thing," Janus says. "Now, if you'll just excuse me."

"Be my guest."

Janus goes into the bathroom, shuts the door.

Palmer leans his back against the chair. His eyes close slowly. He smiles. He wonders how many locker-room lies about Janus and his women he'll have to hear now. He figures: enough. Enough to whittle at his self-esteem, his self-defenses, his pride in his knowledge of the world—enough to take from him everything but his fantasies. And it will not matter if Janus lies. Janus will lie, in fact, and Palmer will disbelieve him. But in the end, it will be the overall image that will settle on Palmer's stomach like the truth, rattling him, calling him the lesser man.

He sighs. He will bear it meekly—it's his momentary image of himself, and it's just as well: Janus would call men vermin to be king slug, and against such determination, Palmer is sadly unmoved.

His head comes forward, and his eyes open up. Glancing discreetly at the bathroom door, he returns to the desk and, having found an envelope, addresses it quickly. He pulls the letter from his pocket, and as he is sealing the flap down over the page, he sees Janus's wallet lying on the bed.

And might there be a portrait of my love?

*And might*

And might there be a glimpse of her?

The idea comes as suddenly as the sight, like a flirt, sweet, silly, impossible to resist. The wallet holds his eyes. The leather seems aglow with the compulsion of it . . . He feels entirely corrupt . . .

He pounces on the thing, seizes it, spreads it open to the picture case. His fingers fiddle with the snap; they tremble with the deed. The case breaks back; the plastic folders fall.

There are five $100 bills inside, each folded neatly in a separate case.

Rushing water sounds behind the door. He snaps the wallet shut and throws it down—it was bait, he thinks suddenly, placed just so; Janus will notice the change—and strolls away from it as casually as from a murder.

The bathroom door bursts out, and Janus is there.

"Okay, hand-job, let's hit the road."

They gather their belongings and step outside. The whole world's white; the blizzard swirls. But Janus walks through it surely all the same, gabbling over one shoulder as he goes, "I ever tell you bout that girl I met swimming in this river just a bit west of here? Man, she and I went at it like nothing you'd even *think* about in front of your mother—sister . . . "

Palmer follows him to the car.

# · 24 ·

And—

Tales without mystery; visions, dreams, spoken as if whispered in a kiss, and Palmer listens well. Women by waters and of dark lands, fallen on the grass like dews, rising from the earth like downs: foreign figures, somehow, smiling, knowing how to smile—they all knew how to smile. They smiled deep secrets for a tease, lingeringly licking them away to have them chased uselessly by other tongues. No recess of them is unexplored, is unexplained, and Palmer listens well, none meeker. But all to the teller goes the tale.

They are driving now through Denver, blind. Frost, white, lacing the windshield, frames the snow. Snow, deep, curtains the headlights, retreating, always reluctantly, before them, regrouping, always, implacable up ahead.

They've replaced the Volvo's headlight with another and taped a square of cardboard over the backseat's broken pane. The board is wet and dark now, starting to sag a little, starting to drip. Palmer can feel the cold air seeping through it, but he dares not turn. The road, or the faint indentation in the snow that he assumes is the road, holds his complete attention. While Janus has his ear, it keeps his eyes; the steering wheel grips his hands, and clearly all's not well. No other traffic passes, no other lights go by—the lie is at the window with the wolves—but Palmer is unsuspecting. He thinks the eastern highway must be better off for the authorities to have opened it. In fairness to his intelligence, he is concentrating on the road.

Janus keeps on talking, unconcerned: five hundred women, fifty loves. His hands are sweeping in broad circles, causing the thin line of smoke from his cigarette to shiver and break and widen until a white mist forms about his face. The words roll out of it, tainted by it, white and misty.

Palmer listens well, thinks of nothing but the delicate mechanics of controlling the car. It goes all right in the city, for the roads were plowed earlier on, and the skids are light and easily contained. The walls of buildings keep the wind at bay, keep the blizzard in a slanting sheet, solid and furious, but constant and plain. Palmer can predict it here, outguess it, and he does.

It is late afternoon, the stations of the sun invisible. Everything's lit with a pale, odd bronze, a result of the yellow streetlamps mingling with the snow. It's an eerie medium, that color, and so is the full, utter quiet, waiting beyond the engine, the hollow howling of the wind, Janus's voice. The car is approaching the highway.

Soon, dreamily, Denver dissolves. The winds turn bad. The bad winds worsen, whipping the slanting sheet outside into a frightening whirlpool, long and deep. Each inch of it seems a storm itself, a full-blown blizzard in a handful of air, working and churning on its own continuous formula, creating and devouring its own continuous time. The car rocks. The headlights snatch at every vortex, then, as if dazzled, turn away, letting it sink into the common darkness. All around, dead gases swell whence, from their greater, lesser diamond droplets die—all around, all one, all motion, and the edge and the guts of the blizzard converge, invert, become everything.

Janus falls silent, his mouth hung open between two words. His eyes are wide. Slowly the cessation of his voice travels across the car to Palmer. Palmer thinks vaguely of the money, the $500 folded neatly into the plastic picture holders. He thinks, vaguely, that is why Janus is running from the law: He has done a robbery, probably of the gas station where he worked. On the other hand, he thinks, thinks vaguely, $500 is not all that much, just enough to fritter really, not enough to hoard. Unless you have some specific purpose for it. Palmer considers.

The road turns secretly, hidden by the snow. The car goes plowing into the shoulder, plunging into a terrible skid, spinning around and around and around until, with a jolt, it buries itself deeply in a drift.

"Did we turn around?" says Janus.

"I don't know."

There is a long silence.

"We ought to," says Janus.

"What?"

"Turn around."

"Why? What? . . ." Palmer looks at his companion, at the taut jaw and the widened eyes. And finally, quietly, surprised: "Why, you lied. About the road being opened. You lied."

"Christ Almighty, man, I always lie!"

"Oh," says Palmer. "Great."

"We gotta get out of this."

"Great."

"We got to, man."

And Palmer, with righteous anger, in a high-pitched, squeaky, almost feminine voice: "What am I supposed to do about it? I don't know which way we're pointed. How can I? I can't see. It's not my fault."

He turns from Janus to the gearshift, throws it angrily into reverse, and hits the gas, throws it into forward, and hits the gas, and again, rocking the Volvo back and forth until it starts to dig its way free and move. They roll forward slowly, delicately, and feel the crunch of the gravel shoulder beneath. And then a bump, and then the road. And they progress.

Outside, the thing is in full fury. At every window it batters and whines. The car weaves back and forth, its passengers silent and staring at the swirl and blur.

Then, ahead, a patch of snow glows yellow for a moment and sinks again into the white.

"What's that?" says Janus.

"What's what?"

Once more the yellow flashes—less diffused and brighter, a single floating circle—and disappears. Both men are silent. It's as if—the circle blinking now again—they were approaching the whirlwind's center. It's as if—again, the light goes on, goes off—a lazy, sallow eye were in the storm's core, watching, without motion, passage in passage, as everything around it whirls madly.

It is the yellow light of a roadblock. It comes on a foot in front of them. Palmer spins the wheel. The Volvo swerves. A vast white screen whips by them, and the vast white explodes in red. Their fender scrapes the block; their tail swings out, swings past the wood by inches. All through the sudden scarlet, there is thunder: "This road is closed!"

The red around them rolls, and Palmer sees the police car only as they skitter by its hood. He glimpses the officer at the microphone, booming.

"Go!" screams Janus. "Just go. Cops."

Palmer's throat is tight; there is a pressure just below his chest. Quickly, silently, easily, through an atmosphere like a dream's, the car is drifting. Behind it the police are still in sight, the voice still thundering, almost overhead. Palmer's foot hovers above the brake, and he glances down. Janus is holding a knife to his ribs.

"Go," says Janus in a strained whisper. "Just fucking go."

Strangely Palmer is neither surprised nor frightened. Calmly he shifts his foot and hits the gas. The car shoots forward, sliding, keeping speed.

"Hold it," the cop yells out at them.

They travel forward for several yards, the impetus of the start maintaining, the back wheels grinding round and round in the surface layers of the snow. At last, they fly into a skid, sideways, circling end about end. They drop down into a virgin drift, and the back wheels thrash in it, and they can't move.

Words indistinguishable in distance and wind, a soft pink glow that rises, fades tell them the police aren't far away. The words grow louder, the light grows red, and the tires keep turning—the car won't move.

Palmer looks at Janus, then down at his side. The knife has been taken away.

He sighs wearily.

"Get behind the wheel," he says. "I'll try and dig us out."

Flinging the door out quickly, pushing against it to make it push the snow, he steps out into the blizzard and sinks into a drift as high as his knees. He curses and kicks forward, holding car door, trunk, and fender for support. He sinks in up to his thighs and stops and shakes his head at the wind. It stings his eyes. It is freezing cold. His fingers tighten; his face goes numb. He hurries—to beat the stiffening of his limbs, to beat the cops—and clawing the snow with his hands and ramming his thighs ahead, he gets to the car's back end.

Wind and water thrash him as he kneels and starts to dig away. The tires are fully covered, and the snow beneath them is soft and wet. Palmer plunges his hands in and starts yanking out white heaps, his fingers more and more brittle with every try. He pounds the snow beneath the tires to make it more compact, easier to grip. But his hands have curved and tightened into claws; his face has screwed and tightened like a mask. He has to get inside.

Stumbling, he rises up; in pain, he pounds his knuckles on the trunk. He hears the engine roar as Janus hits the gas. But the car won't budge, and when Palmer looks down, he sees the tires spitting snow up at his legs—his legs are numb, feel nothing.

Stiffly, quickly, he wades around the car. The air is crimson, and in the wind is the giant voice coming nearer still.

"What's your location? Stay where you are. What's your location? Stay where you are."

Palmer tries to open the door, but his hands won't close. He pounds against the window. Janus lets him in.

"Oh, God," says Palmer softly, throwing himself inside. He leans toward the heater, and his joints start to thaw. He says, "Oh, God."

But there's no one to hear him. Janus has leaped out into the snow and is pushing his way around to the back. Palmer climbs slowly across the seat and straightens behind the wheel.

Now, finally, breaking through the snow, the headlights of the police car shine, nearing the Volvo slowly, steadily advancing, staring.

Palmer hears Janus pounding on the trunk behind him, and he lowers his foot gently, and gently the car begins to move, pushing against the drifts ahead, drifting from the headlights and the crimson and the shouting voice. Palmer edges it forward smoothly, neither increasing nor dropping the speed, changing direction in a simple glide, and in seconds, with a single jolt, reaching the highway.

In the howl of wind, a siren howls, and in the siren's howl, a howl: "Higgs!" It is Janus. "Open the door."

Palmer's eyes are on the snow; his hands are on the wheel. He doesn't move; he doesn't slow the car. He listens well.

"Open the door," yells Janus, running behind him, slipping, out of breath.

In the depths of the rearview mirror, Palmer can see him: his skin a leprous white with cold, his outline aglow with flashing lights, as if on fire, crackling, folding, consumed. As the car keeps moving away from him, his running form seems swallowed by bloodred snow, by bloodred lights, by wind. The corner of his mouth's agape; his single eye is terrified and pale. He seems to disappear in pieces, like a nightmare in a shaving glass, in parts . . .

Palmer leans over and opens the door. For Mary—he tells himself it is for Mary: so he can hear her story's end and find her. It seems so possible. It seems so near. But even as Janus grabs hold of the car, hoists himself up and into it, Palmer's vision of his love, so close at hand, slips back, away, forced back, away, as by a curse falling echoless from the Denver ranges: that he may glimpse her in description only and, hearing of her, lose her for all time.

The world behind them, crimson, fades to red, to pink, to bronze and white, a white that blows through the empty distance, circling endlessly. It seems a long time before the blizzard breaks.

They travel slowly, skidding often, often stuck for a half hour at a time. But the storm is at its worst in the mountains, and once they descend, it turns to rain and then, close to the end of Colorado, to a blooming night of stars and all the rest, and it is finished.

"State line! State line!" yells Janus. "Whoo-whooee, we made it. We made it, boy."

Without a look, without a word, Palmer stares sullenly ahead. He has grown furious while he drove. And now, remembering the tickle of the knife blade in his ribs, he starts to feel afraid, too, with an odd and oddly familiar fear. It is like a house cat, stalking in the dark, and it is like the dark. It has a terrible gleam. Like eyes. He shudders.

They travel more quickly on the open highway. The state ends, and then the day.

# *Friday, December 23*

# · 25 ·

There are fragments of a rainbow in the sky in the morning. Then they fade. The dawn comes, white as tin. The sunlight spreads out slowly, fans across the surface of the land. The land, flat, fallow, brightens, void of color, melancholy under frost. It runs wide, long past the coming spring and out of sight, beneath a road as empty and as flat, as long. This is Kansas now—the Volvo cruising across it quickly, gathering the highway underneath.

Sleepless, the passengers are at their posts. Palmer, driving, is silent, in a brown study, angry all night, frightened all night, dreamy and nervous now, homesick, lovestruck, dull. His encircled eyes, his broken nose, his unkempt beard reveal him, as he picks and pictures thwarted fantasies out of the territory passing: bright citadels in the white dawn, conjured by distance, endangered by spies.

For against these thoughts, these words keep coming, these endless words, these endless lies. Hands flicker;

matches flare; tales tumble into each other, meaningless, not meant to be heard or believed, but only counted, even as a constant drone, even as a god hears prayers. Janus is talking.

And something happens in the car. Sounds mix. Liar's hum, engine's rumble, driver's fancy—voice, piston, dream—combine until a tale's a dream, and a dream, no vision but a myth, and all converge on one, a woman, on Mary. She stands at either ocean, just out of either's reach; she calls behind and before, she beckons, and with a rhythm like the waves she commends all other rhythms to her own. Liar's hum, engine's rumble, driver's fancy—voice, piston, dream: these and the like of these blend in a sound formed in the underseas, washed to the ground.

Falling from the hoboes' house into the mixed colors of the end-day, Janus was confused a little, sick a little, angry, and ashamed. What he imagined to be his blood cried out for blood with a noble savagery nearly Greek, and his line might have been the line of Agamemnon, its fists clenched forever. But as he stood in the warm dusk, breathing deeply, he grew calm. He could not completely understand the feelings that had drawn Mary here, to this degraded, this corrupted place. But he was sure, in his heart he was sure, that she was blameless. Yes. It was that fool Yarnell's fault, and that bastard Harve Perkins', and the fault of these filthy, these filthy—bums. But none of them had touched her—in his heart he was sure. And he would not trouble himself with revenge now. He was in a hurry now. Because now, at last, he knew where she had gone.

He went to his car, made its engine thunder, made its tires screech as he started down the hill. West as always, faster than usual, he pushed the Chevy as if it didn't matter—and it didn't matter—if he tore the crate apart. This was the final journey. He'd found her. This was his last trip home.

Ahead of him the thin orange glow that held the farthest rim of land settled under a cloudless violet, and night fell. There were nearly three hundred miles between him and his hometown, but he covered them quickly, looking blankly into the dark. The road rolled back, and fields rolled by as if they moved against him, but he didn't notice. The wind at the window and in his hair, though it was fine, blew hard, but not for him. The land in its blackness and under the moon were nothing to him, and he didn't see the pavement or the lines of it or the lights of other cars. He stared, instead, at one distant portion of the night, a spot always beyond illumination, though Indianapolis passed him, and Springfield, a point in the darkness where his own town would be.

It was only midnight when he came to it, knowing he had reached it more by instinct than by sight. He slowed down and, watching the outskirt streets, the unlit houses on them—homes of the middle clan class, too small for all their children and pictures of Christ—felt a twinge of bitterness at being here again.

It was not that he'd been so unhappy here. Though he'd left it readily enough, this town had always had its better features. There was always the river here, the Mississippi, and by it, a boyhood of beer and boredom, sitting on the shore with his friends, drinking, complaining, philosophizing, longing after the mystery of the passing barges. As a child he'd bathed there, too, in the warm water, in the cool evenings, and his mother, a sturdy, kindly-looking woman, had taken him as a babe to play there. He remembered the yellow ball that bounced between them glistening where the morning sun struck its side. It was not at all that he'd been unhappy.

It had been nothing that substantial, in fact; only a

vague, bitter restlessness, a panic in the blood, a fear that life was passing like the barges, with him onshore. No matter how much of a hero he'd become—and he became quite a hero in his best seasons—there had always been a nagging sense that he had been cheated by his origins into seeming less than he knew he could be. He might have been an emperor if his hometown had been the world. Instead, a field of anythings beyond its borders called him to go where he was unwanted and unknown. Of course, he'd become a hero in college, too, but it was easy there; it was just like high school. It could not go on forever.

When he reached the main drag, he turned onto it and began to cruise. It was, to his great satisfaction, as of old, as if he still might reach out and slam his palm against the car door to attract the inattention of a passing beauty and drive beside her for a time, quickening the click of her heels. But the street was dark, closed down—rolled up, they used to say—and no one passed by him. A stranger would've said the night was over. Janus, however, citizen that he was, knew better.

At the end of the streeet there was a bar. Its owner was a former high school football man himself and, by winking at the phony proofs of age of the present lot, peopled the place with the town Turks. The bar stayed open into the morning, and there would be yellow lights inside, and yellow beer. Janus drove to it, parked his car.

As he stepped out into the soft air, into the river breeze, muddy and wet, and the night, he noticed a strange silence coming from the place. There was music enough, and through the pebbled glass window he could see vague, wavering human forms, and yet—something was missing; some sound that should have been there was not. It made Janus pause before entering.

Of a sudden, a voice exploded, and another met it, and there was a crash. Over the music, through the pebbled glass, Janus heard and saw a great commotion rumbling indoors.

"A brawl," he whispered, smiling.

It was nothing else.

For the first time in what seemed like ages, Janus felt a rush of joy. He doubled his fists. He set his face. And striding forth like Ajax on the ships, he charged inside.

Two factions were clashing there, amidst yells and a rumble of tables. On one side, the larger side, were the high school football players. The smaller group was of older boys, and it was they who seemed to be winning.

With a great shout, Janus rushed in. He punched some guy in the face, but it hurt his hand, so he punched someone else in the stomach, and the fellow punched him in the face.

"Take that!" yelled Janus.

He turned and grabbed someone by the shoulders and hurled him into a table. He began to laugh.

He was trying as much as he could to fight on the losing side, and battling almost wholly with the older boys, he began to half realize that they were all acquaintances: old teammates or old friends.

He punched Joe Healy, famous for his golden mustache and French cuffs. Healy had been with Janus the night he was struck blind by a jug of bad rum. Healy had seen Janus clutching at a commode and trying to bite it. Healy had seen Janus weep. Healy had cared for him. Janus did not return the favor. He knocked Healy to the beer-stained floor.

Next, Janus flung a roundhouse at Jim Patterson, the renowned warmer of benches. It was Patterson who, in this very bar, had shilled for Janus in his beer-chugging contests. It was Patterson who had convinced the suckers to take the dumb wager again and again. It was Patterson now whom Janus slugged in the chest, just below the right nipple, sending him to the floor, where he crawled off, like an ant looking for its contact lenses.

Then Terence Law, who had all the intelligence of a stick of gum, leaped at Janus from a table, smacked against the boards, and slid beneath a chair.

Janus laughed and laughed.

After a few minutes the fight paused, and the factions, smaller now, pulled apart. In the lull, Janus saw Ben Noble. He grinned. Ben Noble, the outcast, the artist, the sculptor. Ben Noble, who had introduced him to Mary. Noble Ben Noble, the best of his friends.

"Ben," Janus cried out, "Ben! Ben! Isn't this great?" and was hit from behind with a beer mug. The scene slipped away from him, and he tumbled down.

Friends dragged him to the open air, where he lay awhile unconscious, waking in time to see the final high school football player punched out.

He started laughing again. It was not the echoless laughter then—it had not become that. And he didn't laugh alone. The sidewalk on which he lay filled with the sound, and the street filled with it: deep, men's loud laughs. His old friends had surrounded him. Bloody and breathless, they looked down at him.

"Laughing. He's laughing," said Healy, laughing. "He comes in here and kicks shit out of his old buddies, and he thinks it's hilarious."

Janus laughed.

"Didn't you know you were on the wrong side?" Patterson said. "Fucking broke my ribs."

Janus laughed.

"They were losing," he said.

"Well, Christ, that doesn't make them right," said Law.

Janus kept laughing.

"I think you just felt like cutting up," said Healy. "You didn't give a shit who you hit."

This was close enough to the truth so that Janus turned red as he laughed.

"Jesus," Healy said. "You broke—I think you broke my tooth."

Janus slapped the sidewalk convulsively, and Ben Noble said, "Come on. Let's haul this drunk out of here."

With great difficulty, they lifted the laughing man to his feet and started walking with him along the sidewalk.

"Jesus," said Janus, wiping his eyes. "Who hit me? What'd you hit me with?"

"Beer mug."

Janus laughed.

"Christ," Ben Noble said.

They moved in a pack, centered on Janus, talking, asking questions, laughing, all together, all at once. Janus slipped easily into the familiar role of leader, lying with the old flair, new lies, commanding with a new authority his old comrades once more.

They strolled the town for more than two hours, slipping off one by one then, heading home happy and vaguely disquieted by their hero's return. At last, only Janus and Ben Noble were left, and they turned back toward the main street, silent.

When they came to Janus's car, they stopped and leaned against it, hands in pockets, staring into the closed bar before them, glancing at each other when they spoke.

"So how you been, boy?" Janus said.

"Not bad. You know," said Noble.

"Yeah. How'd you get mixed up in this brawl anyhow?"

"Just a-drinkin with m'old buddies, Duke."

"Well, you held your own for a little guy."

Noble shrugged. "It's all in where you hide."

"Yeah, right. Just don't wantcha to damage them expensive hands is all, I mean."

Noble looked down at his hands, sliding them out of his

pockets and laying them softly over each other. They were unmarked.

"Dem bones, dem bones, dem dry bones," he said.

Janus didn't answer. He did not understand. Noble had always been odd to his clan, slight and taciturn and a standout amidst the big, wild folk. His thin face, its thin Roman nose impressively jutting, its skin as white as neglected marble, was almost unearthly in its quiet and calm. Even at his maddest, his drunkest, his worst, he never seemed more than a rowdy monk, a learner of tongues, elevated above the rest. That perhaps was why Janus had been proud of their friendship and had expected great things of this strange, inscrutable boy.

"What—what've you been doing with yourself?" he asked him. "Thought you'd be famous at least by now."

"No," said Noble.

"Did you finish college?"

"No. I didn't go."

"No kidding. You?"

Noble nodded. "Even I."

Janus turned this over for a small space, considering it carefully. Then he said, "Well, what're you doing? You working somewhere? You making statues still?"

"No. I work at Wilson's."

The two men started strolling down the street again, hands in pockets.

"Wilson, the grave guy?" asked Janus. "The guy who makes markers?"

Again Noble nodded, his face so peaceful that it seemed an image in a still pool.

"You make those markers? For graves?" said Janus.

"Yup."

Janus considered some more, his eyebrows knit and his eyes turned down.

"Let me get this," he said. "You're working at Wilson's making graves."

"Markers," said Noble with a laugh.

"Markers," Janus repeated. "Yeah, I get it, I get it. To make money while you're a sculptor."

"Nope. I became a gravestone cutter to make money while I was a sculptor. Now I'm a gravestone cutter."

There was quiet between them at this, Janus thinking, thinking hard, Noble looking down the street ahead, his eyes, deep and sad, growing deeper, sadder, bottomless, tragic after a while.

"Are you staying with your folks?" he asked Janus suddenly.

"Hm? No. Not if I can help it."

"I can put you up."

"Great. We'll get the car."

In the Chevy, moving down the main road toward the edge of town, Janus thought silently a long while more, then, striking his palm on the steering wheel, burst out, "Now hold it. Let me get this straight."

Noble raised his hand. Janus said nothing else and waited.

"Ever hear of Rodin?" Noble asked.

Janus shook his head. "No. French guy?"

"Yes. A sculptor."

"Rodin?"

"Yes. 'The Thinker'?"

"That guy? He did that?"

"Yes," Noble said.

"Yeah, sure. So what?"

"There's some of his work out in San Francisco. It isn't a bad collection, for the States . . ."

"This guy's good?"

"Yes. He's great."

"Okay," said Janus, "so?"

"I went to Paris to see more."

"Yeah?"

"His house is there, with his sculpture in it."

"You just go in his house?"

"Yes. It's magnificent, the work. It's everything." He paused. "It's everything. The bastard stole my mind."

"Well, hell," said Janus. "You can't say that. You got your own stuff. Maybe you can even get this guy to give you some pointers. You can't . . ."

Noble raised his hand again.

"I don't think you understand. It's not a matter of quality. It's a matter of meaning."

"I don't, I don't get that," Janus said.

"My tradition is exhausted, Jay. It reached a truth past the level of action, and it just—died." He paused, his eyes closing for a moment, as if in sleep, as if in thought. "A passionate mind can only murder or create. And to—to extend your thought beyond a completed art form is to lose the moral complacency, the courage maybe, that it takes to do either." He looked at Janus calmly. Janus looked confused. "I'm afraid, I suppose. I'm afraid to try to be the best and to find the position filled forever, no longer extant."

Janus frowned deeply, leaning close to the wheel.

"No, no, no," he said. "I don't get this. I mean, let's say, I mean, you're gonna laugh, but let's just say, like, you take westerns—those books or western movies? I know, I know, I mean I know they ain't the kind of stuff you mean, but let's just say."

"All right," said Noble.

"I mean, that stuff is—the exact same every time—zact same. Fellah comes riding down the trail, right? Dark secret, he's a gunfighter or something. Always a little boy slobbering over him and a pretty girl and her maw and some kind of dangerous stuff. Same thing, right? Howdy, ma'am, bang-bang, ride off into the sunset."

Noble laughed. "Okay."

"Well? Folks keep reading it. Folks keep going to the

pictures, don't they? I mean, I know—I know it ain't the stuff you mean, I know that. It's just . . ."

He stopped. He wasn't sure what it just was.

"Man, that's just the way it is," he said finally.

Noble nodded.

"I know," he said. "I told myself that. It's the method, I thought. It's the method we lack." He shrugged. "And now I'm a gravestone cutter. Here."

He pointed to an apartment building, and Janus parked the car in front of it. They got out and walked, without speaking, up the path to the building's door.

Noble was living close enough to the railroad tracks to smell the wrong side of them. His apartment, four hard flights above the ground, looked out over thin roads and white houses, old white houses, dirty, run-down, where the town's blacks lived, and its other poor. Trains ran under the window. Freights passed sometimes, too long to take in at a glance, too rhythmic for the sadness of the river barges, but romantic still. They improved the view.

The apartment itself was small and spare. Its main room was furnished with a sofa, some chairs, and an aged bureau with a mirror on it. The walls were bare. There was one other room and a bathroom, neither of which Janus could see; both were very dark, and both appeared to him to be very small.

There was no kitchen, but next to the sofa was a box: a little refrigerator. Noble knelt by it, opened it, and pulled out two cans of beer and a bag of pretzels.

Seating himself in a battered recliner, Janus accepted the food and drink quietly, impatient to resume the conversation. Noble settled himself on the couch. He looked out of place here, an icon in rubble, white on the gloom.

"Not bad," said Janus, gesturing around him.

"It lives," said Noble.

"Yeah. Could be worse."

Noble took a light swig of beer. "So you haven't told me about yourself," he said. "Passing through just or looking for work?"

"Nope," said Janus. "No." He didn't want to talk about this yet. He wanted to drink and philosophize with his old friend. But the fridge was full of beer, and they both would be eloquent ere long, and he did have a mission, so he drank and leaned forward and drank again.

"No. I'm looking for Mary," he said.

Noble paused mid-sip. Light flickered and passed in his peaceful eyes.

"Mary," he said.

"Mary Williams."

Noble sipped. "Nice girl."

"Oh, hell," said Janus. "Great broad."

"She was. You were very lucky."

"I was."

Noble grinned, a pale sort of grin. "You're shit. You didn't deserve her."

"Hey, no joke, my friend."

Both men were quiet and looked at the floor; both sighed. Noble closed his eyes very tightly. Janus said, "You remember when you brought her to my place that first time?"

There was a slight inclination of Noble's head. His eyes were still closed.

"I knew her before that, though, you know," said Janus.

"Yes."

"When we were kids. But she was really—I mean, really a tomboy then. Used to go around in these big, baggy sweat shirts—I think she was hiding her boobs; I think they were huge already."

Noble raised his fingers to his shut eyes.

"Man, when you brought her over," Janus went on, "I thought I'd cream, the way they grow up on you when you're not looking. So pretty and really shy all of a sudden. And you were perfect. 'Uh, can you two deal with each other for a while? I have something to do.' Shit, that was great."

"She was very understanding, very kind," said Noble, looking up at last.

"Yeah," said Janus with a suppressed laugh, nodding. "Yeah."

And the night went on from there, and they got drunk, a little buzzed, friendly and somber and worried for the world. They both had been too long without a confidant, with ideas festering in unnatural solitude, going bad, so each now talked his fill, fretted for the other, pitied himself, and it felt good. By and by they fell into a deep silence, their heads leaning on the backs of their seats, their eyes staring up at the ceiling.

"Thing is," Janus said in a while, as if the subject had never changed, "thing is, I think I still love her."

"Mary."

"I think I love her still."

Raising his pale face forward, Noble shook his head: a definitive comment on the state of things.

"This is very bad," he said.

And Janus: "Naw. Well, hell . . ."

"No. This is bad." He looked around his apartment, pointing to it with his eyes as an example. "This, for instance, is squalor."

"Well. Hey . . ."

"No, no, no." Now Noble was in earnest. "Somewhere . . . I mean, Jesus, Jay . . . There are bright things . . . Money."

"Aw—money is for children."

"I know, but . . . where the barges go, New Orleans, say, it'd be happier there . . . brighter."

"Hell, no. These places—all the same. Man, you gotta shit some of this stuff outta your system. You been alone too long; you don't talk to nobody. Things get blown all outta proportion."

Noble's slim frame convulsed, relaxed. "I know," he said.

"Petty fears and points of honor." He wrote a word in the air with his finger, studied it thoughtfully, biting his lip. "I like to spell 'honor' with the *u,*" he said. "It's a word that should be done up right." His eyes moved as if the word were dissolving, turning into points of light that sprinkled to the floor.

"You've lost her, Janus," he whispered. "I can't tell you how completely, how utterly you've lost her."

"What do you mean? She been here? She's been here."

"Drop it," said Noble. "Forget it, Jay."

"Hey, no, wait a minute, has she been here? Is she still here?"

"Janus, I'm telling you. Listen."

The intensity of that white, chiseled face stopped Janus for a moment. The two stared at each other without speaking, and had it not been for a small collapse, a barely noticeable crease of weakness and defeat on Noble's brow, Janus might not have gone on.

But the gravestone cutter was weary and no longer strong.

"I gotta see her," Janus said. "I gotta, babe."

Noble sighed. Unsteadily, slowly, he lifted himself from the chair, jangling the beer cans around his feet. He walked to the door of the other room and posted himself at it like a guard. Janus also stood and joined him.

Noble reached in and switched on a light, and Janus entered the room.

It was hardly a room, though: a closet, almost, with a single bed covering half of the floor. Janus looked at the dirty, crumpled blankets, the yellow sheet and pillowcase. Noble came in behind him. For a long time neither moved. Then, swiveling only his head, Janus looked at the cracked wall directly before him, moved his eyes across it to the corner, over it, onto the opposite wall.

The breath in the big man caught. Noble turned away. A

reflex brought Janus's hand to his mouth, where, the reflex gone, it dragged down over his lips and chin, falling again to his side. He tried to turn to his friend, but his eyes were riveted and wouldn't move.

At last, the breath in his lungs poured out, cold with the touch of bad blood; iced. A whisper came with it, harsh as a shout.

"Oh, God," he whistled. "Oh, God. Oh, Christ."

In a single instant every light on the Volvo's dash comes on, and steam seeps out from under the hood. The engine tugs twice, stalls once, stops dead. Palmer, cursing, guides the broken car to the shoulder of the road.

# · 26 ·

Steam pours out in a thick white sheet as soon as the car comes to a halt. It gathers around the windows for a moment, shutting off the view, and then dissipates gently in the cold plains breeze.

Palmer hits the steering wheel with his fist and curses again. He yanks hard at the hood release. Violently, he flings out the door—it bounces back twice, and he finally kicks it still—and gets out and walks to the car's front end.

He lifts the hood and sticks his head under it, while Janus steps out and comes to stand beside him.

"What's up?" he says.

Palmer sneers at him.

"There's a big hole in the radiator, I don't know whatall's wrong with the generator, and we're out of oil."

Janus considers the engine, shrugs.

" 'Tain't so bad," he says.

"Yeah, yeah." Palmer shivers in the wind.

Other cars pass, and trucks, large trucks with a suction after them that rocks the air. The cab metal rushes, the trailer rubber pounds, and the whine created by proximity and speed exhilarate Palmer. He looks at his engine, sizzling, dead, and feels left out and eager to be on.

He slams the hood shut.

"Damn it," he says.

"Hell," says Janus, following him around the car. "We can putt along till we find us a station, easy."

"We'll tear up the car," Palmer mutters.

"Naw . . ."

And spinning, Palmer shrieks, "We'll tear up the car, we'll tear up the car, I'm telling you."

"Hey, now, calm down, fellah."

"Bullshit, bullshit!" Palmer spears the air between them with his index finger. "Calm down, shit. I didn't say we should go through that blizzard. I didn't say that."

Janus darkens. He is not afraid of that high-pitched scream, this little man.

"Now you just listen . . ."

"Just shut up," yells Palmer, starting to pace in a circle.

"Hey," Janus growls. "You been driving. You been driving almost since we started out. You're the one behind the wheel, mister."

"Yeah, yeah."

"You take too much on."

"Listen: fuck you," says Palmer.

Janus grabs him by the arm, but Palmer pivots swiftly and knocks the arm away.

"Keep off me," he says.

Janus is quiet. "Calm yourself, son," he says. It's meant to be a dangerous sound.

"Just keep your hand off me," says Palmer.

He strikes a threatening pose, but no more. He's forgotten the methods of violence and the flowing kill—the smooth strike from eye to groin to nape of neck—which always felled his phantom villains in the past. He's forgotten the handbooks on self-defense that taught him how to dispatch the insolent bolster pillows in his room at home. Fear, honor, and the wish to have won garble in his mind, restraining him. He wants out of this badly.

Janus grabs his arm again—it is mostly to show he won't be ordered about. This time Palmer throws the arm off and pushes him in the chest. He uses both hands, but it's like hitting mud. Janus pushes back, one arm shot out, and Palmer falls two steps, trips, and almost goes down. Regaining his stance, he stares at the other. Janus is still, sure, waiting, maddeningly sure. Tears of frustration fill Palmer's eyes.

"I swear," he says. "If you pull—ever pull a knife on me again, I'll bury you. I swear it to God."

"You do that," says Janus, sucking in his cheek.

Palmer stomps back to the car and slams his way inside. Janus saunters to the passenger door and, swinging it back slowly, lowers himself to the seat.

The tough old, hurt old car starts up, with some trouble, on the third try. Across the dash, the warning lights, red, yellow, green, flash on again, and every meter needle, out of whack, clicks to the meter's end and shivers back and clicks again.

Sputtering, barely traveling, at the slowest speed it will, the Volvo gets about a quarter mile farther before it overheats. Palmer stops it, waits while the thick steam billows up and around them and clears. He lets the engine cool and with a delicate touch, of no particular use, turns the ignition key, and they are off a few more yards.

They reach a gas station this way, in steam and starts and short distances. It takes almost forty-five minutes for them to travel a mile and a half. Mostly they spend the time in silence—they curse sometimes, and once, engulfed in steam, Palmer says, "We ought to get a tow."

And Janus answers curtly, "Shit of bulls."

In the end they are poised atop a hill, looking down at a junction of little roads. There's a gas station on every corner but one; there's a diner on that. Engine off, they coast down quietly to the nearest garage.

The last trickle of steam coughs up and hangs above them, like a cloud. Through it, a mechanic strolls over to them, wiping greasy hands on a greasy rag. Palmer steps out to meet him. The mechanic, looking the car over sadly, sadly shakes his head.

"What is it?" he says.

"It's dead," says Palmer.

The mechanic huffs, walks around to the front, and tries to raise the hood. Palmer reaches through the window and pulls the latch. The mechanic looks down at the engine.

"Fern car," he says.

"Volvo," says Palmer. "Swedish."

"Volvo," the mechanic says blankly. He shakes his head again. "Thas quite an engine, quite an engine," he says.

Palmer is used to this; it happens often. The hick mechanic and the foreign car, circling each other, neither admitting defeat.

"Quite an engine," the mechanic mutters again.

Palmer nods, saying nothing.

"Best bet," says the mechanic, scratching his nose. "Yer best bet would be to get a tow to K.C. and find yerself a dealer."

From inside the car, Janus is watching, his eyes held narrow, his lips pressed tight. He sees the mechanic walk into the garage and Palmer follow and both disappear. The steam holds over the open hood, and the hood obscures his view.

After a while he steps outside and begins to walk away from the car. He seems to walk aimlessly, but his course runs straight. He reaches the junction quickly, and there he stands.

In three directions, the land is flat, and the roads grow small between wide winter fields. The roads are empty to the end of sight and seem to head nowhere, through no one's land. The fourth road, to Janus's left, is the hill, the one the Volvo coasted down. Cars come over its peak sometimes, stopping at one of the stations or the diner, then head back the way they came. The interstate's behind the hill. Janus looks away from it at the borders of flat earth and sky.

It is wistful, wistful country, with wistful clouds, hung low: thin, breaking, white. Janus even sighs to see them and shuffles restlessly on the station drive.

"Janus," says Palmer. He's come up behind him. There's no more anger in his voice, but it isn't friendly; it's a little stale.

Janus doesn't turn around.

"Janus. Listen. Go," says Palmer.

Not turning, Janus shakes his head.

"I'd get"—he snorts—"I'd get—five miles." He comes round, smiles at Palmer sadly. "I guess you better use the phone here."

"Listen, just go."

"Naw. Hell. 'Taint no good."

"If you keep your mouth shut, you'll be all right."

With a short laugh, Janus spreads his hands. "I can't, Palmer," he says. The hands fold. "I just can't do that anymore. Was I you, I'd go and use that phone."

Restless, shifting his weight foot to foot, Palmer looks out to the end of the road: at the flat and long land and the blue and bright sky and the delicate clouds passing steady and slow.

His gaze returns. The two look at each other, both visibly disturbed. Janus makes a movement with his shoulders, or half of one, given up then and let go.

"The mechanic will try with the car," says Palmer.

"Oh, yeah?"

"He isn't sure he's able."

"Oh. Yeah."

"Jesus," says Palmer.

"Yeah," Janus says.

In a stiff stride, Palmer is standing beside him. They seem in parade as they start to move. Side by side, they cross the road, steps slow, pace measured, echo even and slow. It's a walk like a walk to a sacrifice when the acolytes mimic the powers that be; it is metrical, like poetry, and fatal, but fatal as prescience is, like a thing before fire in the mask of God. They sit on the cold ground, bask in the cold air. Palmer leans back, and he looks at the sky.

It's a beautiful sky. It is deep; good; deep; and the hard earth's in the smell of things. Palmer breathes long. He aches, and aches . . .

*You would have that border.*

I would have that border, where the blue comes down, at the eye's last acre, deserted and bare; in winter's last hour, when the sun is born, I would have horizons and see beyond: the world, the water, and my own true love. I would go to the river to meet my dear, where a thousand indiscretions melt into virginity and many's the time we'll think on desolation with a smile. Brats in the belfry, half a dozen at least, and she the queen of all and me; captain of seven at the river's side.

*In a sugarcake house in the woods?*

Ah. Smedley. Unless I miss my guess, which I doubt, I would say we are nearing the end of this little adventure. I believe, at the conclusion of the case, we will find Miss Williams has come home to stay.

*But you said that Janus never found her.*

Yes. It would seem that having seen the world and having made her share of, shall we say, errors in judgment, the young lady returned to the place of her birth and retired into temporary seclusion with the intention of thinking things out. Noble, who, no doubt, was aware of her hiding place . . .

*I don't want this to happen.*

. . . kept her secret from Janus. By this time even our pigskin-headed friend would have suspected something was amiss and would have abandoned the search with, perhaps, even a small sigh of relief.

*Or else Mary* is *dead. That would also explain why Janus never found her.*

Quite. Quite right. Shut up. Now—the problem for us is discovering what Janus could not: where exactly our girl is gone to.

*But how?*

Well you may ask. I suspect we will find a clue to her whereabouts in what Janus saw on the wall.

*And what was that?*

A painting, no doubt. One of Mary's again.

*Of course. But—he gasped when he saw it. He was quite shocked. Why?*

Something to do with the subject matter, I presume. As it happens, I've developed one or two little theories about this aspect myself, but I would prefer not to reveal them until we are in possession of all the facts.

*C'mon, you can tell me. I'm your pal.*

Sorry.

*Cough up, shithead.*

No, we must wait for more proof. The game's afoot, Smedley.

*We're hunting a foot?*

No, no, the game's not a foot; the game's afoot.

*Oh.*

In the meantime . . .

*I don't want this to happen.*

In the mean . . .

*I don't. I don't. Oh, please ...*

Calm yourself, Smedley.

*It doesn't have to.*

It only seems that way.

*No. It was you who brought him out of the mountains. It was you who brought him out of the snow.*

It was also I who couldn't fight him.

*Does he have to be there? Does he have to see? Does he have to watch it rise and bloom?*

I'm tired. I need her so much. I'm so tired.

*I don't want this to happen.*

It doesn't matter, my dear fellow. Death is before and behind us—we must take a stand.

*All right! All right! You think you're so clever, Mr. Palmer Higgs. But there's one thing you forgot.*

Palmer grunts. Janus looks at him, murmurs, "What?"

"I forgot my sister's letter."

"Hm?"

"In Denver."

"Oh."

"I forgot."

Janus nods and watches the road. "Yeah. Hey, what's old Sister like? No, really."

Palmer, who had turned in anger, turns back calmly and looks at the sky. He thinks for a moment, and after a moment, in a small burst of words, he says, "God, nice."

Neither says more. Janus swings his face away. Then suddenly, softly, he coughs a little, and then he is chuckling to himself.

"Nice," repeats Palmer, and grimly he nods.

He continues nodding for a long time as the other continues laughing.

# · 27 ·

They sit just so a little while, till nod and laughter lapse and they are still. Palmer shifts position to his side then. Janus stirs a bit. Palmer grunts, and Janus coughs. Palmer grows uncomfortable with thoughts of Mary and Yarnell. A cloud goes lightly across the sun, and the cloud and the sun turn silvery white. Palmer rolls full over on his stomach.

"So what was it a painting of?" he asks.

"Which?" says Janus.

"On the wall? At Noble's."

"Now who said anything about a picture? Boy, you keep on thinking all the time; a man can't hardly build up no suspense."

Palmer says nothing.

"Bet you couldn't tell me what was on it," Janus drawls.

"Yes. It was a painting of some handiwork of Noble's," Palmer drawls back. "Say, a sculpture."

Janus slaps his forehead. "Whoooee. Whooee! I say. I do

say. No fooling you for all the world, is there? I bet I don't have to even go on. I bet you know the ending here and now. Dontcha?"

If I did, you think I'd be here, you insufferable fuck? Palmer thinks.

"Well, try me. Tell the rest," he says.

Leaning on his elbows, Janus shakes his head. "Hell, what's the use? You might as well tell it to me."

Palmer smiles nervously, scratches his beard. "If I did and I was right, you'd change the ending," he says.

Janus laughs. "Reckon I would at that." His eyes glisten with laughter, and when the laughter ceases, without an echo, his smile remains, an echo in itself. But something in the lines of his face, in his forehead and the curve of his lip, is tense and troubled, haunted, deep. The smile relaxes, slips, grows dimmer, falls, and, in an instant, dies, all traces gone, and yet a glimmer of it lingers in his eyes.

That frightened, that haggard, that hopeful face was what he turned from Noble's wall. Those eyes, those gleaming eyes, unfocused, hooked themselves on Noble's eyes and held.

"Is that it?" Janus asked him.

Noble shook his head, as if in the negative, but there was no meaning in his placid face. His slender shoulders shrugged, and hardly changing his expression, he began to weep. He didn't utter a sound. Just once his delicate body jerked and his face fell slightly, but he soon recovered and only wept, with his face calm and even, and his swimming eyes serene.

Head down, looking at the floor, Janus went into the other room. A little dazed, a little numbed, he sat. He lit a thin cigar and smoked it through a long silence.

Finally, he sensed Noble stir; he heard him sniff and thought he turned.

"Sorry for that," he heard him say.

Janus shrugged. "Forget it."

"I never thought I'd hear her name again . . . or that I'd see her here."

Janus nodded.

"I'd hoped . . ." said Noble, but his voice broke. Wearily he shuffled to the sofa, sat down, rubbing his brow with his fingers.

Now, distracted, his eyes flitting from one spot to another, seeing nothing, Janus began to speak, almost incoherently, as if to hear his own voice.

"I don't know, I don't know," he said. "I always kinda remembered you really stern and pure. She was very shy; I remember. But where the hell is everybody? I mean, that's what I want to know. When it comes down to it. Damn it." He kicked the air before him angrily. His lips grew thick, and his eyes filled with tears. "Everyone's sure been flailing hell out of themselves around here," he said. "That's what I say anyway." A tear rose over the brim and fell, running a track down his cheek. He raised a thick finger and rubbed his eye. He sniffed. "What happened?" he said hoarsely. "That's what I want to know. Anyway. What happened?"

Noble didn't answer.

"It was cause of me," said Janus, trying to sound calm.

"I can't tell you what I know," said Noble. "Except to leave it alone."

"You'll tell me. That's for sure." Janus did not know what he was saying. "Anyway, it's because of me she would do it. You'll tell me. I can make you anyway."

"She said not to."

"Not about me."

"Especially you," said Noble.

"Cause it was me. That's the way I see it." One great, terrible sob wracked the span entire of his chest.

He threw his hand up over his face and said, "God!"

"Jay."

"Oh." The hand slipped down. "That's it," he said wearily. "So that's it," he shouted. He slapped his hand down on the chair, shot up, and paced around the room. Noble watched him silently till at last he paused by his chair again.

"Damn," he whispered. He kicked the chair and stared at it. His lips trembled, and his hands did, too, and he stood there looking sad and guilty, afraid he felt relieved that it was at an end.

He felt relieved and tormented and helpless, and he loved her so much. He wasn't sure what she had suffered and didn't know what she had done, but instinctively he felt that she never would have been what he'd come after and never had been what he'd left behind. He was empty forever now, as he saw it, guilty and afraid that he had made it so, guilty and afraid that this alone was peace.

He sighed out his anger and walked to the bedroom, pausing at the doorway, then striding through. He stood before the painting on the wall as before an adversary poised faceless on the lists to charge.

The painting was huge, taking up almost the whole wall. It was a landscape, shimmering with the strokes of abstraction, mad strokes like a dissembling wind. In the background were woods, and the river and the sun, caught in the gold of an afterdawn. From the river and woods, savage brush burst forth, running to the fore where flowers grew wild. Overhead, insects, unnaturally large, swarmed, flew, and dove, sovereign.

Everything leaned toward the middle ground; everything grew to one central point, where a greater growth rose above the rest. It stood in the brush, a god among kings, lord of the flowers and of the flies. It was stark and grand and unaffected. It was Noble's handiwork. It was Mary's grave.

The headstone was large and broad, the lettering high and deep. It was just her name and a date in June and the date in December when she died. It was spring in the painting; six months were meant to have passed.

Janus felt frightened. It was six months past December now. The picture depicted the time, and Janus felt afraid.

Because, at the center of the overgrown mound, in the deep green brush, amidst the flowers, a last pure color grew up with the rest, a final bud sprung forth with the rest: the rising finger of a human hand.

It was digging free. The suggested motion of it made Janus queasy. Again he heard himself say, "Oh, God," and he turned away, and he left the room.

Noble was still on the sofa, composed now, the eyes under control.

"Rodin does something like it," he said.

"Yeah, well, he doesn't sound so dead sane either." Janus dropped to his chair and sat there, his gaze on the floor.

After a while he leaned back and sighed. His eyes grew wet with tears again, and his mouth was working as if he would cry. "I guess that finishes it," he said. He thought some more, and his mouth kept working, and a tear rose higher, but he brushed it off quickly with his fingertip.

"I guess it's done," he said.

Noble looked thoughtfully at his friend.

"You were lucky to have loved her," he told him. "She was very good."

"Was she?"

"Yup."

Janus nodded. "I spect she was." He rubbed a knuckle at his nose and snuffled, pulling himself erect. "I guess I'll go and see the grave and sort of say good-bye to her."

Slowly Noble leaned forward, toward the other. His voice was gentle.

"No, don't," he said. "Mourn her where you are; leave her where she lies. That's for the best."

But Janus covered his face with a spread hand, engaged in a struggle which, like the struggle of conscience and purse, was surely ill-fated either way. When, at last, his hand came down, he stood, walked to the window, and looked out at the lighted rails.

"You'll have to take me there," he said.

"Don't, Janus."

"I want to go tonight."

"But don't."

Janus turned around. His voice was firm. His tears were gone.

He said, "I want to be with her awhile." He smiled. "I want to be with her at dawn."

# · 28 ·

The mechanic shouts again, waving at them from across the road. Palmer and Janus stand and walk to him.

"What's wrong?" Palmer says. His voice is shaky. He bites it back.

"I fixed it," the mechanic says. "I think I got it fixed."

Turning, he leads them back to the car, shaking his head and chuckling, proud. He yanks open the hood, and the three peer inside.

"Now was I you," the mechanic says, "I'd take her to the dealer in K.C., get her looked at. I patched the radiator okay, but I was sorta making the rest up as I went along. It's a fern job, you know."

"We heard," says Janus.

"We hain't equipped to handle em. I done my best." He stands back, waiting for approval.

Palmer keeps staring down at the engine. His face has a deathly pallor, and the circles beneath his eyes seem black.

He grips the rim of the car so hard, his hands pale, and red spots pop out on the knuckles, rise to a peak, and sink away. A word, barely a whisper, tumbles from his lips: her name.

"Is there water?" he asks.

"Yep," says the mechanic. "It was dry as sand, but it's good now."

Palmer slams the hood, steps back.

"Nice job," he says.

The mechanic shrugs. "She's an odd one all right."

"I know it. Thanks."

The mechanic nods. Palmer follows him into the station and waits while he labors to figure the bill. Through the window Palmer can see Janus leaning against the car. There is something strong and arrogant in his movements, something Palmer watches with envy, remembering the story of the barroom brawl, hearing the jolly crack of bone beneath knuckles. Janus fixes a cigarette in his mouth. A fire flares; the thing is lit. Palmer turns back to the mechanic.

The repairs are costly. As he pays the bill, counting and re-counting out the cash, he notices his funds are growing short. Soon he will have to work again, in a store somewhere or a field somewhere. It will not be romantic. He considers wiring his sister for money. That will not be romantic either. This must have an end.

Walking to the car, hands in pockets, he is mightily depressed, terribly confused. Like a wife receiving word of a husband dead in a distant land, he is beleaguered by a loss without a face and a guilty thrill that swirls and will not clear. His brain is humming, and his steps are quick. Without even knowing it, he has swiveled from his path and, with a stiff-arm, batters back a bathroom door, locking it behind him and checking the lock. He steps to the toilet and leans down over it, closing his eyes. There, before his eyes, behind their lids, that grave, its ground, deep-grown and wild, the hidden pit she dug before she graced it, paints itself piecemeal, stone, finger, sand, described as by its tenant's hand, and he, come naked to the tomb, will lie, in a grass embrace, hips rising for the thrust to mud and the mud will squeeze between his thighs and she will be beneath it and he'll grip the stone and kiss it where it meets the earth and hear a hollow sighing under as his buttocks rise and push in a rhythm that will have come to this as he will come to plow this savage ground, to reap the rising hand, to dig his body down to sow the virgin land until, head falling forward, he vomits. Mary is dead.

When he stands, he stumbles, and he staggers when he walks in an attempt to bring some dignity, through romance, to this unlooked-on scene. He winks at the mirror and tries to smile, and washing off his face and rinsing out his beard, he whistles. Arranged, finally, he goes outside and struts to the car, where Janus is still leaning.

"Let's hit the road," he says.

He gets behind the wheel, and they drive off. They both are silent. Palmer sometimes sighs. It is not the tale he thought it was. Poor Mary. Poor Janus. Poor me. Poor everyone. Deep, but not so very deep, a beast, not cruel or kind, but beastly, perverts the power to deduce into the power to dissemble. Aye. It was not the tale I thought it was. But almost. The retreat more permanent. The shame and the love and the life more lost. Nearly as I thought, with but one exception.

She loved Noble. Back in the beginning of it, if it had a start, before this travesty, invented to be told, was lived, it was he and she.

It must've seemed perfection, too. They must've strolled to school and talked, and the town folks must've looked and smiled, and the schoolgirls must've envied and admired, and the schoolboys must've made their jokes and laughed and felt lonely. Girls, who had ignored Noble before, would have seen him suddenly as a romantic figure and loved him in a way for loving Mary. And boys, who'd seen in Mary something a little too niceish and prim, would've recognized all at once the sexuality of her and the chance they'd missed. As much as we exist in others' eyes, as much as we find our pride there and our being, it must've seemed just right for them. They themselves reveled in the imagery, I'll bet—a sweet, pretty painter and a thin, pale sculptor . .

*Much like . . .*

. . . and a thin, pale sculptor, done where I am unbegun, but not just then, not yet. Then he had potential: a spark and a real passion. He was stern and handsome and pure and, oh, the grand torment he endured at his elders' hands as they refused to understand the wild, budding genius that possessed him—Mary must have thought him a great man. And with someone to believe in and admire him, his adolescent ego broke leash—and he must've thought so, too.

Ah, aye, a great man. A man so great, in fact, that that little town, that small-town girl seemed a burden to him after a while. How could he have all there was before him, do all there was for him to do, when already he was shackled to a single smile? Sure. It is a curse to find your love so young—and in a town that size, the illusion that she is the only one, the one above all others in the world, must strain the power of belief to its limits. Her words of admiration and encouragement began to nettle him—she was just trying to hold him down, to hold him back, to keep him from his destiny, to smother him in placidity, sweetness, and self-content. Yes, yes, yes. He grew bored with her and cold with her but had neither the courage nor the conviction to rid himself of her, so . . .

So. He done his only work of art—he sculpted her a Janus.

He met her, say, one afternoon, when school was out.

And she said something like: "Who is this boy we're going to see?"

"Janus Quintain. You know him."

"I used to."

"Well, he's a big football hero now. Real handsome guy? Really nice, a great guy, you'll love him."

"Okay."

"Don't you want to?"

"Well, I thought we could spend some time together, but it's okay."

"You'll really like the guy. All the girls love him."

"And will you be jealous?"

"No. Of Janus? He's a good friend."

Maybe there were weeks of buildup like that: molding Janus's fidelity, his physical prowess, his wit, until she saw what Noble made of him, none else. And Janus, of course, would have been at his best, free, because she was another fellow's girl, to flirt with her safely and therefore well.

So they met Mr. Quintain, who was big and muscular and handsome, and he told his tales and made them laugh, and he used his friendship with Noble as a license to make insulting cracks about him, and they laughed some more. And he grew livelier and more entertaining as he grew more and more entranced with Mary, and suddenly, "Can you two deal with each other for a while?" Noble said. "I, uh, I have something I've got to do."

And he left them alone.

Probably it took weeks or months, but life seemed long then, and things went quickly. Mary found herself between a scrawny, anemic braggart, who was bored with her and cold with her, and a broad, dashing hero, who fawned and wooed and made her laugh.

She took her choice. She chose her Janus. But she loved Noble, and it killed her in the end.

Because in time it began to seem to her that the business

between her and Noble had not been finished. She began to remember their better days, his better mind, his hands. She began to remember him better wholly than he was. And when Janus left her, and when she went away to college, she went with an antique passion rattling around her brain and a hope that it might one day be fulfilled.

That was why, when Yarnell said:

"I love you,"

she paused, and when he said:

"I love you, Mary Williams,"

she paused, too wise to try to go back, too frightened to try to go forward, and so trying, instead, to make a stop, with a little boy like Janus, in a little town like home; to find the starting place again and begin anew.

Then there was the crash and Yarnell torn apart and Mary kneeling by him and the degradation of that place, that house. Until, unhealthy with lack of food and proximity to death and pain, she remembered the old love and made her way back to him, stumbling against his door, in the night, pale, ill, so that he, thinking someone knocked, called out, pulled back the knob, and caught her as she fell. In his white hands.

"Ben."

"My God, girl," carrying her to the bed.

"Ben, before—just—I love you, I do still . . ."

"Hush." His eyes away from hers. "Let me help you. Lie quiet. Hush."

She might then, even then, have lived, if he had loved her—but he was not fit to have her now. He was a failure, and a coward, and not so noble as he once seemed. And she was witness to his crimes against himself, privy to his intimate baggage. When she looked at him, he felt the weight of his old grandiloquence and bravado heavy at his neck. He was a gravestone cutter. He had come to that. And she had seen him. And he could not love her now.

So he kept his eyes away from hers.

"You're not sorry I came back. I didn't mean to."

"No. Of course not." But he kept his eyes away.

Until, finally, hopeless, she died not of love, but in its name, unable to wait for the thin, pale drifter who might be anything, but is her man.

So mourn her.

*Mount her high and weep.*

Weep for Mary and go home.

*Woe.*

Woe.

*Woe-de-yo-doe.*

Woe is me, and I am woe.

*This is the loneliest life ever lived.*

This the loveliest lady lost.

*Woe.*

Woe.

*Woe-de-yo-doe.*

Mourn the morning that meant her end.

*Mount her high and weep, and weep.*

Weep for Mary, and go home.

*Go home.*

I will . . .

*Go home.*

There is . . .

*There is . . .*

No cause.

*No cause to stay.*

I will escape him in Kansas C. I'll weep for Mary and then go home.

He can see it clearly; he has it planned. Taking the car to the dealer for repairs, leaving Janus at a motel in the morning, just going out as if to pick up the car and bring it back around, then driving off, away from this folly which has detained him so long.

Thus, he plans to avoid the end, to see again his sister and the sea, to watch her watch the waves he never loved come in, great breakers banging on the rocks, mighty, steady, seeming to him, at first glance, powerless against the high brown cliffs, until he knows them better and begins to fear for the sweet green hills beyond on which the house is built . . .

I'll ditch him in Kansas C, he thinks. He's sure of it; it makes him glad. It seems to him a final kindness come from the woman he loved who died, some guidance whispered with a fading breath, some soft hand pointing through a closing paw, some good womb, giving through a barren maw a proof of affection on the edge of death, so that mightn't he find her at the brink of dark? He will, just as the night appears; no, as the day is going, at its end, a cloud-enshrouded sun will ride its cover to the west horizon, putting on light in bits and parts till beams pierce through like solid fire pillars into lake and mud and grass, and then the outline of a disk and then a disk and then a ball of flame will break forth, sinking to an earth full gold with a flash on the water and a glow on the grass and a bright, blind thunder to chase all eyes away, pulling in light like a breath as if to hold then to expel a dawn that is the spirit of the day renewed with manifold works of color brought without labor to the labor of men lost in a dark like dying and a night of lions and slithering things.

They will lie; no, they'll be kneeling; no, she'll kneel, he'll stand before this spectacle as before a shrine. She'll even clasp her hands, the bones, the fingers linking in a reverent way until she raises one hand in an utterly feminine gesture, utterly composed, as if to block the light, yet utterly feminine, utterly strong, as if to hold the sun in check, as if to pledge, as if to vow that it shall set no more, and he'll stand straight tall broad firm manly watching, trusting, loving her so much he would not be surprised to see dusk hold, stop, and reverse into a weird and west-east rise that lights the world again.

They'll pose, pause, stand a moment thus, she kneeling, arm bent, hand upraised, he standing, and the sun will turn to orange and silhouette them and as shadows, and as if by chance, she'll lift her free hand, he will raise a hand to hers, and they will join, weld, melted, as if melted by the last good heat of day, till hand is indistinct from hand one, the single star that links the May twins, and with an oath untold, she'll grip the firmness of him, he will feel the soft decay, the yielding that is yielding that is he will feel until in just another instant under just another dark beneath the suffocating sky; beneath the purple sky she'll raise that skull, that flesh, that lovely face to his; how can he say good-bye, how can he say good-bye to that? But she will, let her, she will pause, they'll join hands, she will raise her face, the sun will break from clouds to set, but let her pause, this dream must have a mystery, this mystery must have an end unless time's patient, but she'll raise her, raise her, her face up, and in that smile that now is lost, that will be there no bared grin but a smile, she'll say:

"I love you, Palmer."

And do the words or will the words that taste so sweet be swallowed and thus bitter for he will be silent and it will grow dark for how to say I love you to the dead but she will be, but she will be, the sun and she will be so he will say, why did he pause how dare he and she'll lift that lovely . . . and she'll raise, she'll raise . . . she'll rise up . . .

Mary!

# · 29 ·

Kansas City startles from the land. Revealed by a gentle turning of road, a small dip in the almost flat horizon, it juts suddenly into the white sky of a bright and changeable afternoon.

Palmer makes a noise, and Janus, head hung down upon his chest, snorts, looks up, squints against the light.

"What's that?"

Palmer glances at him. "Kansas City," he says.

"Mm," says Janus. "Go around it."

"Can't."

"Why not?"

"The car needs fixing. I need sleep."

"The car's all right."

"I've got to sleep."

"I'll drive."

"We're stopping here."

Janus grunts again and stretches. "Think we'll hit New York by spring?"

You might, thinks Palmer, but it's quite a walk.

He smiles. He stops smiling. He's unsure, and he can't clear his head. The thoughts of the previous moment escape him, and he tries to reassemble them, but they are gone. He has almost remembered when Janus breaks in, chasing all thoughts away.

"Good town, Kansas City: knew a girl there once, a purty lil thing . . ."

Across the expanse of land, above the city ahead and in its midst, is a coming fury of darkening clouds, a suggestion of snow and a threat of it near the sun. The durty lil story of the purty lil girl carries them down the highway, wrapping them in a peace of rhythm and sound and nonchalant lusts meaning everything quietly and mixing in the motion under the arc of sky. Neither man seems troubled now; both are weary of the ride. Each, with a hint of resolution, sets a face forward to the time ahead, eyes mellowed by his decision and lips tight against consequences and conclusions and irrevocable change.

They enter the city on level ground, slipping into it as if it were a sordid romance. The traffic tightens, grows thicker, and they make their way slowly to the streets and through them, sputtering by signs and signals, looking for a spot to leave the car.

By the time they reach the dealer's garage a flurry of snow is already falling on the city. Palmer gives instructions to the mechanic; the mechanic says he can be finished by tomorrow; on foot, Palmer and Janus huddle off through the winter evening.

Lost in talk, Janus doesn't seem to notice that Palmer is lost in thought and so talks on in a sort of catalogue of lies. Stories run to one another linked by the simplest of threads, joined more by the fact of noise than by a common tone. It is all without exuberance, without hesitation or joy: a habit of speech.

Soon they are at a plaza in the center of town. It is a square of buildings built to look like a Spanish city. Its outline is lit, its edges surrounded, by bulbs of yellow and red and green: Christmas lamps, some blinking, some steady, strung for the remembered season, the forgotten god.

Palmer frowns. "It's Christmas almost."

"Hm?" says Janus.

"It's Christmas soon."

"Oh. Yeah. That's right."

They wander through the plaza slowly, weaving through the crush of shoppers, making their way to the windows of stores, and peering in, noses pressed to glass. The snow keeps falling, lightly still, turning to water as it hits the ground. The two approach the restaurant and stand before it, lost looks on their faces, balancing the price of a meal against their cash and coming up on the wrong side of hunger every time. They keep trying until, in a sudden shift of his glance to the window, Palmer sees, superimposed on the activity inside, Janus, behind him, staring at him, reflected eye upon the real. Palmer turns around.

"I've been planning to dump you here," he says.

"Yeah?"

"I was going to sneak away."

Janus smiles and nods.

Palmer hoists his shoulders up around his neck.

"Uh—but I'm going in the morning," he says.

In a soft, lackluster voice, Janus asks, "Dontcha wanna hear the end?"

Palmer tilts his head for a shrug, says, "No."

And Janus: "Okay." He sighs—as if he were relieved, as if a burden had fallen from him—then he catches it, makes a sucking sound, to retrieve the sigh, it seems, to call it back.

"Goin home to Sissy, huh?" he says.

"Yes," says Palmer, nodding. "That's right."

"Yeah. Sure, sure. Purty lil Sissy. Can't blame you a bit for that." He nudges Palmer rudely with his elbow. "Well, you gonna leave me high and dry and starvin half to death on top."

"I'll buy you lunch," Palmer says.

He leads the way to the restaurant door and, as he reaches it, hears Janus coo behind him, "Purty Sissy."

And he thinks that this has all the signs of a very unpleasant meal.

So they eat—they eat well—and walk out into a heavier snow and out of the plaza, hurrying along streets, trying to find a place to sleep.

They get good rooms in a cheap motel and plunk themselves on lumpy beds, hands locked under heads in a manner of rest, neither resting. Neither speaks. The quiet goes a long way, although Janus mutters into it sometimes, some half-formed narrative that doesn't quite flesh out until, in the end, the silence advances, surrounds, succeeds, and leaves the two men tracing shapes of light and tricks of vision against the shadows on the wall.

For Palmer, there are confusions of snakes: tangle, purple, ugly, cursed. There is a peace of mind he can't remember and a dream he lost and confusions muttering, "These are they," and a faint disgust at what he thinks he sees. He wonders if he has told Janus about his plan to leave him and recalls he has. He wonders why. Talk draws talk, he guesses; yet it seemed then, seems now, the braver way to do it. It made his adrenaline rise to tell him; it made him excited; it made him afraid. He'd been scared (he is still) that Janus would stop him, that Janus will yet, drawing him into a flat, dull cowardice that suspects itself but never ends. There is a force between them that he cannot accept, that he must not ignore if he's to get away, a power that links them in an interplay, that might be used to keep them knit and might drag Palmer down into a place unspecified and a time unclean. He fears himself. He calls up unclean wonders on unclean configurations on the wall, tangled, ugly, cursed, things meant for thinking and left unthought, stray bits of mind he had planned to conjure but recoiled from under the brand: unclean. He is left with calm façades and phallic structures shimmering like boiling cities in an August sun when all an empire is is half remembered guiltily and named unclean. They rise as high as written record and wrong surmise; they smother that little oracle of history, each man, beneath imaginings lined with saints and reason, birthing lies that are not lies, that cannot be, though they attempt it, of a wedding in the leaves and a set sun, of Decembers and Decembers and December's end, and a shortening of eves, and a day done . . .

He remembers . . . He remembers and begins again.

Yes, yes. We'll have her lovely in the dusk, solid, a *peraten,* a perates kneeling there, and when she turns, her face upraised to catch the last light,

"I love you, Palmer," she will softly say.

And he will answer, will answer at last, "Oh, Mary, and I love you," and he will lower himself in silence to her and lie the length of her, all lines hard and all words merely fire breathed from mouth to mouth as witness to this passion, and he'll lift her dress, see nothing, though, not spurred by outer visions but the need to be inside her and to measure the matrix and make it real, he'll lift her dress, see nothing, nothing, and with all things all true, he'll fail first, falling, dying, or he'll say he'll fail and she will understand and it will bring them closer or, what the hell, it's his dream, he'll forgo the ritual of impotence and ascend and enter, seeing nothing, aching, blind and the ground like thunder, and erect they'll stand like figures on a cake, otherworldly, like icons chasing curses, unafraid, and their hands, surrounded by clean faces, crowded by dead eyes who bide their time, and he will turn to her as it is told him, "Say your vows."

And he will say, "My Mary, mine, for time that is, for days gone by, for the moment coming when we will meet and love and save each other . . ." but solemnly, no dry eye in the house, all dead, no dry eye in the house, he'll hear her say, "I do," through tears and he will say that resonant "I do," that lets them know that this is no beast captured but a good man pledged and he'll lift that veil of well-deserved white and she will lift her face up to him and he'll lift her dress before the minister, Janus, and alone together, he'll undress her as she whispers, "Gently."

And he'll say, "I shall."

"Wow!"

Let us—let us begin again.

"It's late."

Let's just . . .

"It's too late."

"Mary?"

"Oh, Palmer, don't leave me."

"Is the sun down? Can't we? . . . The fire. It's cold. Chill winds."

"Oh, Palmer, don't go now. Not now."

Chill winds. Lightning, voices, rain. Whispers that are thunder and a coming quake.

"Palmer!"

Vipers whisper thunder. Wash me in the river with my woman till I

"Wake!"

Palmer sleeps.

# · 30 ·

A young girl's scream, desperate, pleading, distant, growing louder and more real, becomes a broken ring. Palmer sits up and blinks his eyes, shakes his head at the window, where the day is growing dark, and turns to pick up the ringing phone.

The voice coming over seems a legion of voices—the scream has not fully gone away—but Palmer gets the sense of it: The mechanic has checked his car out, and it's ready. Palmer answers with a grunt, hangs up, and lies back down.

He is dozing, even as his eyes close, but he suddenly sits up again and blinks again and shakes his head.

*How?...*

How did they know where I was?

*We came ...*

We came here after giving them the car.

He grunts. He thinks: Janus called them. And he looks

around. The room is empty. Sitting on the edge of the bed, he tries to clear his mind.

*Why.*

Why? To get the car, Mahoney. The bastard's got the car. The idiot. The poor bastard.

He jumps to his feet, strides to the door, then, stumbling groggily, reconsiders, and turns back to splash some water on his face. Reaching the bathroom, he yanks at the knob. The door won't budge. He pulls again.

"Hold on. Hold on," yells Janus from inside. "Can't a man whack off in peace around here?"

Palmer hears the toilet flush, and Janus comes out, buckling his belt.

"The mechanic called," says Palmer.

"Shit, I thought the crapper was on fire."

"How'd they get our number?"

"I called up and told them."

"Why?"

"So I could steal your car," says Janus.

"Pardon?"

"Sure."

"Are you crazy?" Palmer says. "I have the registration."

"Yeah, I figured. I was going to cut your throat while you slept. I may still do it. Go back to sleep."

"No," Palmer says. "The girl at the front desk saw you."

"Yeah, that's right, that's right. I could knock you out."

"I'd wake up."

"Tie you down."

"I'd get free. You'd be caught."

"Mm. Yeah," says Janus.

"They would look for you."

"Unless I lied to you bout my name."

Palmer seems shocked at the idea.

"Did you?"

"Uh—nah. Forgot."

"Mm," Palmer says. He walks back to his bed, sits on the edge. He rubs his face. "What time is it?"

"I don't know. It's close to five. Hey. I could take your body with me. Put it in the trunk and ditch it somewhere on a lonely road some lonesome night."

Palmer thinks a moment. "That might work."

"It's perfect."

"No. You could be seen."

"Well, damn it, a fellah's got to take a chance now and again."

"That's true, " says Palmer. "But there'd be blood."

"I could get you in the bathroom."

"I would lock the door."

"Forget."

"I can't."

"Why not?" Janus whines.

Palmer stands up; he stretches. Janus is watching his throat.

"Because," Palmer says, "then I'd be an accessory."

"Oh," says Janus, and he sits down on his own bed, stumped.

Palmer, standing nervously, with his hands shoved in his pockets, looks at the other sadly.

"Well," he says, "I'm going for the car."

"Yeah," says Janus, not raising his head.

"It shouldn't take—well, I'll go and get it."

"Sure."

For no reason, Palmer glances around the room. He puts out his hand for no reason. Janus shakes it.

"Go get your car, good buddy," he says, and letting go, he jangles backward, like a severed marionette, upon the bed.

Palmer treads quietly to the door, and at the door he pauses. Though now he is eager to be going home, he knows that once there, the excitement of reunion will slowly fail him, and in its stead, the threat of commonplaces, the danger of reverting to childishness under his childhood roof, will encroach upon his peace and happiness day by peaceful, happy day. It's sad.

It's sad—outside, through evening and a wall of winds, a quiet conqueror approaches, slender footsteps blooming under nothing on a sheen of snow. It nears in the silence of a child with an armful of questions, and no one to answer, and no one who can. This is farewell to the country, coming; this is good-bye to the long, good land. With all the hankerings still intact, an armful of yearnings, this is the end of a sweet, useless motion over hills and the brave seeking of disappointments. They christened it rightly: wanderlust. They knew it when they named it, and they named it well.

Pulling back the door, Palmer steps out into a drizzle of rain. He stands with one arm inside the room and his feet on gravel.

Janus calls behind him: "Hey, wait a minute, what about strangulation? . . ."

Palmer shuts the door. Almost on tiptoe, he creeps from it until, as the crunching gravel flattens, becomes the concrete sidewalk, his feet fall. He walks, walks faster and faster, and then he is running, feeling foolish, feeling observed. He was always quick on those long, lanky legs, and now distances approach him rapidly and pass into periphery, and peripheral vision blurs and what has passed is gone and he runs on faster, and he grins and he starts laughing, and he knows he's just doing it for effect in a phony performance of joy, and he can't stop laughing, and it takes his breath till he slows down, stopping in the drizzle and the breeze.

It's still before five, but the streets are jammed with traffic. Palmer, leaning over, out of breath, remembers again that it's the Christmas season.

Astounding Higgs, he thinks. Is it not true that counting on an average speed of fifty miles an hour, maybe fifteen hundred miles to go, fifty into fifteen hundred, it would be . . .

Yes. When dinner's finished, and the drinks, too, and the rest, and she's shown friends to the door and she'll be up in just a minute, dear—my Beth, kind, kind, kind sister, who might, in the spirit of the time, forgive a fool prodigal boy—and when she turns to the tree, the big tree, lit prettily, pretty lights glowing; when she kneels to click them off, and rises in the darkness and pauses as she shifts to go, and moves almost slyly, so to fool herself, to the window; when she stands by the window, the woman who waits, and gazes till long-sought-for travelers, as ghosts, return to love her . . .

Look, Beth! Lights on the long drive! Look!

He rubs his palms together like a crafty villain: hee, hee, hee, hee. And on Christmas Eve, too, I'll come back to her.

He stops a pedestrian to ask directions; then, grown chilled and damp, he starts jogging through the rain toward the post office. The place is packed with last-minute senders of presents and cards, and he has to wait a long time, first to buy a stamp and then to pick up his mail. The stamp he places on the crumpled envelope of the letter he wrote in Denver. That letter, tenderly, he puts in the slot. Finally, squeezing past queues and queues, he takes his mail to a corner, rips it open, reads.

*Dec. 14*

*Dearest Palmer Higgs,*

*I have managed to steal a few moments away to write to you. There is so much activity in the house, though really very little is being accomplished, that I've hardly had a second to be by myself. It's just the usual holiday planning and panic—all needless, but it gives me something to do. Richard's family will be here soon, and while they are all very dear, it is hard to work up much enthusiasm. Last Christmas was a gloomy thing and I missed you. There were all those subtle digs about my not having any money, and Richard's mother did a whole song and dance about her children's accomplishments and then said, "And what is our Palmer doing these days?" As if she understood you in the least. I would have liked to have you there then. You were always the clever one between us, and you could always make people feel vaguely insulted without knowing exactly why. I love to watch them get shocked when you talk. Oh, Palmer Higgs, I'm not happy at all. I want my brother back. Have you seen him?*

*I can't help thinking about how long it will take for this letter to reach you. Here I have saved up all sorts of wonderful nagging and cajolery (something I'm sure you enjoy no end) to get you to come home, at least for Christmas, and by the time you get this Christmas may already be over. If you would call me and let me nag and cajole you in person (as is my wont), I could be much more effective, and we might get somewhere.*

*Anyway, I have already bought you your present, and it is very special, but this time I refuse to send it to you. You will just have to come and get it.*

*Duty calls. I have to go. Take care, sweetheart.*

*I love and miss you,*
*Beth*

Palmer's face has blanched. His eyes flick back and forth between the letter's text and the date up top, and his cheeks keep whitening more and more. As he folds the letter carefully and puts it in his pocket and walks out into the dark and the rain, his posture fails, his shoulders sag, hang heavy, as if physical sense has left him. His mind spins, races, and his stomach turns, for he can't, won't say what bothers him . . .

*What, what?*

Not sure.

*Keep walking then.*

Can't.

*Let's go then.*

Can't.

*Go on. Go on.*

I want to go. Would I stop without a reason?

*What is it?*

Wait.

*What, what?*

Shut up, shut up, shut up.

*What, Higgs?*

Be quiet.

*Think, think, think, think.*

Be quiet, damn you, and let me think. It's like a ghost on the road when a horse rears, like the angel of death—an animal thing. It *is* her painting; it *is* her grave. But it's him, it's him—I'm not without him at the end of this. And damn him, I can't curse him now.

*Sure you can! Get out! Go on!*

I'm sorry.

*God.*

It's just awhile. It's just awhile.

*Aw no.*

It's just a little while.

*Oh, woe. What's to become of me?*

You shall go with me. We shall go to the grave.

*No.*

Yes. We shall go to the grave with Janus. We shall go to the grave at dawn.

## *Saturday, December 24*

# · 31 ·

Leaden, languid, dull-eyed, Palmer's body bows behind the wheel, one arm extended to it and the other raised to grip the window top. Nothing seems to stimulate or move him. Even his anger's just a half idea, souring his stomach lazily. His eyelids droop, giving his face an expression of sordid weariness, like a whore's face. His eyes flick to the mirrors, to his side, then rest on the passing road.

The road must travel far to the horizon, for the land is level and hardly ends but fades in a distant shimmer somewhere ahead. A pale December sun, hung in the center of the sky, seems cold.

Janus is quiet now, too, but his eyes are alive, taut, waiting. He seems scared to speak. He smokes a cigarette tensely and sees a haze collect before it and file out through the slightly open window in a stream. He sees the road.

The road must travel far to the horizon, for the land is flat. The fields around are sterile, dead; not even ghosts would grow there, and the ghosts that grow there are risen at the living's call, a call as ephemeral as themselves . . .

Palmer calls them: auburn, in decay, imagined dripping with the mire of the grave, and dull for all that. Janus and Beth in adulteries and violations, and an urge to lunge, plunge steel in both, lie unexciting on a land in motion, and the land, in motion, doesn't whisk the images away and so seems motionless beneath them and beside the moving road.

At last, a minor irritation, a small impatience, nags at Palmer. Begrudgingly he lets his glance go oftener at Janus, and his jaws move as to chew the words he wants to spit across the car.

He says, "Let's hear the ending."

Janus sighs, relaxes, takes his time. He holds his cigarette up to the window, watches as the ash flies off and as the red tip underneath it glows more brightly. Then he stuffs it out. It flies back, hits the road, and shatters, sparkling. He can see it for an instant; then it's gone.

"So, the rest of it," he says.

And without embellishment, as most good lies are done, he enters on his own.

And on the lean land, where dreamt travesties unfold, unfolds the tale: two figures told to the two imagined, action laid on action until neither is a separate one, till each suggests the other, is the other, both the same; a visionary harvest and a crop of lies with no real difference but to different eyes.

There was a river, the Mississippi, and two men sat by its side. From a slope of grass, which rolled down to the muddy banks, they could see the reflected stars rippling, and barges passing on the great dark mass, and an elegant moon in a dapper sky shattered to sparks of silver by the barge's wake. Janus was silent, watching, legs outstretched before him, limp, elbows propped beneath him, head up, chin pressed down on chest, with only his eyes alive and in motion, scanning the water end to end. Noble sat with his legs crossed and his arms thrown backward, hands to the earth. His head swiveled slowly, and he was silent, watching.

They had been an hour without a word. During that time the river had done its work on Janus: It had made his sadness seem romantic and had almost quieted his wild thoughts with its own quiet flow. He felt partially restored, and sometimes even a fullish satisfaction rose in him, and he sighed. Sitting here, he felt, was communion with something big, with the Real Thing, and only minor annoyances—an allergy to the grass, which made his nose stuffy, an occasionally full bladder—kept him and the universe from an ultimate togetherness.

He looked over at Noble. He needed to speak, desired the old, youthful conversations, the philosophy and instant understanding of them.

"Pretty," he whispered.

"Yeah," Noble said.

"The same. Like I remembered it. I missed it in the East."

Noble shrugged. "I don't come down that often."

"Shoo. I would. You ought to."

There was a small movement of Noble's eyes, unintentional and swift. They went over in back of Janus, glanced at a dark line of forest, and glanced away. Janus brought his head around and looked up at the trees.

"Oh," he said, and then said nothing for a while. He put his hands behind his head, lay back. He remembered he was depressed, and he was afraid of crying.

"I'll miss her fiercely," he said. "I guess I will." He coughed, rolled his head to the side to see the other. "You too?"

Noble nodded.

"Yeah," said Janus. "You liked her some, dintcha?"

"Yes," Noble said.

"Well. Can't blame you. She was something again."

Suddenly Janus made a strange sound, like a sneeze, and he sobbed once and caught his breath.

"God," he said. "Sorry."

"No, it's all right."

"It comes and goes."

"I know. Forget it."

Lifting his head, Janus brought a hand up, wiped his eyes, and settled back down. They were silent again.

The moon, silver and brilliant, was full. Noble's stare was fixed on the spot where its light shown in the water. He seemed to be drawing energy from that reflection, and soon, rocking back on his haunches, he closed his eyes, as if sated and as if to draw more, to draw the whole river for just the moon.

It's a big river, the Mississippi, and everyone knows that it goes to the sea. At night it is perfect. It is perfect and invisible, and any journey on it can be taken with the eyes. The unfriendly heart of it, inexorably Gulf-bound, seems instead mysterious, past fate and past prediction.

Once more Noble looked to the picture of the moon and kept rocking his body back and forth, wanting to speak. Finally, he said, "Janus?"

"What?"

"I loved her."

"I know."

"I'm sorry. I haven't hidden it. If I have, I haven't hidden it well."

"Forget it. Poor bastard. It must be hard."

"It comes and goes."

"I know," Janus said.

The moon arced down and out of the sky and set, and the river turned pitch, and there were many stars. In the darkness the two men sensed each other and, without sight, felt closer than they had, felt close enough to say without regret words they would regret in time. It was intimate and intoxicating and a little frightening by the river then.

"When she came back," Noble said. "When she came back to me . . ."

"Hey?" said Janus.

"When . . . what?"

"Don't tell me this."

"I should."

"It doesn't matter now."

"It might."

"Naw. What the hell's the difference?"

"I guess," said Noble mournfully. "It doesn't matter now."

Janus sat up and dusted his hands. "I better get going."

Noble spun to him, and a spark flared in his hollow eyes, and his hand reached out for Janus's arm, a luminescent hand in the dark, and the voice it carried was dark and glowed.

"She's mine," he said. "She was always mine."

Janus stood and reached down to squeeze Noble's shoulder. It sure was nice to have a buddy. "I know it's tough," he said. "We're the boys who loved her."

"You don't understand."

Janus squatted before him in the dark. "Listen," he started, father to son. "We're buddies, ain't we?"

"Janus, you don't . . ."

"Wait, just—just—are we buddies? I mean, we're buddies, right?"

Noble sighed. "Yeah, yeah, but listen . . ."

"Okay, okay. Now, I'm never coming back to this town—not ever. You wanna go and live with that woman in that pine box in that dirt grave, I ain't gonna be around to stop you."

"Listen to me."

"Wait, just . . . As your buddy I'm telling ya, you can do that. But think about this. Maybe now, I mean, just maybe, you always been a little bit, like maybe there was some things you never got to do that I did: football, travelin around, havin certain women. Maybe it's time you—faced up to that, faced that and just be your own self. Don't try to be me cause it just ain't worth the time. Sure, I been around a little bit, but in the end, you sorta find that one thing's as good as another, and was I you, I'd just go on home and find me a girlfriend and make your sculptures and put that old Rodin fellow out of business."

Noble covered his face.

"Now I'm telling you this as your buddy."

Noble shook his head and lowered his hands.

"Janus, you're right. I admit it. I've always admired you."

"Well, I know that."

"You're a great guy."

"Thanks."

"But don't go into the woods tonight."

"Why not?"

"Because she never loved you. She loved me."

Janus nodded, sighed, and spoke patiently. "Okay. Okay," he said. "You just think about what I told you."

He extended his hand, and Noble shook it.

"Good luck, good buddy."

Noble said nothing.

Janus pushed up and looked down on the other, then looked to the woods and started off.

# · 32 ·

The trees at the top of the slope seemed a black mass, shadowy and foreboding, as Janus approached. When he looked back, he could still make out the river. But while he knew where Noble was sitting, he could no longer see him, not even as a shade. He stepped on slowly toward the trees.

Dawn was near, and there were no sounds, no breezes. The water below was still; the forest ahead was uncannily quiet with its bloom deep and lush and still. Janus's footsteps were muffled in the grass, and the grass grew thicker as he reached the woods, and the ground about seemed darker for the grass and for the looming blackness ahead.

He was frightened as he neared it; as he entered it, the fear grew worse. He was sorry he'd come—the whole idea seemed stupid and sentimental now—and if it hadn't been for Noble, a witness to his dishonor, his honor would have meant nothing, and he would've turned back. With the sky cut off, and the river hidden, and a sense of movement in the corners of his eyes, and a great, stationary forest when his eyes spun round, he felt exposed and defenseless, as if his whole massive bulk were but a sheath for something fragile, small.

It was too dark to find the way. He didn't want to touch the trees. He tripped on roots and didn't want to touch the ground, felt terror, in fact, at touching the ground and, once upon it, clung to the space he touched for fear of finding some terrible thing close by. He thought of goblins as he walked—not laughable, peak-capped trolls, that is, but carnivores, small and awful, near, watching, deadly, dead. He swaggered for assurance and swung his arms to feel the girth and strength they had. He cursed the stares that scared him and the eyes he had invented and his own.

He stumbled, screamed.

He lay, feeling foolish, on the forest floor and listened. There had been another sound, beneath his shout, and lying still, he could hear it: just a current of air, so like the silence that it and the silence seemed the same. He stood and tried to follow it slowly, pausing to listen and going on.

The presence of the wood bore down as he moved for the presence inside the wood. For a moment, unthinking, he leaned his hand against a tree, and something crawled across it. With a shout, he jerked away and brushed at his hand, though the thing had gone. And then he laughed and choked on the laugh and gurgled spit, and a gurgle answered. This was the sound he'd heard, grown louder, and he stumbled toward it again.

Breezes began to filter to him from the Mississippi through the trees, and he turned toward what he thought was the east and bent down some, straining to see light. There was none, not even a patch of sky. The gurgling sound grew louder.

Sometimes he thought it a river, and sometimes a child in pain, and often he found it easiest to think nothing and go forward with a sort of blind faith that all this fear had some purpose in the end. He made his headway through the underbrush, entangled only when he paused, and at last, when the dark seemed at its fullest, when the slightest hint of a world beyond the leaves was gone, he felt his foot sink into water, and looking up, he saw the sky.

It was a dark sky. The gurgling stream he'd stepped in seemed frighteningly alive. Snatching his foot free, Janus shuddered at the damp settling into his sock, making his foot seem strange, like a ghost limb, strange and cold.

Delicately he leaped the stream and wandered slowly into the clearing. The new freedom of movement here made him feel, if anything, more afraid, for it made him feel more vulnerable than he had before. When he stepped forward, the high grass clung to his wet ankle, making it tingle, making him imagine insects, clustering at his feet.

He took two more steps and was overcome. The man's bravery had gone full course and ended. He spun round to run and, spinning, lost direction and ran only to find the nearest trees, but he never made it.

He was caught by the legs and, with a stiff jolt, tumbled, rolling, terrified, into the grass. He felt all manner of hands come clutch him and fought to his knees only through the vigor and strength of his fear. Finally, he tried to stand and, putting his hand before him for a guide, touched stone.

Janus had reached the grave, and it was the grave of Mary that had pulled him down.

"Mary."

He spoke the name but shivered and shut up right after. It sounded like a greeting. He gripped the headstone with the hand that touched it and, holding to it, grew calmer and looked upon the name.

Such winter nights this summer seemed to have: it still was dark. And Janus, in the dark, as he grew calm, grew sad. It was a strange sadness, almost animal: a sensation that a comfort was lost, that the warmest place in the world—Mary's breast—was grown cold. Later he called it selfishness—blaming his past as one transfers his own faults onto others—but it was not that; it was less than that. It was as instinctive as the hurt of a suckling at a dry teat: just grief, is all.

Little by little it numbed him, and little by little it let him go, and when, at last, he wept, he wept for the memory of it and all the time left him in which to remember.

His wet eyes lifted, and the sky was gray. He could see clouds, moving in the predawn dark with predawn breezes, and he felt the wind. He rose and stepped back from the tombstone quickly, removing his hand as from an unclean thing, and he stared at the dirt before it with wide and expectant and horrified eyes. The breezes grew stronger, and the trees around whispered, and the small brook gurgled like a giggling girl, and Janus watched the grave's grass stirring and stared at the dirt beneath the grass.

Even with the thick woods, the sun's first rise pierced through to him, gold pillars like reaching hands. They seemed to push the winds that made the forest whisper. The whisper grew with that wind. The stream's giggle strengthened to a feminine laugh with that wind.

Janus tried to look up, but his gaze was fastened to the restless grave. Out of fear, out of pity, he wanted to reach out and dig at the earth's surface with a helping hand, but his arms were plastered to his side, trembling.

And the winds grew stronger, and the sun rumbled up, and the laughter seemed the laugh of many, mocking, hammering at his ears, and Janus, mouth open, eyes still fixed down, went to his knees and raised his hands as if he thought they caused the dawn, and in the shriek of water and the burst of light, he made his eyes, with an effort, shut, and with a full sun slashing through the rest of night, he brought them up again . . .

•

"Then what?" Janus says.

Palmer doesn't answer, doesn't turn around. He has listened to this with no response but a slight shift of his body against the seat that might've meant interest or just an itch. As Janus's lively voice surrounds him, attacks him so directly, he makes no sign.

"Come on, man," Janus says. "Bet you can't gimme the rest of this."

Palmer shrugs, says nothing.

"Boy, you are not displaying the proper amount of fascination with this here narrative. You don't mend your ways, and I'll be damned if I even finish it if this is all the audience I got."

"There's no need to finish it," says Palmer wearily. "I know the rest."

"Oh. Yeah. Aw haw." Janus laughs loudly and joylessly, grinning, wisely and joylessly, slapping his thigh. "I'll bet. I'll just bet. Come on then, you so smart. You tell me the end of it, tell me what I saw then."

"I know what you saw," says Palmer.

"Well, come on then, genius, spit it out. What'd I see?"

Palmer glances at him dully.

"You saw Mary," he says.

Janus stops laughing, and his smile falls off. He tugs on his cigarette deeply, shaking his head.

"Well," he says. "That's right. I did."

# · 33 ·

"Now how in hell did you get wind of that?"

Palmer shuffles position, makes a face that, had it been a sound, would have been a whine; but he is silent, and the torpor's on him still.

Quite simple, my dear Quintain, he thinks. Dull, too. Even to the untrained observer, like certain paperheads we needn't mention, there are two facets to this prevarication which immediately present themselves. First: it works; it pans, that is—that is, it makes some sense. From this, we may deduce—what was I saying?—we may deduce from this that the tale is either true, a fantastically elaborate lie, or true as you remember it, changed but fairly intact.

*Or true or false, the only sense it makes is yours.*

Yawn.

*Higgs?*

Pardon? Oh. Secondly. Secondly, secondly—secondly, what? Ah, yes, secondly: it's nothing like you've said it is.

Not that you haven't said it all, but truth lies in the why of things. And from this—from this, we deduce—what?—we deduce that everything is true after a fashion and ... What am I talking about?

"The date," says Palmer. His mouth works like an insect on its back. He yawns.

"What're you talking about?" Janus says, annoyed. "What date?"

"On the grave."

"Well, damn it, what of it?"

"It says that she was born in June."

Janus thinks a moment, seems to try to remember, closing his eyes with the effort, then ending the effort, opening his eyes.

"It did," he says. "It said that. I remember."

"She was born in the winter."

"She was?"

"You said so. You said her father found that farm in Pennsylvania in the winter, and that's when she was born."

Janus thinks again, then lifts an eyebrow.

"Yeah. So what?" he says.

"Why lie on a tombstone? Is there no death?"

Janus stares at him. Palmer shrugs.

"That's how you figured?" Janus says.

Palmer nods.

"But what if I lied?"

"Lie or no, it's been consistent."

"Wull, what if I just forgot it, huh?"

"That," says Palmer, "would be inconsistent."

Resigned and sighing, Janus shakes his head and falls into a reverie. Palmer wonders mildly if it's fake, but he doesn't turn to look, looks outside, instead, and guides the car along the interstate, across Missouri plains, rolling land studded with lone dead trees and clusters of them. His hooded eyes fixed forward, he rests his gaze upon the great distance and is passively drawn on by horizons and miles, unrevealed flats past hills, and hills, and the ache to have the hidden stretch and the stretch beyond when the first one shows.

Finally, Janus's brown study ends, and he looks at the driver with interest and concern.

"So why'd she do it? Figure that," he says.

Palmer shrugs again, and then considers. A joke between artists. Yes. A way of cutting off the past. Sort of.

But he says nothing, lets the shrug stand.

"Well," says Janus, after a while. " 'Sgood thing I'm making this up, or it'd worry me."

Palmer smiles. "Good thing."

"So, genius, you wanna hear the last chapter of this exciting tale of danger on the high seas—or did you already figure that out, too?"

As it happens, this is the one thing still confusing our wizard: the story's end. Up till now he has considered the fact of Mary's lost—and lost and lost—virginity rather a secret, suspected at best by Janus, known only to the men who slept with her—and to himself. From this he has deduced, as he would have it, that the football player and the lady never met or, having met, shared neither confidences nor a bed.

But here, to his unending chagrin, which he reveals to the observant by a drooping of his right eyelid sufficient to leave him half blind, here she has appeared and in a spot that wants explaining. Rudely ignoring the incontrovertible evidence so ably sifted by Palmer and his trusty mind, Janus and Mary have met. If she tells him much, or sleeps with him and, sleeping with him, tells him everything, then all his figuring was—curses—wrong, and the man who has beaten him everywhere but at thought has now at last outthought him.

It is not a pleasant prospect, but with admirable restraint, Palmer only grunts as if to answer that he'll hear an end if offered and, if withheld, will leave it be.

Janus grunts back and falls again to thinking. Cigarette poised in fist, fist held by his ear, and mouth set firmly in a frown, he ponders grim things grimly and is well occupied for a time.

Lazily Palmer ponders, too. Indolence aside, he is somewhat curious, somewhat thrilled, and if a haze of half indifference buries his fears, the fears are, like the woman who caused them, buried but not dead. To find her, to achieve her in the flesh—he'd rouse for that, surely. To glean from her story a final clue with which to track her down; to grasp—to grasp—that moment when, astride his faithful Volvo, he comes riding over the discovered country, up the uncovered trail, to a wedding night—a night of lovemaking and making heirs—on which this orphan and this lost girl might be saved—this, yes, this would bring him round.

It could all be true for Palmer, with a son pulled from the life he loves to lead the life he lost in loving. A son. A thinker's boy and soldier he would be, a man of his own action and his pa's philosophy, and it will be his pa who brings him forth, yes, he alone, if to be neither womb nor hero, then deliverer at the very least, to share a joke between artists with a laying on of hands and a bringing forth of that first prophecy of breath.

He will rush to the room where she, in pain, will lie, a tidy bead of sweat drawn dimly on her temple, nuns surrounding her, their lips puckered as if this pain were theirs, the doctor frazzled and already this will be ridiculous but Palmer will rush in.

"How is she?"

"I'm sorry, Mr. Higgs, we're going to have to perform a popearian. Nurse, make the incision in her throat."

"Stand back, Doctor . . ." Ah, no. Ah, no, a storm, with lightning flashing like a dragon's tooth and rain, like the wicked angels, falling.

Palmer will rush with blankets and boiled water to the barn, where she, in pain, will lie, a tidy bead of sweat drawn dimly on her temple, and yet her eyes clear and brave, and she'll smile weakly at him, and he, terrified and guilty, scared and guilty, resolute with slight subconscious guilt feelings manifested in heroics, will return a smile more grim and say, "The car is dead! The bridge is out!"

And she, nodding with womanstrength and understanding: "Eesh, I married such a pinhead."

And she, nodding with womanstrength and understanding: "It's all right, darling. It's just a baby coming into the world, and he makes a big fuss and causes a lot of pain, and then he's born, that's all."

What a broad!

"It's just a baby making fuss and pain, and then he's born, that's all."

And the sky will flash and the thunder roar as if to birth, yes, like to birth a god. A god and sundry saints will hasten from the matrix of the moon and stand, projected, wavering on sheets of rain that, falling, rise like ocean waves, and Palmer, Mary, on the shores, at last upon the shores of seas, will lash themselves to courage in the raging winds and stare into each other's eyes and try to bring forth life.

But even stout hearts have a paltry beat beside the pound of waves, and as they labor on the sand, the ocean will belch forth its heir, a leopard, lion, dragon, bear, and Palmer will hear (Palmer hears) the first commandment of the deep: Worship the dragon, bow to the beast, but though, as Mary moans, he'll turn away a little, half seduced, the little man, this little man, our true, small Palmer, is not gone down, and wrenching back to her he loves, he'll plunge his hands deep in her womb and know the ocean's imprecation—"Blood"—and fear to see the blood, but Mary, pretty, courageous, good, convulsed with pain and staunch against it, will cast her small water in the mighty ocean's face for answer. Taking courage, then, will Palmer, wrenching back, plunge his hands deep into her womb and grasp the anus of creation, tugging forth.

And Mary: "Oh. Oh, God."

And Palmer: "Hold on, pal."

And still, the ocean: "Blood."

Until, with one last hard contraction, Mary will fling her babe against the beast, and while the surf screams laughter, Palmer will raise the newborn up and pat it gently, and all the weather will lull to listen to it cry—and it will not, will not, and he will slap the thing again as Mary braces on her elbows, watching, terrified, and Palmer will become aware that it's dead, stone dead, and the dragon laughing all the while, his teeth, like lightning, flashing, and Palmer will slap again and roar through all the roaring world:

"Live! Live, child! Live."

And Mary, wailing, will begin to weep, and the never-living babe, as if the premier lesson from mother to child is misery, will draw in breath and start to bawl . . .

The storm will cease. The child will cry. The ocean will recede. The beast will die.

And "Hey," will Palmer say, "it's a kid."

And Mary still weeping, will laugh and reach her hands out for her son while Palmer does the necessary wiping, tying, cutting, whatever they may be, and gives it to its ma, and she will lay it for warmth between her legs as if the child would give its premier lesson to the man, and all that's heard of the ocean is a gurgled "Curses. Foiled again," and Palmer will collapse upon the sand beside his woman, he'll collapse beside her on the sand and, as the tide recedes, hear nothing but the cutesy burble of their boy, and Palmer will say something fatherly and amazed like "It's really a kid," and Mary will say something motherly and serene like "Of course it is, silly, what'd you expect?" and Palmer, father, dad, pa, pop, popola, will lie back, staring at the clearing sky, and offer thanks to Sydney the Cosmic Oneness, and a star like Bethlehem's will start and glow, for it should be like that, yes, it should, a star should rise for each child born, a light so small seen from the sod it looks to man as man to God.

Yes, Palmer runs over the whole again, his face convulsing with the various emotions of it. Yes, he would rouse himself for that, surely, truly, and he is sure she's truly near, untouched by his companion, ready for a love untouched by measure with another.

Deep, it would appear, in thought, this threat, this Janus, casts a sidelong look at his fellow and, eyes flicking back to place, grunts once and straightens.

The car has crossed the Missouri and grows closer to the Mississip. The sun's behind it, setting with a leaden dullness and no blaze. The Volvo travels slowly, and so slowly the bleakish plains pass by, and both men's eyes are on the road, and both men's thoughts around the bend.

They near the country of Mary's tale, as Mary's tale begins its end.

# · 34 ·

Mary Sue Williams was a pretty young woman, with a fresh, freckled face full of the open airs. Her cheeks were round and rounder for the round pink blush upon them. Her hair was striking, silken, strawberry blond, and her green eyes were witty and kind. But of her features, her finest was her smile, which, opening shyly, broadening slowly, beaming, bunched her freckles and wrinkled the bridge of her small nose.

She was dressed in a blouse and slacks, light spring wear, each a different shade of green. Slim legs, full hips, slim waist, full breasts tightened and softened the surfaces of the clothes.

Standing by the trees through which the dawn had broken, she was caught by the sun, and Janus saw her first as a radiant specter, the source and center of a circle of light. He would have, in that moment, dubbed her Aurora had he known the name, but instead, thinking her a goddess, ignorant of the goddess he thought she was, he only stammered a little and stepped back from the grave. The picture he saw then—a glowing lady behind her own tomb—only confused him more. With a silent movement of his mouth, he came to a stop and stood and stared and awaited the descent of the rest of heaven or the rise of the rest of hell.

Mary must have been bewildered, too, because she paused before coming forward out of the sun and peered at him cautiously as she approached.

"Jay?" she said. "Is that you?" Her voice was rural and flat, soft and slightly nasal. "Jay? Are you all right?"

Moving closer, she rested her hand on the gravestone. Janus shuddered, and Mary, perceiving it, looked down blankly at the thing on which she leaned. She stared from it to Janus, and she realized what was wrong.

"Oh, poor Jay. Didn't you talk to Ben? Didn't he tell you?"

Shaking his head, Janus gulped.

"No," he said, and he spat out the word.

"Oh, gee, I must've frightened you to death."

Janus did not nod or move. It was the sight of her touching her own grave that held him, but it was the woods that made the illusion last; the deep seclusion and the sudden light that made the strange corollaries of the image seem possible so long. Even here, however, sense, sight, sound, the common knowledge that folks don't stroll about much once you get them good and buried worked to break the spell, and finally, warily, Janus found his tongue.

"Bleeding Jesus. Is it really you?"

"Course it is." Mary let the stone go and came within a step of him. She smiled. "Who else? It's my grave, isn't it?"

"Ugh, please."

Mary laughed, then tried to stop and giggled; she took his hand—he pulled it back once, but she, with a kindly insistence, retrieved it—and tugged him after her as she walked.

"Come on, we'll get away from here," she said.

Janus followed her to the edge of the trees and to the stream. Nimbly she leaped across the water and plopped herself down on the grass beyond. Janus stepped over and sat beside her, facing away from the clearing so he wouldn't see the grave, still visible behind.

As his thoughts began to clear, Janus began to tremble. Tears welled in his eyes, and he spoke harshly to drive them back.

"Well, what in hell is this anyway?" he said. "I mean, Jesus!"

Mary shook her head and laughed through her nose. "I'm really sorry, Jay," she said. "I really am. It was just . . ."

"I mean it," said Janus. "Was that supposed to be funny?"

"Kinda crazy, huh? Well, I was feeling kinda crazy at the time."

"Jesus."

"But didn't you talk to Ben?" she asked.

"Yeah, sure I did."

"He should've told you."

"He knows."

"It was him did it."

"The bastard."

She laughed outright. "Poor Jay. I really am sorry. I guess he was just protecting me, is all. He didn't mean anything."

Janus grunted sullenly; he had not rallied yet. She was different, this Mary, from the one he remembered; even with allowances, she was not the same. The softness, the kindness, the pity—and she was a woman men lived to be pitied by—were all there, in her voice, her breasts, her lips, all there—but different, changed somehow. He could see it in the smallest thing. A thin row of perspiration just below her hairline—it had not been there when he left her. A motion of her head that whipped her hair back and over her shoulders—a motion that made him breathless—a motion she'd never made before. Her eyes, her green, her glittering green eyes, were fathoms deep now and had a new humor in them; her glance seemed the record of the follies of a man—this, too, was a transformation.

And Janus, who wanted to weep to her, plead to her, confess, couldn't, was afraid to.

She gazed along the forest floor, quiet, thinking.

Janus was afraid of her. And that made him angry. But he had not rallied yet.

So, plaintively, he said, "Well, what's going on, anyhow, Mary?"

"Well now." She smiled. "That—is kinda a long story."

"Yeah?"

"Well, I don't know. It was kinda bad for a while. I was sorta in a state when I came home. I'm only a small-town girl, as the saying goes, and I guess I just hadn't counted on a lot of things. I don't know, Jay, everything just seemed to go wrong somehow; nothing was like I meant it."

"I guess it was all my fault," he said hopefully.

"Aw, no, of course not. It had nothing to do with you."

"No, I shoulda wrote to you," he insisted.

Mary answered nothing, sat with an amused patience that made him angrier still; jealous, too. When she sighed, so calmly, he found himself almost shouting at her.

"I mean, that way you coulda come out and gone to school with me and everything would've been okay for you. Right?"

She looked at him, and his face flushed scarlet, and he grew angrier as she turned away.

Janus let out a deep breath. Mary was pensive; her green eyes turned down upon the grass, and her teeth worked at the corner of her lip, her brows pulling prettily together. In that instant, with her sitting so, her small shoulders relaxed and her breasts in the rise and fall of steady breathing, Janus wanted her and loved her wholly. And he was angrier still.

She sat like that for a long time. And then she spoke very softly. "See. I had kinda a bad go of it for a while, Jay."

"What do you mean?"

"I don't know. Just everything." Mary's flat voice was steady, very soft. "My folks—poor Mama and Papa, you should see what's happened to them."

"I saw them," said Janus.

"You did?"

"Trying to find you."

"Then, see how it is, they're sorta—gone. It was all different in that old house, and nothing was there for me, so—I went away to school, and I had this friend, this real sweet friend, and then, he, he got himself good as killed really."

"Yarnell."

Mary seemed only mildly surprised.

"You know?"

"I talked to him. Trying to find you." Janus looked down at her lap. He set his teeth. "You love him, did you?"

"I don't know."

"I mean, well, I mean, what was, what was between you?"

"I don't know, I don't know, Jay," she said impatiently. "That's not the thing."

"And, and that place, that place with them bums in it."

"Yes. Then that."

"What about it?" said Janus, growing angrier. "Were you, I mean, what were you . . ."

"Jay, no, stop." She shook her head, tousling her hair, then made that unconscious motion that whipped the hair back. "Just—I just wasn't ready. I wasn't ready for a lot of the things that happened."

The two looked at each other silently, and Mary tried then, earnestly, to explain.

"See. When I was little?"

"Yeah?"

"Well, when I was little, I was—well, I was—a—good girl." She laughed at herself. "But I was. Really. I was a good little girl when I lived here."

"Not now?"

"Well, now, see, that's just it. It gets so hard. It gets harder and harder. Just to know what you're supposed to do, I mean. And I kept wanting to get—get hold of when I was a good little girl again. So's I could remember what to do and figure things out. So I could—I could get at the truth of the matter." She shook her head. "I tell you. Plenty of things don't come in handy in this world, and one of them's knowing the truth of the matter. Not the whole of it anyway. I mean, you gotta start somewhere, you got to just take hold of something, else—else what're you gonna *do*? All I did was miss when things were right and picture when things'd be right again—when I'd meet a guy and all . . ."

"And me?" Janus couldn't help but say it. "Did you miss me? Ever?"

Mary looked at him frankly. She was very serious—but for her eyes—and her voice was very soft.

"Yes," she said. "Sometimes I'd miss you. And this town. But mostly, I just missed being young."

"But hell, kid, you're plenty young."

"I know, I know, I'm just trying to tell you how I felt."

Janus didn't get it. He shook his head.

"So how'd you feel?"

"I felt not as young as I used to be," said Mary.

"Who all is?"

"No one is. But neither was I. Don't you see?"

Janus did not. She was full of ellipses to him. To him, it seemed the heart of her story was gone. He kept looking at the way her cheeks were—soft—and her thighs inside the pants, and he wanted to know, to *know.* He was so frustrated by it, so angry.

She went on. "And—and—I wanted to be young—but I wanted to be old, too, with kids, and with my husband."

"Mary . . ."

"And . . ." Her body had tensed for a moment, but she relaxed again now, as if she had stopped trying to make him understand. She smiled, kindly. "And—I finally worked myself up into such a snit over the whole thing that I was likely to go crazy. Did you see that last picture I did?"

Janus nodded. "Yeah."

"Well, then you know."

But he did not. Mary's soft and soothing voice was pleasing to him, more than that, but the words made no sense—she was withholding the sense—and he felt pushed off her and lonely. Angrier still.

Mary went on.

"Ben, when I came home—here—he reminded me of the Crawford shack, up yonder." She gestured toward the woods. "And I came up here to sorta get away, think things over and all. It was Ben made up that stone. Sorta a joke between us. But I sure wish he hadn't. He said it would make me feel like all the bad stuff was over and I could just start fresh whenever I wanted. He got it from that awful painting, but it was all a mistake. That's just what I didn't want at all." She considered a moment. "I guess that's why I kept it, though," she said. "I guess it served its turn."

Jealousy and anger and adoration full beyond their mark in him, Janus came around. The situation was as Noble said: He'd lost her—not to death or another man, but to an unexpected, an unknowable calculation of her own, cut off from him and his considerations. All the sins he'd brought here for her pardon, and the love he'd dragged along for her delight, were nothing to her. So, of course, he was incensed. He knew she couldn't love him if she couldn't forgive him, and how could she forgive him if she blamed him for nothing?

He looked at her hair, falling, silken, over the round cheeks; and the witty green eyes, deep, bright, flashing, and out of rage and love, out of spite and desire, he resolved to win her back. It was only the old game after all: to make of himself a creature she could not help but love, evoking pity, petty anger, passion. And he had—who has?—no scruple in the getting of her but the gain because, simply, this was not the way he was going to let it end.

As she gazed into the running water, Janus stretched out on the grass beside her, dreamily plucking blades out of the ground.

The early-morning sun was already golden, already warming the inner wood. Birds were creating a row above them, and insects in motion gave a motion like a breeze's to the leaves and the grass and the air. Janus took a good, long breath of the day.

"Ah, it's nice," he said.

Again Mary raised her head suddenly, her hair whipping over one shoulder and spilling back, and she smiled. "Isn't it? I love it here."

"Don't blame you. I sure missed this place when I was gone." He made his eyes seem tragic, just for a moment, and then courageous and resolved.

But Mary didn't go for it, or else she wasn't watching, and Janus said, "Yeah, I missed the old town and the river."

Mary gave his arm a patient and lackluster pat.

"Poor Jay," she said. Then—though he was not sure whether it was to elaborate on or change the subject: "So now you have to tell me what you've been doing all this while."

"Oh, I don't know," he said, sad and brave. "Just wandering around—place to place, I guess. Seeing some things."

"Did you finish school?"

"Yeah. Yeah, who'd believe it? I squeaked through." A bitter memory filled his eyes—but that! for it, and a jaded smile.

"Did you play football?"

"Football," he snorted. "Yeah. Yeah, I've played some football. Got an offer from the pros."

"And you didn't take it?"

"Nah."

"Oh, but, Jay, why not? I thought that's what you wanted."

"Aw, hell, Mary." And with one of the deftest ass-swivels in courting history, he dropped his head into her lap before she even saw him coming. He stared deliberately past her, into the treetops. "I don't know, I don't know," he murmured. "I want—I want—something else right now. Just to get away for a while, get everyone off my back. This travelin around all the time, no home, it gets to you. I want to cut it out, to settle down. You know?"

And here he looked directly at her with the eyes of a blue vagabond on a league full of sorrows.

"I been trying to find you," he said.

Mary reached down and touched his cheek and smiled. "Listen, poor homeless child, head off my lap."

"Hm?"

"Come on, and we'll go for a walk."

She lifted up a little, and he had no choice but to rise. They stood, staying for a minute to brush the earth from their clothing, then strolled slowly into the forest, through the lifting angles of the beams of sun.

"What about you, Mary?" Janus asked. He was the shy kid now, shucksing and shuffling, broken twig in hand and on his lips a faltering smile. "What's exactly a person do out here?"

She laughed a bit. "There's a good question. Read mostly. I'm quite the educated lady these days."

"Yeah? What kind of stuff you read?"

"Oh, old things. Poems, novels."

"Whoo. I guess you understand that stuff better'n me. Jeez, they almost bounced me outta school on account of them."

"Mm."

"I guess you're too smart for me now, huh?" There was real charm to his grin.

One corner of Mary's mouth turned up. "Hm," she said. "I think I'm being wooed here."

Janus shoved his hands in his back pockets. "Yeah," he said. "You are."

"We better talk, huh?"

"What about?"

"Well, you been trying awful hard, it seems, to find me."

"Yeah," he told her gruffly. "Cause I love you, Mary. I always have, see, and now I know I do."

"Oh, Jay." She gave him a smile of such honest friendship that he wanted to knock the teeth out of it.

"I love you," he said again, furious that this alone didn't subdue her.

"Oh, I don't know." She smiled at the ground. "I'm not sure you'd want your old Mary now."

Janus stepped to her and took her by the shoulders. "Mary, I'm telling you, I do. Why won't you tell me anything? Tell me what's happened. Another guy? Is it another guy?"

"No, there's no other boy."

"Ben?"

"No."

"He says so. He loves you."

Mary didn't answer.

"Is that it?"

"No, Jay."

"So what then?"

"Can't it just be over? That's all."

"No," said Janus. "It can't. I love you."

Mary freed herself from him and walked over to a large white oak, leaned against it, patting it like an old friend.

"Know what I did when I first came here?" she said.

Janus shrugged gloomily.

"It was just summer, and I came up here and sat down under this tree, and I cried. Gee, did I cry."

"Over what? Who the hell? . . ."

"Jay, it doesn't matter. It doesn't concern you."

Janus almost choked on that.

"I sat under this tree all summer, and every day I cried. I don't remember eating or sleeping, just bawling like a baby. I felt so bad." She looked melancholy for a moment and then only wistful. She looked at him directly, still frank and straightforward. "Then, Mr. Janus Quintain," she whispered, "you won't like much what I did then."

"What?"

"I—I took off my clothes. And I sat, spread-eagle, in the brook and let the—water run up into me until I—I was finished"—she looked down and colored—"until I finished. And it was better after that. Oh, Jay, I was just all ready to start with that and—and leave here and go and get it right."

Janus stared at her. Once, in school, he and a friend had ganged up on a kid they didn't like. Janus's friend had dropped a blanket over the kid's head from behind, and Janus had knocked him cold. Disgust dropped over him now like that blanket. Disgust that this should be she, that this should be Mary. The very solitude of the woods, which gave her peace, whispered his anger on: No one's watching.

"Then I came back and messed it up," he said. "You mean that?" His whole appearance darkened. He was downright frightening now.

Mary clung a little closer to her tree.

"Jay?" she said.

He took a step toward her.

"Ben says you never loved me."

"Jay, don't you remember what it was really . . ."

"Shut up!" He had lost control, and he screamed it. He took another step, coming closer, and for a second she cowered from him, hugging the tree. But then she straightened, and with that glance that so infuriated him, and that smile, she shook her head.

"That's not fair," she said quietly. "You're playing on my . . . politeness."

"What does that mean? What's that supposed to mean?" He was right up to her, towering above her.

Without pleading, without even a doubt, she said simply, "You are. Now come on, and let me get away. I'm nothing to worry over. Let me just find some man somewhere and have some kids, and don't think about me." He could see the children in her eyes. He hated them. They weren't his.

"You—blame—me," he growled.

"I don't. You want me to, so you won't have to. And you can't, cause . . ."

"What!"

"Cause then you can't blame me for it anymore," she whispered.

It was a broadside, and she took it because he scared her and she lost her temper and because, here, she was invulnerable to all but physical pain.

Janus slapped her.

# · 35 ·

Janus was too big a man to go around slugging women like that. His arms were too thick and muscular, and his hands were too thick and hard. It was a light backhanded blow, flicked at her without much force, and she was a sturdy girl of country stock; but it toppled her, and she fell beneath the oak and lay there.

Even as she stumbled, even, in fact, as he threw the slap, Janus regretted it, would have pulled it back. His fury was released, relieved, in the movement of his arm alone, and when he actually connnected, he was shocked and, seeing her fall, horrified.

"Mary!"

He dropped to his knees beside her, shouting her name. "Mary. Jesus, are you all right? I'm sorry. Jesus."

Mary was dazed for a second but regained herself in another and her green eyes were brilliant, calm, and filling with tears. One drop rolled over, rolled down her cheek to wet the red mark rising there.

Janus shouted again and took her by the arms, but she seemed so delicate to him now that his grip was limp, and he feared to jolt her.

"You're okay," he pleaded.

She sat up in his grasp. Janus looked close to crying, and he brought her to his chest and held her gently, rocking her back and forth.

"You're okay, you're okay," he said.

Holding on to his shoulder, Mary started to stand, and he helped her, standing with her, guiding her slowly to her feet.

"Are you okay?"

"Yes," she said.

"I'm sorry. I'm sorry. I didn't mean it."

She pulled free of him, walked unsurely back to the tree, and leaned against it, looking off into the woods.

"I know," she whispered hoarsely. She bowed her head, and the tears came freely, and yet she seemed somehow at ease, crying more from the slap's sting than from sorrow. In a while it stopped.

Coming up beside her, Janus propped himself against another tree. He was smart enough to keep silent and did, as the girl snuffled quietly, quietly struggling to be composed.

Now that he knew she was not badly hurt, he began to feel better about having hit her. Perhaps what he'd done in anger, out of control, had been an inspiration. It was sensuous, wasn't it? Force, when the pain was gone? It showed he was a strong man, didn't it? A man deserving of her love and her pity. A mighty man. He still felt terrible to have bruised her, it's true, but hadn't he, hadn't he happened on the precise, forceful nature of a man she'd love?

But it didn't work that way. She faced him, not passionate, not angry, without tears. Revenge—whether in itself or on him—seemed beneath her. And although the welt upon her cheek was rising large and ugly, Mary might have been untouched for all he noticed in her eyes.

Her voice was quiet, steady, and it was kind, and that made Janus fear her all over again. He was as furious as he'd been before.

"Anyway," she said, "it's like I told you. And maybe I better go, huh?"

"Mary. I'm really sorry. I don't know my own strength."

"I know, Jay. I know." She stepped to him lightly, stepped up on tiptoe, kissed his cheek. "Take good care of my old Jay," she said. "Good-bye."

She was walking back to the clearing when Janus's hand shot out at her, grabbed her arm. His fingers made the circle around the slender limb, but they did not tighten. He was afraid of hurting her again. His hand dropped back.

"I love you," he said.

She had turned when she felt his hand upon her, slowly, as if expecting it.

"No, Jay. You don't love me."

"God damn it!" he yelled, and again he stood over her, his arms trembling with the urge to take hold. "I want to make love, to make love to you."

She looked in his eyes, but only as she'd gazed upon the grass, reflecting in that maddening manner, self-involved, and utterly—he finally saw—utterly, utterly vital.

Then, very gently, she nodded once.

"Yes," she said. "I think that's the thing."

He stared at her.

"Well, I mean, hell. Well, I mean, hell. I don't want it that way," he lied.

But she, perhaps none too eager herself, did not help him out by convincing him otherwise. She simply stood there, saying nothing, and with her hair stirred in wisps by the wind and her bruise lending her a fragility that made her wholly adorable, she was convincing enough.

Janus was terrified, hated her, wanted her, began stalking around in a circle like a beast. Like a beast, he whipped his head up, lashed a finger at her.

"What're you doing? What've you been doing?"

"Jay," she said.

"No. Now, what've you been doing? With that Yarnell, huh? And in that godfucking, fucking, fucking house?"

But she only turned her palms outward and raised them a little, as if in supplication. She had explained everything.

He broke from the circle of his stalk and lunged at her and grabbed her to him as if he were grabbing her from the brink of a pit, but her eyes—her eyes were tender ones—slowed him, and when he plunged to kiss her, he kissed her gently and was surprised, was delighted, when she did not resist. Her lips were so soft, and her breasts were so soft, and she seemed, in whole, so little near him that he wanted—more than just this—to possess the total of her, the essence and the vitality and the essence of that, and he couldn't let her go when the kiss broke off but held her, his arms around her, her hands on his arms, and kept kissing her cheeks and her hair and her eyes and the purpling mark he'd made.

Of a sudden, though, he pulled back from her, and she saw his face: the face of a child afraid of the dark, of a dark where ghouls devour saints and Christ's unarmed. She reached up and laid her hand on his cheek.

"Oh, poor Jay."

"Mary?"

"Don't you see? Don't you see what you've done?"

He pulled her down with him to the earth and laid her back on it, her hair splayed out all gold around her head. She smiled at him. But Janus shivered. And now, from the deep beryl solitude of the wood, a sound tolled, sonorous, grisly, and just for him.

It echoed and fleshed behind his brow, once tolling never

ended, source and its reverberation simultaneous and the same. There was no peace in gazing at her, no respite when he looked away, for something of her sprang to greet the bell, the bell immortal or ever dead, a hollow drum, a clapping to, the final slamming of a vault. The woods shut, locked. The echoes rung. He looked—and, in her eyes it hung:

By my fault. By my grievous fault. By my most grievous fault.

With a hard, quick yank to the right, Palmer takes the car to an exit ramp, its tires screeching in the turn. His body's recklessly relaxed; his eyelids, drooping still, droop over eyes on fire, intensely dead.

The sun has had a leaden set, is gone, and night is blackening. They cannot see thė river, but it's there, just where St. Louis glows and just ahead.

"Where we going?" Janus asks him.

"This is all a lie," says Palmer very quietly.

"Well, now. I am deeply shocked to hear you say that. I am."

"All of it," says Palmer as if he were in a trance.

"Too true. You want to hear the rest?"

"We're camping here."

"Aw, what for? It isn't even late."

"In the morning I want to go up to the woods."

"What woods? There's no woods here."

"Shut up."

"It's cold. I ain't got a sleeping bag."

"I've got a blanket."

"Shit."

Palmer takes the car along until he spots grounds not far from the city. They are almost empty; a few collected trailers, strung with lonesome Christmas lights and figures, huddle in one sector, but the rest is brown and bare.

They pick the lot that's farthest from the others and

come out to make camp. The night's bitter cold, and they scramble for wood, moving in a jump and shiver, artlessly piling twigs together, then stooping down while Janus torches a can of Sterno and shoves it in. The cold twigs are dry, catch fast, soon blaze, and fed with snapped-off limbs of trees, the fire surges to a billow, holds.

Palmer makes a final dash for the car and brings back his sleeping bag and a blanket roll. Then the two men squat by the heat with raised hands.

"We'll have to keep it going," Janus says.

Palmer nods. He stares blankly at the central flames and blankly throws a twig in, settling from his haunches to his seat. Janus follows suit, watching him, but Palmer stays at gaze, gazing only on the fire, his face expressionless, his eyes dull and wide.

He is thinking of his lady; he is picturing her face, with amendments started in the name of truth abandoned in the name of pleasure and a mind at peace. He sees her in the forest, and he paints her by her grave, and he wonders what she wondered by the trees and tries to understand what, naked in the brook, she knew.

His brain's not up to it. His stomach aches. And hazily, behind the flames, he knows the shape of Janus flickers, making fear of fire, introducing pain to this, his love.

So did she take him, like the water, for a lover in the leaves? Was there not another lie like this? He is too tired to think back.

Smedley! Come here. I want you. For I think . . . I think . . . What do I think?

*He thought she was a virgin, though he told you she was not.*

Good God, confusion.

*Aye.*

I don't know. I don't know her. Did she send him off? What was she thinking? That's the ticket here.

*What was she thinking?*

Aye. And I don't know. Ah, confusion. Ah, I am confused. What was there suffered, and what said? Ah, I am confused.

*Poor ba-ba-loo.*

I have a sense of things, that's all. Perhaps that's all I've ever had: a sense of things, proven with deductions after the fact. One can build palaces with an imitation of reason and never find the truth. I have a sense of things. That's all, that's all.

*And Mary?*

I love her.

*I'm sorry, old boy.*

And I'll find her. Tomorrow. Soon. I'll track her from the woods. If not, I'll go see Noble. And if not, I'll go see Tom Yarnell. If not, I'll see her parents, but I've got to find her cause I love her.

*still*

And maybe in this Christmas I will find her if she isn't far. She wouldn't let a stranger have his holiday alone. Just let her discover me, give me time.

*To know you is to love you.*

Well, just let her give me time.

His eyes flick up and break the spell of staring. He is looking at Janus, and through the fire, Janus looks at him.

"The end then," Palmer says.

"All right, the end," says Janus. "But you sorta screwed me up. I mean, you cut into it just as I was getting to the good stuff."

"All right. All right. The end."

"Yeah, yeah. Well, after I fucked her, we sorta talked for a while, and I, I sorta realized she was right. She hadda go her way, me mine, as they say. But it was good, I tell you. It was sweet as pie to have her one last time." He chuckles. "Man, let me tell you about what sweet means."

That laugh, that laugh without an echo, coughs into the fire and blazes and burns. Palmer knows what is coming now. It is Janus and Mary together now, flesh and dream sweating in the June wood. He has to listen carefully. He must listen very carefully. He must know the truth of the matter.

"Whoo," says Janus. "Old Mary. Yeah. Man, it was frightnin as lightnin, cause when it's the one you love, boy, when it's the one you really want, it's really on the line. Maybe that's why I was so rough about it, you know how you get. But I don't know, she liked it, I think. They like it, you know. Hee, you shoulda seen her when I whipped it out: Her eyes got all buggy, and she started shaking her head like no, and man, oh, man . . . She squealed something when I put it to her, wriggling and screeching like she'd bring the woods down. O'course, it was all right, no one around out there. Just me a-puttin it to her. Whoo! And her a-holdin on. Christ, a-holdin and holdin on." He laughs and wipes the sweat off his face. "It was like the first time, for both of us. I mean, it was like the first time! Women, they sorta tighten up when they're without it awhile, and like I said, I guess I was a little rough, but she was squealing and crying, and there was blood. Yeah. Man, oh, man. Sweet as pie."

The fire crackles, sways with a frosty wind, and rises greater in its wake. Palmer stares, though now not at the flames, but at Janus or the shadow of him, orange, wavering, malevolent. He feels very sick and gulps once, and his mind races but is empty even so.

"Well, then we were quiet after that," Janus went on. "Listening to the birds. I told her things, I told her things, lying there next to her in that wood, like I never told anyone before or since. Heh, I sure ain't gonna tell you either. But still, like I said, we hadda split up; it was obvious, the only way. I helped her pack up her things, what she had—

it wasn't much, she was living like a regular hermit—and we walked outta the woods to that hill I told you about, looking down on that big, old river, that big old Mississip rolling from the day God was born till now, rolling till God dies, I swear . . . And I wished her, man, I wished her the best . . . The best guy, the best world . . .

"I loved her, man, that's what you gotta see. I loved her, and I let her go because I loved her. And I went westward and she went east, and I looked back once and saw her disappearing over the crest of the hill, and then, well, then I walked away, into the sunset."

His voice, unlike his image, doesn't trail off but stops short and simply, giving a finality to the aftersilence, capping the tale.

Palmer says nothing. His face is white. He reaches behind him for his sleeping bag and lays it out beside the fire. His stomach knots, and he's afraid that Janus will speak again. He kicks his shoes off but, remaining dressed, slides into the bag on his side, closing his wet eyes and raising the down above his mouth and nose.

Janus stays quiet, but Palmer hears the flames go on, hears him adding wood to them and hears them growing. He makes a muffled noise and tries to muffle it further with the bag's top edge. He's afraid he will not sleep, he feels he must, and in fact, he's hollow and exhausted. Already his thoughts are becoming nonsense, and he wonders vaguely from where they came. Only these visions keep him from his rest, and these just barely. But even on the edge of nightmare, he knows the place; he names its highways: streets crammed with the damned, trodding on lanes paved with the saved, where beds like slabs are up for grabs and girls like saints are weeping . . .

He knows the face of nightmare for a moment, then is sleeping.

•

There'll be a footstep in the hall; there'll be his name, half whispered and half heard; a knock; the door will open, and his sister's husband's haggard, ghostly, ghastly face will enter, framed with blackness, white.

"Palmer, are you sleeping?"

"No."

"She's dying."

"Why?"

"Impotence."

"What?"

"She's gone."

"What's wrong?"

"Beth. She's left her room."

"She was asleep."

"She's gone."

"She's dying, she can hardly . ."

"Palmer, she is gone, come quick!"

He'll step from bed and come into the darkness of the twisted halls.

"She can't have gotten far," he'll say.

"I've checked the whole downstairs," his weakling brother-in-law's voice will whine.

"Hang on. We'll find her. Look up here. I'll go down to the basement."

"Jesus."

Palmer will leave him searching to slide through the unsure pathways to the stairs. Down them, and it will grow quieter as he goes, and darker as he goes, until his foot comes to the lower floor, and all the large front hall is black and silent.

Eyes near glowing with the effort to see, he'll slide on, reaching out for balance, touching nothing, seeing nothing, growing sick, afraid.

He will hear the ocean as one submerged, a soft dash on a distant shore. He'll find the basement door and pull it open, frightened that no light divides the formless threshold from all else, and stepping over, he will think: This horror. This horrible thing.

This horror is mine alone.

He'll move through total darkness as if through time, like tragedy, from pain to greater pain; from fear to greater fear, he will move on, descending. And at the bottom, chill and fear at his throat, he will reach out again, his fingers at the wall—then, suddenly, withdrawing. A slimy, living damp is there.

He'll jump back and back up; his eyes will widen, useless, staring at the wet and empty space. He'll reach out, in a panic, for the light; it will come on, and he will see the terror that he knew he would:

Beth, his sister, cancerous, with just her eyes' whites showing, clung in sex to one in black, and violated deeply with a pound, she'll grin and turn her darkling johnny round, giving up her last breath in a kiss—

To this, dear Palmer Higgs, to this. To this.

His heart beats heavily against the earth as the nightmare seeps away. Squinting at the bright and blinding light of flames, he gets his vision back by grades and starts to trace the image of his fellow traveler across the way. The face of Janus burns, the eyes burn in it masked by fire so, and in another instant all the terror of his sleep is back in Palmer's stomach, gripping him.

Our great detective sees at last the way the story ends. The sense of it is dazzling, and the flaw, without which all is flawed, is clear.

Impotent.

*What?*

Impotent.

*Janus?*

Impotent, impotent, impotent all along.

*But . . .*

Yes.

*But then—*

Yes.

*But, oh, Jesus.*

Yes. Dear Jesus.

*Not her.*

You know my methods, Smedley.

He peels the bag away and stands, shaking his head from side to side slowly, making a small and miserable sound somewhere inside his throat. His eyes are suddenly deeper, sadder; his scrawny body huddles to itself. The orphan seems finally orphaned by all.

He looks at the ground, and his eyes are filling.

"Janus."

Something maybe in his tone alerts the other. Janus stands up, too. He's blazing, massive.

"The whole thing, huh?" he whispers.

"Janus."

"Now just—just cool down, buddy."

"Janus. And I loved her so."

"Take it easy," Janus says. He stands, tense, one arm out in warning, waiting. "It's just a story out of my head, just lies."

"You could've found a way to tell her."

Janus snorts. "She knew. She knew."

"She could've helped."

"I lost my head."

"My God!" Palmer roars.

Instinctively, quickly, Janus whips the knife out, flips it open.

"Don't get dumb," he says.

This confirms everything, finishes everything, for Palmer. He is done with grief, with pining, left only with some sad fury and the loss, his loss.

For it was murder in the woods, he thinks. A hundred years of impotence erupting, so that Janus, furious, tear-blurred, crazed by even her understanding, drew that knife and plunged beyond himself, in her, in her, in her, who cried out like a virgin, like a virgin bled, while the birds scattered and the humus drank and Janus felt, for just an instant, free of the years like nights, the nights like years of remembering Mary.

Mary.

Lifting his eyes from the earth, Palmer stares across the fire at him and at the blade that killed his love, his hope of love. His voice chokes with the rise of tears.

"Now," he says. "Now, now, now—you will deal with me."

A wind blows in an updraft, and the flames inside it swell.

Janus smiles like a devil. Palmer hasn't a chance in hell.

# · 36 ·

There must be death somewhere in this. There will be courage, so there must be death. It will not be the bravery of soldiers (though this attracts him still), but some, there isn't time, but there will be some peaceful confrontation with a violent end, a martyrdom, if you will, in which this Palmer and his bride, armed only with a word, will meet the ends that men bring on each other. He'll stand before crowds that roar like oceans and make his speeches for the better cause. He'll stand before the guns, beneath the rope, astride the pit, at death, and talk it back and brave it down, and live to know his glory and die inside his fame.

And she, decked in white, his wife, his wife, will be beside him, will be braver even than himself. She will battle a mighty nation and prove herself truly a woman of the soil; she will battle a mighty religion and prove herself truly a woman of God; she will battle the powers that tear lives asunder and prove herself, truly, a woman.

And if by history they are forgotten, they will be resurrected by a time more virtuous than this, for they will have left a record with their tongues, and scrawled truth with their bodies, and given breath away to make a world, and disallowed their own apotheosis, though apotheosized, so that the race might be aware that in the midst of Oedipus and in the den of fear, that in the halls of the worst, one might yet make a creature who is worthy of all the earth. There is no time. There will be, though, and time to make a universe of nothing. There's no time, and yet in that time he will stand, afraid, courageous, at the very mouth of fear. He will stand, afraid, courageous—even as he's doing here.

Palmer and Janus confront each other, motionless, staring, across the fire. Janus remains tense but smiling, a bit incredulous perhaps that Palmer has stood, thus far, fast, and waiting still for him to break. Palmer, however, is keeping his small body rigid and erect, his eyes pinned on his adversary, his arms tense at his sides.

So Janus realizes he must do something, save face, at least; he can't back down. He figures he knows men, and he figures if he makes a frightful-looking rush, the other will turn coward and take off, leaving him to stop short, start laughing, and leave his opponent humiliated. He relaxes his muscles slightly—the muscles gone somewhat soft, not as responsive as they used to be—just enough to help his spring. Then, without warning, he lets out a shriek, a hoot heard clear across the yard and leaps directly through the fire, brandishing his knife.

To Palmer, in that moment, Janus seems a demon draped in flame. His legs go weak and almost buckle, he shouts in panic, but he holds his ground. Janus is upon him and already stopping on his heels, preparing to start laughing when Palmer punches him in the mouth.

Janus goes, "Oof," drops back, and angrily jabs his hand out, stabbing Palmer in the chest. The blade hits no obstruction—it sinks deep.

Palmer feels an obscene intrusion, a tearing of essentials

## *Sunday, December 25*

# · 37 ·

I see a shining many spheres away.

*By the river.*

Just a pin of light. Strip a shield of vision back, and see it pulse a little, watch it glow.

*Oh, the obscurity of vision! To be blind!*

Approach the river; gun the engine some. I see its beams extend, reach with a latent power at the outer rims.

*What light is this?*

Follow that river. Gun the engine some. It is a star and, like a star, is small but from a distance, giving off an ancient day to fields left unbeheld to this, the puny eye of man.

*Yes, I imagine it.*

Hold back, have faith, and gun the bloody engine. Don't you see it, can't you see it blow, or is it our perspective as we near that makes a nova of it? Even then, it breaches the perimeter of stars, sets off so fierce a glow it brings the lids down for protection . . .

*Cast your eyes away!*

Not yet. Like blood, you still can see it through the lids. It blazes—wait—it rages with a light. Approach it. Know it for the sun, and ride the river to it, gazing wide-eyed at its center till your own light's scorched away. And now—be blind! In blindness, see that in the seventh sphere . . .

*Yes! In the seventh sphere . . .*

And in the seventh sphere—naught but a rose. We die.

*We do?*

We really do.

*Well!*

Merry fucking Christmas.

*Yeah.*

Come on, guys, let's play something else.

*Ahem. Ahem. I'll wait.*

Sorry, Professor.

*Ahem. Now, as I was saying in my last excruciatingly illuminating lecture, the world is divided . . .*

Uh, Professor.

*. . . into . . . What is it, Mr. Higgs?*

Uh, Professor, may I be excused? I've been stabbed to death.

*Can't it wait, Mr. Higgs?*

Uh, actually, no, sir, I don't think I can breathe anymore.

*Settle down, Mr. Higgs, it can wait until after the last bell tolls—I mean, rings. Ahem. Now. As we see on our map . . .*

Meat. Give Higgs meat.

*Why? What would you devour?*

Meat.

*And keep it on your belly till you puked it up a god? No. Nay. Never. When he overleaped the flame, the spark was yours.*

But you saw. You heard.

*I saw a man shouting myths at a mountain. I heard an echo, endless, that he never heard. But, ah, Palmer, I am wiser than brave, and philosophy, like the universe, is finite and unbounded.*

Like a pit covered with paper.

*Aye. And if I am a tragedy, then you at least are dust.*

Swell. That's nice. But I can't breathe.

*Aye. And Beth.*

And Beth. What have I done?

*Aye.*

Beth. Dear Beth. Dear Mrs. Hayden. We regret to inform you that your brother, your little brother, that child but for whom you might have looked less wistfully at college doors and entered through them, but for whom you might have had your fill of poets and engaged a mind born just to know their work, and but for whom you could have looked up with your poet's eyes into another's and seen a man you might have loved, and had a man you might have loved instead of this pragmatic spouse you got to gain the money that would give your loves and lovers to an ingrate boy, who raised his haughty pockmarked face and ran; I say, ma'am, this young brother—for whom you gave your life—has squandered his. Vagabond, rootless, gutless, dead, we found him in a hobo camp, a victim of murder most foul by person or persons unknown, undoubtedly another of his drifting kind who killed him for a piece of bread. The entire state police force of Missouri wishes you a happy holiday and extends their heartiest sympathy, even though it's a blessing you won't be burdened with the little sucker anymore. Oh, Beth. I'm frightened now.

*This isn't jolly.*

Hey. Are you kidding? *Are* you kidding? What could be jollier?

*Living.*

Hey, now. Hey, now. Buck up, spunky.

*Smedley.*
C'mon. Everybody, sing:
Let's do a dance to death.
Let's do a dance to death.
Stick out a tap shoe
And clack cross the floor:
Quick or perhaps you
Won't be here anymore.
*I love it.*
Let's keep on dancing just,
Until we turn to dust.
And then we'll rest in peace forever stead of work and toil,
So let's shuffle till we shuffle off this mortal coil.
Here's to our final breath.
Let's do a dance
Toooo
Death.

Yes. And Mary. And black curtains, they will be there. In a drab room, yet much kinder than the woods, hung with death and purple curtains keeping out the sun. Mary. Mary, there you'll be, laid out on the velvet bed, wasted, stretched out, loving me, your ivory life ebbing and your eyes calm.

Lift the haggard face, and look on him who loves you still. You will.

"Palmer."

"Yes. I'm here."

"Dear Palmer."

How can I help weeping? I think I'm weeping now, to know you're gone, such a girl as you were, gone from me forever, and I, your knight, too late upon the lists—but understand, my darling, lies become flesh, too. I'll weep.

But "Hush," you'll say.

"I'm sorry."

"Hush. I must to my father, dear."

"But he's in Pennsylvania."

"Well, uh, no, not that father, but that Great Father who watches over us all. I will be with my ancestors."

"But they're all dead."

"Yes, well, you begin to get the idea."

"Mary . . . Mary, please don't . . . "

"Palmer."

"Yes."

"Palmer—dress me as I married you. Dress me in my wedding gown."

"I can't breathe."

"I know. Hush. Dress me, sweet."

I will. I'll bring the white gown forward, lay it over you and watch you brighten slightly when you are so dressed and watch you quietly, serenely, slip away. I'll weep.

"It's all right," you will whisper, smiling but unable to lower your eyes to me anymore.

I'll move to you that I might see them, come to you that I might see them. Weep.

"Poor Palmer. My poor sweet. It will be fine."

"All right. All right. But don't you be afraid."

"I'm not, love. I'll be around, won't I?"

"Yes. Always."

Then a frightening silence, and: "Mary?"

"I love you, Palmer."

"Mary? Say it, please, again."

"I love you, Palmer Higgs. My husband."

That, at least, could be the end of it. I could've taken heart. Can Roman soldiers guard the tomb of spring or boulder-bar its entrance to the world? We would be part of it. No sanction but a smile to summon sex, no sacrament but sex to bring on birth, no prayer, no incantation, and no hex, no baptism but time on the face of the earth.

*Are you quite done?*

No, by jinkies, not yet. I've got to speak: a speech to the reeds and an oratory to the corn; a prayer to the river and the wheat and sea.

*May I be excused?*

Let me talk to the winds of a woman. Let me tell her tale. Of her unrequited first love and how, when it finished, she fell in with a boy already wrecked, already overfathered and destroyed, who demanded she give him what he couldn't receive.

And I'll weave a story then of her confusion. And I'll tell of a good man, who loved her well enough to let her go, go until she found she could love him, too. And of how she beckoned him, and of how he died, and how she gave him back what life she could and faced despair alone.

Mourn her—Mary—she was a simple girl and a good. And she sat, quietly, with her tragedies in a wood (pursued, though she didn't know it, by that wretched boy, poor boy, who could not help himself) and rose courageously to meet the world and so met death.

Oh, Mary. Me—*I* loved you.

*That's the corniest . . .*

Stop.

*Oh, please.*

I'm weeping.

*Oh. Hurumph. Well, yes, I do believe you are.*

Follow the river, Smedley. Gun the engine some. It's hard to breathe.

*I know.*

Look there!

*What?*

There. A barge, at the river's mouth, and on it . . .

*What?*

A woman.

*Ah.*

Get closer. Toward the ocean, man. My God, that light, that seventh sphere . . .

*Naught but . . .*

It's her.

*Oh, Palmer, Palmer.*

So gun the engine—hard.

*Sorry, old fellow. Afraid I can't.*

But it's her, it's her, I see her. I can see the color of her hair. What's wrong?

*Looks like I've had it, old friend.*

Smedley!

*Ah, Palmer, I have to go.*

Smeds. Not you. We were five and six together. We were alone, and when my sister came . . .

*Good-bye, old buddy.*

. . . we . . .

*Good-bye.*

Ah, Smeds. We were five and six together. We were alone. We always were. And alone, one needs a little man dancing, or the tragic music ends. You were the man.

But on, on, on. On, on and all alone.

I see her clearly now, upon the barge and almost at the sea. Yes, it's her, it's her. Her hair, that hair, blows back and bares her shoulder and . . . I'm sure, I'm sure it's she. Taken now by the ocean, caught by the powerful plash and surge, out in the great glowing promise. . . Oh, hell, my darling. I can't breathe.

Lillian?

# *Epilogue*

In the room at the end of the hall, two little boys, one six, one eight, are having it out in whispers. The younger is insisting that the North Pole is another planet, citing as comparisons such other planets as China and Holland and New York. The elder is defending the concept of countries, all put together to make one big planet, not counting the Pacific Ocean, and is slowly gaining ground as the younger, suspecting he is wrong, is now arguing only out of pride. Both, however, are strangely patient with each other, neither wanting to lose his temper or otherwise misbehave. That, of course, would scotch the whole deal at the last minute.

In the room beside them, their parents are lying in bed, listening to the sound of the children's voices. The father has already boomed out to them his best stentorian predictions about what will happen if he has to come in there, but perhaps his heart was not in it, since it didn't take. Now he is lying peacefully beside his wife, listening and smiling. It is Christmas Eve, after all.

In the room beside this is a youngish man, undressing, and in the room at the other end of the hall, is an elderly couple, asleep.

A grand staircase winds away from all of them to the first floor, and wandering through the rooms down there is a woman.

She's a beautiful and erect figure, clad in a white nightgown, her rich hair spilling over its back. Her hair is auburn and swallows the lamplight. Her step is slow as she proceeds.

She passes into the main den and kneels beside the Christmas tree, to rearrange the presents underneath it with a careful hand. When all looks right to her, she rises, pauses, listening to the wild sounds of the winter ocean, beating at only a small distance beyond the walls. She goes to the window and stands there quietly and looks out intently, though it is very dark and she can't see far. Her lips begin moving rapidly, but the only word she says aloud is the last one: ". . . safe."

Then she turns and moves away, to the sofa, and sits down slowly, and peers forward for a moment, as if in a trance. Finally, she bows her head; she raises one hand to cover her eyes. And, Reader, we leave her weeping.